"I know it's difficult to say, but would you have considered his actions within the parameters of your husband's character?"

Julia listened to his language and was impressed by the man. Then she thought about the question. "Absolutely and utterly out of character."

Armand Jones held the letter out to her, and she stepped closer to take it. Now he signaled to her chair. "I'd like to share some more information with you."

His expression had shifted from blank to serious. Julia sat down quickly. Her stomach plunged into a state of nausea. She swallowed.

"A young woman, a research assistant in Dr. Streatfield's lab, has been found in her apartment." Mr. Jones waited, gauging her face to make sure she was ready for the rest. "Murdered."

Why would this have anything to do with Wilson? Mr. Jones seemed to be waiting, expecting a question, but she had no questions.

He finally spoke again. "The police have traced her last hours, which appear to have been spent with Dr. Streatfield."

BOOKS BY JODY CARR

No Regrets

My Beautiful Fat Friend

Monday's Child

HarperChoice

MONDAY'S CHILD

JODY CARR

HarperPaperbacks
A Division of HarperCollinsPublishers

HarperPaperbacks
A Division of HarperCollins*Publishers*
10 East 53rd Street, New York, NY 10022-5299

This is a work of fiction. The characters, incidents, and dialogues are products of the author's imagination and are not to be construed as real. Any resemblance to actual events or persons, living or dead, is entirely coincidental.

ISBN 0-06-101381-1

HarperCollins®, 🔥 ®, HarperPaperbacks™, and HarperChoice™ are trademarks of HarperCollins Publishers Inc.

Cover photograph composit © 1999 by Phil Heffernan
Cover photograph © 1999 by FPG International

First printing: March 1999

Printed in the United States of America

Visit HarperPaperbacks on the World Wide Web at
http://www.harpercollins.com

❖ 10 9 8 7 6 5 4 3 2 1

For Elliot, Rachel, and Daniel,
with love

ACKNOWLEDGMENTS

I'm a lucky woman. Thank you, friends and family, for waiting through the long years with me.

Jo and King Carr, Jean, Jacy, and Celie Carr and Este Armstrong, George and Sarah Carr, Jackie, Artie, Stuart, and Richard Schein, Karen, Allan, Lewis, Esther, and Laura Gibofsky.

Rami Levin, Carol Voorhees, Aniko Racz-Muth, Charles and Sallie Schaeffer.

I'm luckier still to have found talented professional colleagues.

Independent editor, *Dave King,* who taught me so much about the craft of writing.

Andrea Brown, for believing I could do it.

Carolyn Marino, always eager to read whatever I wrote: a heartfelt thank you.

Jessica Lichtenstein, a truly gifted editor, for whom I say *dayenu*!

Et, enfin, a mon ami sans nom: a notre pont sans nom.

MONDAY'S CHILD

TEN YEARS BEFORE

A wet summer dawn wrapped around Julia like the sleeping bag she'd crawled out of sometime in the middle of the night. Naked from the waist up and her skin as cold as the damp, packed earth beneath her, she rolled over and opened gluey eyes to gaze at Wilson.

His handsome, tanned face, turned up to the sky as he lay sleeping on his back, swarmed with the black bristles of a three-day beard. Lush eyelashes trembled on the upper cheekbones. He'd kicked the sleeping bag down around his ankles, and his body, covered only by white cotton boxers, shone with a sheen of sweat.

Julia lifted her right arm, making a weak fist with her hand, and reached across the small space to touch the black hair on his chest. Her fingers dangled and tickled. His skin seemed to shiver, and a shudder crept up her own legs. Goose bumps exploded and she felt the hair on her legs stiffen. Julia crawled toward Wilson, and then crept on top of him. She tucked her nose against his ear, breathing hard. Her hands cradled his head and she scratched lazily, watching him wake. And so she searched him and so she found him.

When she thought about it many years later, she couldn't remember that she and Wilson had spoken at all. She knew they must have. She remembered looking down at his beautiful face, his eyes screwed shut as if in horrible pain, a grimace on his large, gracious mouth, and no words of any kind. There'd been the language of his body's movements, a language she understood perhaps too easily, but no other.

At the time, she'd been grateful that he invited her along on the project. His research focused on the development of antipsychotic drugs, and he usually worked in his lab at Columbia University. But for the last year he'd been reading and thinking about the hallucinative effects derived from sources in the natural world, particularly opium and its derivative, codeine; so he'd decided to spend this two-week vacation camping in upstate New York to look for unusual fungi, plants, and growths. Neither of them expected that Julia would be of much use.

By eight o'clock in the morning, they'd wound up their sleeping bags and lodged them high in a crook of a pine tree, with the backpack of food dangling from one branch. They were hiking to a swampy section of the forest, noted by other scientists in various journal articles as being rich with fungi.

Wilson led the way, his strides about four inches

longer than hers. She quickened her pace to keep up. For the first hour, she didn't mind, but in the second hour, nearing ten o'clock, her glare focused on his T-shirt where the faded words *The Metropolitan Opera* undulated in a harassing, boring motion.

Forty-five minutes later, Wilson found the area. They balanced gingerly on a fallen log and glugged water from canteens. Wilson's breath came ragged and hard. He dropped to his hands and knees, then lay full-length on his belly. One hand snaked out to lift a leaf, and he stared intently. He gave her no instructions.

Julia wasn't even sure that he wanted her to search with him. She scooched around on her butt, lifting her thin brown legs over the log until she faced in the other direction. She stared idly down at the forest floor and saw nothing at all. Now, that was annoying. She knew there had to be all kinds of things down there, if she'd just concentrate. Both hands held the log while she lowered herself to the ground. Julia glanced at Wilson. He was inching forward on his belly, just like a combat soldier, she thought crazily. She leaned over and stretched out on top of the brush. Sort of comfortable, sort of not.

She crawled across the forest floor, eyes about a foot from the underbrush, her long fingers gently turning over leaves and branches. Sweat trickled down her thin cheeks, scattering like raindrops. Julia knew only vaguely that she was looking for the fungi that feed off of insects. So, first, she searched for bugs. She crept even more slowly, lying full-length on her belly, staring at the ground and easing aside the brush so that the black earth, glinting with granite, worms lying languid and lazy, sent a dizzying, rich smell to her nose pressed so close. Music ran through her head, or maybe a prayer, sounding and repeating, balanced and classical in structure, a call for the ground to give her what she needed.

A discovery for Wilson.

She was beginning to get light-headed, and wondered about drinking more water. But there was a piece of wood just an arm's length away, its decayed bark covered like fine gauze with mold. Julia crept forward and touched the wood, lifting it away from the ground's hold. A beetle grub scooted to the safety of a nearby leaf, swollen with moisture and decay.

She saw something sprouting from the head of the beetle grub. Her hand shot out and snatched the beetle. It lay still in her closed fist.

Julia sat up slowly and looked over her shoulder for Wilson. He was about twenty feet away, only the top of his head visible.

"Wilson," she called out.

His head rose higher. "What?"

"I think I found something."

"What's it look like?"

"I don't want to open my hand in case I lose it."

No answer. She could feel him thinking, something she'd become curiously adept at doing with him. Feeling him thinking, and then even feeling the unspoken thoughts.

"It was some kind of beetle with a growth popping out of the head."

Wilson sat up and then stood. He covered the space between them in seconds, crouched next to her, and cupped his larger hands around hers. "Lemme see."

She opened her hands as little as possible. Her heart was beating fast and she had an uncanny sensation, almost like love. His face was close to her hands, peering in, and she could smell the sweat and pine sap that mingled on his skin.

Still Wilson didn't speak.

He moved, liquid and sleek, grabbing from his waist pack a small wood-framed box with screening attached to three sides. Wilson opened the lid and Julia heard a faint squeak of the hinge. He scooped up a handful of dark earth, scattered it in the box, and added leaves and some moss. From the canteen, he dribbled in water. Then he cupped his hands beneath hers. "Just let it go."

"Why shouldn't I put it in myself?"

Wilson glanced at her, green eyes wondering and excited. "Yeah, sure." He bent to pick up the box, and held it beneath her hands.

Julia opened her hands. Nothing happened.

"Shake just a bit. It's made a home in there," Wilson said.

She shook them harder and the beetle tumbled into the box.

It lay still, a shiny greeny-blue color, with the muddy brown growth nearly its own size sprouting out of the head. They watched as it disappeared under a leaf. Wilson replaced the lid on the top of the box, stood up, and returned the canteen to its sling.

"We'll walk back to camp and eat lunch there, okay?" Wilson said.

"Do you think it's something?"

Wilson took a step up onto the fallen log, but swiveled on one foot to look at her. He was poised there for a moment, beautiful in his long, thin body. "Yes, I do."

CHAPTER 1

G eorge McDuff couldn't believe his luck. He'd been an illegal Irish immigrant, working nights at that godawful fish market, when he was tapped for this new line of work three months before. Now he was on his way to being an American citizen, and all he had to do was some running and fetching and watching. He was virtually an errand boy for a group he figured imported drugs from Asia. They didn't tell him for sure, but it was the only explanation for all the money and subterfuge.

He just got word that today he could quit the tail he'd been doing for the last two weeks. He'd followed some guy, a nobody kind of guy, and this nobody hadn't done a blessed thing for the whole two weeks, so far as George could tell. He seemed to have a city job, where he went Monday through Friday, disappearing into the large, nondescript building at Twenty-eighth and Lexington every morning at 8:55 A.M. He never came out for lunch, not even to grab a dog from the street vendors, and only reappeared at precisely 5:05. Then he'd meander the eighteen blocks home. He stopped at a Korean market exactly halfway, where he'd buy a big salad for his dinner that night.

George had never seen anyone eat so much salad. He figured the guy had a terrific case of the runs from eating all that lettuce. Still, he'd become familiar, almost like a friend. You could tell he wouldn't hurt anyone, a real wimp, if the truth be known, and though George was grateful the surveillance would end today, he felt a small puff of sadness.

He didn't wonder what his boss, Mr. Wong, wanted with this man. It wasn't his job to wonder, or even to do much thinking. George had never considered himself much of a thinker, anyway. He dropped out of school in Form Two, when he was thirteen, mostly because it was too hard and there wasn't anybody around who cared whether he did the work.

Of course, they say you never really stop thinking, and George was what you might call a Big Thinker about all the little stuff he saw on the street. Just yesterday morning, when he'd been standing in his usual spot after the guy went into the office building, he started watching this old lady shuffling along the sidewalk. She was far away when he first caught sight of her, but he noticed her because she was all dressed up, like she was on the way to church. She stood erect and her arms were held still as her legs took small careful steps. He quite admired that old lady. And he didn't even think once of grabbing her pocketbook, which, back in Dublin, he would've done.

He stood all that long, last day in the position he'd chosen on the first day because if the sun shone it would hit him square in the face. The October weather was changeable, and there'd been plenty of days when that sun made all the difference. Then there were the days without sun, and instead a hard, driving rain in a cold wind. But today, the last day, it was glorious. The sun beamed out of the blue sky like it was some kind of joke or tease, like it was saying to George, "Hey, son, you like this? Well, don't get too used to it."

Around about three o'clock, when he knew he still had two hours to go, his eyes started shutting. And then, finally, he gave in and let the drowsy feel of a nap steal over him.

His eyes flew open ten minutes later, blinking and watering in the sun's glare. He checked his watch. Yeah, 3:10. So why was the nothing guy coming out of the building? George straightened and got ready to move.

The man turned to the left, a direction he'd never gone before. George felt his heart speed up, though not too much because, after all, this guy had so far been too boring to inspire hope of anything else. They walked at a fast clip and George started swinging his arms at the pleasure of actual forward movement. He even felt his lips purse up, ready to whistle, but he reined in the impulse.

The man turned down Tenth Avenue, walked three blocks south to Twenty-fifth, and turned again so that he was heading for the river. The neighborhood was getting a little scarfy, and George stopped swinging his arms. At one of the busier wharves, the man started walking straight out where it jutted into the river. Enormous ships crowded either side of the wharf, blotting out the sun. The wind whipped along the tunnel made by the looming ships, and George quickly buttoned his coat all the way to the neck.

They were nearly to the end. George wondered whether he'd better slow his pace, then immediately did so. The man whirled around and looked at him. His expression was hopeful and pleasant.

He took a hesitant step toward George.

Before George could decide what the hell to do about this, a small Chinese guy appeared behind the man, lifted his gun, and shot him in the back.

The man tumbled forward without a sound.

The Chinese man stared at George, then gestured with his gun, shooing him away.

George turned and fought the urge to run. He expected to be shot, and nearly hoped for it.

He was in over his head.

After the killing, he went to his room in the cruddy boarding house he'd found the first night he arrived in

New York City, six months earlier. The bathroom, always damp and fungal, was down the hall. He shared it with six others. He carried a can of Lysol disinfectant along with soap, shampoo, razor, shaving cream, and towel to the bathroom. George wore rubber beach shoes on his feet so that he wouldn't have to touch the floor. He sprayed the bathroom liberally, holding his breath, then stepped back outside for a moment while the spray dissolved. He tried not to breathe as he shaved and showered.

His room was more pathetic than disgusting. A single sagging bed crouched in a corner, and a bureau of fake wood, missing the lower drawer, was next to a closet the size of a child. The floor was filthy linoleum. George had tried to scrub it, but the dirt was permanently baked in. A turquoise dinette table was in front of the small, grimy window. Someone had hung a plastic window shade and painted a picture of a tree on it. If the shade was up, he looked into a dark elevator shaft. Usually he kept it down, and suffered with the sorriest looking tree he could've imagined.

He hated the bathroom and bedroom so much that he knew he couldn't tell Mr. Wong to go take a hike—or, smarter, to disappear himself—which was what he felt like doing for a good hour after the shooting. Finally he accepted that if he was in over his head, then so be it. He needed money to get out of this place.

Fifteen minutes later, George rang the doorbell at Mr. Wong's Upper East Side mansion.

The door was opened by another young Chinese man. He wore black cotton pants and a white T-shirt. Though the man was small, shorter than George's height of five feet nine inches, he was bulked up from weight training. His black hair was buzz cut and added to his overall look of a tough.

George avoided making eye contact with anyone in this house except Mr. Wong himself.

The man opened the door wider and George stepped in. It was four o'clock in the afternoon and the setting sun was still strong. Streaks of sunlight shot across the marble entrance floor and George was tempted to bend over, place the flat of his hand against the marble, and feel its unexpected heat. He did not.

"Mr. Wong will see you," the man said.

"Thanks."

George started up the curving, elaborate staircase. His hand glided on the smooth black walnut banister, which should have felt warm but instead was cool. Nothing in this house felt like it should. Everything was backward, and it made him nervous.

What was especially backward was how beautiful the house was. In George's experience, crime was an ugly business. Ugly people, ugly places, ugly, ugly, ugly. George had an eye for beauty. It calmed him as well as a neat scotch could. The truly weird thing was that for an Irish boy with an eye for beauty, he needed a life of ugly crime to ever hope to make life beautiful.

On the second-floor landing, he turned right and walked quickly down the hall. He didn't know for sure, but he thought Mr. Wong had been notified of his arrival, and it seemed wise to move fast. Good impressions and all that. He glanced down at his shoes, which he'd polished before leaving the boarding house. Still, they were old brown loafers, the cracks filled with leftover polish. His blue shirt was clean and ironed with spray starch. He used an iron belonging to his landlady, a tiny Hispanic woman who oozed meanness out her skin and had the gall to charge him fifty cents. She made a man want to kill her.

He knocked on the door of Mr. Wong's office suite. It was opened immediately by a young Chinese woman George had never seen before. Her head bowed low as she glided backward to allow him space to enter the office. He could not see her face. The top of her head showed sleek black hair swept straight back and gathered into a bun at the nape of her neck. She gave off the suggestion of beauty, and though George immediately looked beyond her to Mr. Wong standing in front of his desk, he felt his body pulling toward her. The urge to see her face was strong, but not so strong as his fear of Mr. Wong.

Despite the bright sun outside, the windows in the office were covered with heavy wooden shutters, and over them red velvet drapes had been drawn. Small lamps shone, spilling pools of light on mahogany wood tables and the massive desk belonging to Mr. Wong. George rapidly blinked his eyes, adjusting to the dark.

Mr. Wong suddenly placed both his hands behind him on the desk's surface, then lifted himself up with a small hop so that he was sitting on the desk, swinging his legs. He wore a sweat suit today, made of some graceful cloth that looked like cashmere. George had only met Mr. Wong a total of four times, and at those meetings he'd been wearing elaborate English suits of herringbone tweed and starched white shirts.

He was a young man; George guessed about thirty years old. His black hair was worn long and pulled back into a ponytail, giving him a more traditional Chinese appearance. George thought of him as Chinese, but he'd actually been born in Birmingham, Alabama, and he spoke with a slight Southern accent. He was so thin and bronzed with color that George thought he looked like he'd been carved out of the same mahogany as the office walls and bookshelves.

"You did a good job, George McDuff."

Did he mean to be funny, the way he said George's full name? George glanced at the woman, who was seated at a small desk in a distant corner and had already begun working at a minuscule laptop computer.

There were no sounds except the tap-tapping of the woman's long nails on the keyboard.

"Thank you, sir."

"Ready for another assignment?" Mr. Wong's hands rested on his knees. George could see his manicured nails, gleaming white. They looked like they had polish on them.

"Sure."

Mr. Wong's face had gone still.

George knew he hadn't sounded enthusiastic enough.

"Perhaps you'd rather not?" Mr. Wong jumped down from his perch on the desk and walked across the room to the young woman at the computer. He bent over her and whispered.

"No, I'd like another job. Very much."

Mr. Wong swung around and for a brief second George saw the woman's face.

She was old, so old that George felt the shock cause a flush to creep up his neck and into his cheeks. Her hair was obviously dyed, and her body, well, George had no idea how her body could look like that. She must work out all the time. His own belly suddenly felt thick and blubbery, though he knew he was actually in good shape.

But she didn't look at him and he was saved the embarrassment of having her read his thoughts from his face. George had tried to develop the technique of withholding information from the person looking at him, but he'd done poorly with the effort. His granny, who was the main person he was always trying to hide things from when he was a kid, said he had the most innocent face in all Ireland, said he ought to have been a priest with a face like that.

Now, there's a joke, George McDuff a priest.

"You see, we have a special need for a young Irishman. You seem to fit the bill precisely."

"Irish?"

"This assignment will be a bit more exciting than the last." Mr. Wong's lips curled up into an attempt at a smile. "You'll be following an Irish nanny, and then you're going to have to strike up a friendship with her, gain her trust, and *convince* her to help us with a little scientific research."

Mr. Wong walked to the built-in bar on a far wall, picked up a thermos, and poured steaming hot liquid into a cup. "Would you care for some tea?" He held the thermos up in the air and looked at George inquiringly.

"No, thanks."

"I thought the Irish drank as much tea as the Chinese."

"I had a cup before I got here."

Mr. Wong cradled his mug in both hands, as if he was chilly and in need of warming, and walked around the back of his desk. He sat down in the opulent leather chair, then crouched over the mug, taking small, gentle sips of tea.

"So what do you think of the assignment?" Mr. Wong said.

"It sounds straightforward."

George didn't bother to tell him that an Irish girl would be more interested in an American, someone who might even marry her and make her legal.

"Jefferson, the man who opened the door for you earlier, has the particulars. He'll tell you exactly what to do."

"Very good, sir."

George was dying to leave.

"The green card he has for you is entirely legal. See you earn the gift."

He couldn't believe it. A green card, just like that!

"Yes, sir."

Mr. Wong stood. His skinny brown fingers played with a round gold ball about an inch in diameter. Suddenly he rolled it across the smooth expanse of wood, right toward George.

George's hand shot out and caught it. He turned the ball in his palm and felt the cool gold caress him. Then he tried to hand it back.

"Roll it, boy, roll it," Mr. Wong said.

George squelched the shit-eating grin that threatened to split across his face when the doorman politely avoided looking him straight in the eye, then grabbed George's two enormous suitcases and placed them on the elevator. "I could bring them up later, on my break," the doorman said.

"I can manage."

The elevator was mirrored from floor to ceiling, and the floor was covered with an ornate pattern of silver and black marble squares. The overall effect was a bit bright, to George's eye, but a helluva lot better than the grungy staircase in the old boarding house. His ears popped as the elevator whizzed upward and he let the grin happen.

The key slid into the lock like it'd been greased only hours before. The room was almost completely dark, so George groped his way down a long hall, somehow having missed the light switch right by the front door. The hall spilled into a large living room, and the lights of New York City lit the room.

He sucked in his breath at the view of twinkling lights from the apartment building across the street. Already he could feel a fascination for watching all those people. He switched on a lamp next to an enormous white hump, which turned out to be an L-shaped seating arrangement.

The apartment was furnished like a high-class hotel. Thick wall-to-wall carpets; down-filled furniture; new dishes, glasses, and silverware; plush white towels in the taupe-colored bathroom; handsome bedspread of taupe, black, and white houndstooth; and a stocked bar.

He very nearly cried.

When he was a child, George had been a pretty boy, so pretty it got him in trouble. You might imagine the girls would like him, but in truth, they were jealous of his lovely face, both jealous and angry that God should give such a gift to a boy who'd no need of it. And then the boys, they were convinced he was a fairy. A real fairy when he was quite small, and the other sort of fairy later on, when all the boys ever thought about was sex. At fourteen years old, he considered that perhaps he was "that way" simply because everyone else seemed to believe it. But then he fell in love, and he knew he was not.

She was French, with the glorious name of Noelle. Not a bit of prettiness about her, only a solemn face, white and simple, and a head of black curly hair. There was no one else in all of Dublin like her; she was the capital letter in the first word of an essay or story: larger, darker, more ornate, the start of all the words that tumbled after.

When he fell in love with Noelle, he couldn't speak to her for two months. Even the possibility of saying good morning—a possibility he suffered over—was unimaginable. He watched her during school, in the play yard, after school. Of course he followed her home and figured out which window in the grand apartment building was hers. He saw her figure move behind the white lace curtains, and seeing her there made him wild. Later he discovered it wasn't her apartment, not her window, not her body.

With all the watching, he slowly realized she was alone. Not a friend at all, and no brothers and sisters. He felt they belonged together. George practiced saying *bonjour* over and over. He even risked asking Gran to tell him how he sounded, was his accent good, did he seem casual and comfortable? Gran being Gran, she made no fuss about it. Said his *bonjour* was right as rain.

He aimed for his birthday, October eighteenth, and on that morning he walked right up to her and stuck out his hand.

"Bonjour," he said.

Her black eyes blinked once. *"Bonjour."*

His hand trembled, but when Noelle reached over and shook it, his hand grew quiet.

He wanted to tell her it was his birthday, but that would've been absurd.

"It's my birthday today," he said.

Now her eyes crinkled up. She gave his hand another strong pump. "It is mine, *aussi*."

Her parents didn't approve. George was a terrible student, a bastard being raised by a decidedly wild granny, poor as a potato, and prettier than Noelle. None of him, not one bit, was right for their daughter. George and Noelle met only once, at the Laundromat near her apartment building, and they talked easily. When he approached her at school the next morning, she turned her back.

He still thought of her. Right at this moment, he wanted to show her his grand apartment in New York City.

CHAPTER 2

A ngela sat up and turned on the bedside lamp. With both hands she reached behind her head and began to unplait her long braid of red hair. She shook it loose and the hair splayed across her pillow, thick and luxurious.

Her room in the large, handsome New York City apartment was small but cheery, painted white with deep blue velvet drapes and a woven blue and white rug. Clothes for today were piled carefully on the small armchair in the corner, covered in matching blue velvet.

Angela stood and immediately turned back to the bed, yanking it away from the wall in order to strip back the spread, blanket, and top sheet. She brushed at the pristine bottom sheet, easing the wrinkles to the outer edges of the bed and then retucking the sheet so that it was smooth. In a minute the bed was made and pushed back against the wall.

Dressed and her hair again neatly braided, she opened her door quietly and slipped down the hall toward the kitchen. She could hear the distant sound of water running and knew that Dr. Wilson Streatfield, her employer, was taking his shower. The lights flared on in the bright kitchen, blinding her for a moment. She hit the dimmer. Ah, better. She crossed to the huge refrigerator, opened the freezer, and took out the Kenyan coffee beans. One of the many reasons to be grateful.

"Angela," Wilson said.

She tossed a grin over her left shoulder and deliberately turned on the coffee grinder to drown him out.

"Do you realize it's only five-thirty?" His voice was loud in the blessed silence.

"I didn't know that, no."

The Doctor sat down at the breakfast table, unfolded *The New York Times,* and started to read. "You're too young to be getting up so early. You need your rest."

"I go to bed early."

"And that's another thing." He gave her a stern look over the edge of the newspaper.

They worried that she'd made no friends.

Angela drifted around the kitchen, setting three places at the table, pulling over Jimmy's high chair and draping it with a clean bib, lining up mugs, cream, sugar, Equal, pouring three glasses of orange juice, plugging in the toaster and arranging butter, jam, margarine, and two kinds of bread in a neat semi-circle.

The coffee gave a final hiss and plopping noise. Angie poured the Doctor's coffee, added a smidgen of Equal, and carried it over to him.

He reached for the mug without taking his eyes from the paper. "Thank you, Angela."

She watched him, waiting to be sure his hand found the handle.

He was always dropping things, spilling drinks, even tripping over his feet. It didn't surprise her that he wasn't the kind of doctor who took care of patients. She and the children had visited him at his Columbia University laboratory where he researched new drugs, and his messy office suited him.

She poured herself coffee and wandered over to the window. Faint light framed the apartment buildings across the street, and windows here and there glowed with light. She took her first sip of coffee and closed her eyes with pleasure.

When she opened them, a light directly opposite her came on suddenly. A man stood at the window, staring at her. He wore a dark business suit and tie. Both hands were plunged into his pants pockets so that the jacket was bunched up over his hips. Now she could see that he wasn't just staring at her. He glared. He looked angry enough to kill her.

Angie took one cautious step backward. The man didn't move. She took another.

"Are you all right?" The doctor's voice surprised her, and she gave a start.

Hot coffee spilled over the rim of the mug and burned her wrist.

She looked at the Doctor. "There's this man." But when she glanced back at the apartment across the way, the man was gone and the apartment dark.

Angela felt two thin arms circling her legs. A small head tucked itself into the back of her knees. She reached behind with her right hand and ruffled Emily's silken hair. "Good morning, sweetheart."

"Morning, Angie." Emily's voice was husky with sleep.

Angela gently unwound Emily's arms. "Give your Da a kiss."

Emily ran across the kitchen, her fuzzy slippers making a swishing noise. He pulled the little girl onto his lap and she dropped her head against his chest.

A tiny dart of pain, like the jab of an inoculation needle, hit Angela. She thought of her own Da, short but muscular, a handsome boyish face, and a way of walking that said *Get outa my way, I'm going places*. So far, he hadn't gotten farther than twenty kilometers from his farm.

Angela glanced again at the apartment building across the street. More lights were on than off, and with dawn, they weren't so obvious. She squinted, trying to tell whether she could see a light farther back in the apartment where the man had stood staring at her.

"Everything under control?" A typical question

from Julia Streatfield. She was a worrier. Angela, a worrier herself, understood.

Again, Angie turned away from the window.

"Could you imagine otherwise?" Dr. Streatfield said. "Angela's in charge."

Julia was still in her robe. Her short blond hair had a cowlick before she took her morning shower. What with the cowlick and no makeup, she looked like an exceptionally beautiful child.

"What time did you get up?" She went to pour herself a mug of coffee and drenched it with cream and sugar.

"I'm not sure," Angela said.

Julia raised her eyebrows, not believing.

"When I came in at five-thirty, she was already busy," Dr. Streatfield said.

"Time for more light in here." Angie pushed up the dimmer so that light blasted through the white kitchen. She opened the refrigerator and took out milk and eggs. "How many pancakes?"

"Me, me!" Emily yelled.

"Definitely you."

"None for me," the Doctor said.

Julia screwed up her face. "If I get fat—"

"You're skinny as a fence post," Angela interrupted.

"You're one to talk," Julia said, "but I'll have two small ones."

That means three, thought Angie. Much as she liked Julia, and she really did, Angie was glad that Julia worked long days as a literary agent in her own business. It was easier to run the apartment and kids on her own, with no interference.

The morning whirled along, gathering speed like a bicycle coasting down a long hill. The baby, Jimmy, woke up with a terrific case of diarrhea and Julia obsessed about that for a while until Angie convinced her that Irish oatmeal for breakfast would do the trick.

After the door closed behind the two of them, Angie always had a small moment of despair. The large apartment, which had been perfectly organized only the night before, was now a mess. She went to the stereo system, selected a CD of Irish ballads, and started the music at a high volume. Singing along, she danced into the kitchen, wiped the oatmeal from Jimmy's face and hands, then plopped him down on the floor of the playroom.

"Emmy!" she called.

Emily appeared promptly, well trained in their morning routine. Angie put the guardrail across the open doorway. She dumped a load of blocks in the middle of the carpeted floor and Jimmy gave a shriek of delight.

"What will you build?" Angie asked Emily.

"A house."

"Good. Make it beautiful for me."

"Okay."

Angie stepped over the rail and headed back to the kitchen.

She flew around the apartment in a peculiar pattern that, for all its apparent confusion, seemed to work. In an hour, while also periodically checking on the children, she had laundry tumbling, beds made, dishwasher humming, and all tidied up.

Time to get the children dressed and to the park.

Julia's office suite was decorated entirely in reproductions since she couldn't see the value of antiques in a well-worked and too small Manhattan office. All the lamps were bulbous brass bases topped with black shades lined in gold foil. The walls were papered in a faux design of leather and gold-stamped books, and the thick carpet was a blackish green color.

Because she loved to sail around on her wheeled desk chair, in her own office she'd put down a vinyl flooring meant to resemble green marble. In front of the one window she'd placed her desk, with her chair situated so that when she was on the phone she could stare out at the city skyline. The surrounding three walls were filled with books displayed on cherry bookcases. A diminutive love seat, covered in a book-patterned fabric that matched the wallpaper in the reception room, was angled into one corner. The final detail had actually cost the most: dark green velvet drapes framed the window. They could be opened to show the view or closed to create a cozy haven.

Julia pushed back on her desk chair and sailed a good five feet across the office. She grabbed the door-jamb of the open doorway and peeked into the outer, adjoining office. "So did you read that novel?"

"*Which* novel?" Her assistant, Margaret, gestured toward the manuscripts that were stacked in tidy piles. She was always neat, or she tried to be, but three hundred plus pages of slippery paper seemed to have an uncanny ability to slide.

"You know, the one about a mother having an affair with her son's best friend." Julia raised her arched blond eyebrows suggestively.

"That one, yeah, I read it."

Julia clung to the doorjamb and swung her chair around, first wildly to the left and then ricocheting back to the right. She waited.

"That book's not for you."

"Why not?"

"It's just ridiculous."

"Sometimes the most ridiculous is also the most commercial, don't forget that."

"I already sent it back, Julia."

"Rats, don't I get any fun?"

Margaret gave her a stern look and shook her head back and forth so vigorously that her cap of sleek black hair fanned out in a sweeping arc. "I thought you hired me to save you from junk like that."

"Was that the reason?"

Margaret had graduated from Princeton three years before with a joint degree in English literature and philosophy. Julia had promised her three percent of any deal for any book that Margaret dug out of the submission piles. So far, three percent of nothing was nothing.

"That's the reason you hired me, yes, that and my exquisite taste in literature, which I've yet to prove to you."

"I have complete faith in your taste," Julia said.

Margaret had turned back to the paperwork piled on her desk, and Julia stared at her. She was definitely getting uneasy vibes from Margaret and she needed to decide whether to say something or not. She tried to keep their relationship both warm and yet impersonal, which probably wasn't fair to Margaret. But Julia had uncomfortable visions of emotional scenes at the office, and she didn't like to get too close.

Suddenly Margaret jabbed the air with the opener. "You gotta call Klein."

"Oh God, I knew I was trying to avoid something."

One of Julia's clients, Jacob Klein, had been a first novelist with promise, but judging from the second novel he'd sent them the week before, his promise had fizzled.

She stood up and stretched backward. Bones cracked. "I really think he ought to throw that book out and start a new one, but he's *not* going to want to hear that."

"Not Klein, no."

"I wish he weren't so handsome."

"Don't let his good looks weaken you," Margaret said.

"Here goes." Julia rushed to her desk, dramatically picked up the phone, and held the receiver high as she punched in Klein's number.

Minutes later, she yelled to Margaret, "I said he could stop by in an hour."

"Couldn't you just do it over the phone?"

"I let his good looks weaken me!"

Julia heard the faint squeak of Margaret's chair pushing away from the desk, and then Margaret's head swung around the door frame, black hair again fanning out.

"I'm throwing him out after ten minutes, tops. You're so behind on reading, it's getting serious."

"Okay, okay."

They smiled at each other, and Julia silently congratulated herself at having, and maintaining, the perfect assistant.

CHAPTER 3

D r. Wilson Streatfield yawned. He was riding the elevator up to the president's office of Columbia University.

He walked down the long corridor and checked his watch. Early, so he ducked into the men's room. Nothing very successful happened. He straightened his tie and smoothed his hair. Though he was forty years old, and pure white streaks shot through his black hair, it was still long, thick, and unruly.

The secretary's office was serene, decorated in mauve and cream with an excess of swirling. Wilson yawned again.

"Go on in," the secretary said.

President Rachel Sebastian was in her wheelchair, shaking food into an enormous fish tank.

Wilson cleared his throat.

She whirled the chair around and delivered a cool stare in his direction.

Her white hair was swept into an elegant French twist, revealing a patrician face. In fact, Wilson thought suddenly, she had a real resemblance to Katharine Hepburn. Despite the constant surprise that the president was a woman in a wheelchair, he was struck once again by her appeal.

"Sorry to interrupt," Wilson said.

"It's something about those darn fish. They hypnotize me."

"You'd like looking at slides under a microscope."

"Why is that?" She wheeled across the room, settled behind the desk, and gestured for Wilson to sit down.

"There's sort of an underwater quality to them."

"I can imagine that." Rachel made a minute adjustment to the brass letter opener that lay precisely perpendicular to the in box. "At any rate, you wanted to see me?"

That was the thing about her. She didn't allow any softness to creep in.

"I know that you're updated regularly about the research being conducted in our department," Wilson said.

She nodded, her grave eyes still disengaged.

"But I think it might be important for the university to capitalize on the drug just starting clinical trials at Dickson Pharmaceuticals."

He wanted to be low-key, but he couldn't control the way his body shifted forward in eagerness. "I guess I could've talked to public relations, but this is so, well, so *big* that I figured we should start at the top."

Rachel sat quietly, her eyes frank and ever so slightly skeptical. "And what is this *drug*?"

Her condescension annoyed him. Wilson took a deep breath and then stood to pace around the large office. "Of course, actual approval of the drug is years off, but, even in its trial stages, it could be vital for attracting government research funds to Columbia."

Hands in his pockets, he paused to peer at a print hanging on a far wall. He didn't know much about art, usually didn't even know when or if he liked something. This was in a dark, mottled brown ink on cream paper, and at first the picture made no sense. But then he saw that it was a man dressed in old-fashioned clothes riding a clownish horse. Both horse and man seemed about to fall down from excess hilarity.

He spoke with his back to Rachel. "I've found a drug that cures all addictions." His hands rose to his hips and rested there. He arched his back, testing the stretch.

Now he turned to face her. There was a long moment of silence as their eyes locked. "It's a big deal—we've been hush-hush about it for a long time, more than ten years since I first began the research— I'm not used to talking about it."

"Try."

"My wife doesn't even know." Wilson's voice

trembled, and he swallowed carefully. The excitement bubbled up and his chest felt all swimmy inside.

Finally Rachel seemed to get it. She backed up her wheelchair, rolled around her desk and across the office to where he stood. "Sit down." She pointed to a small couch under the print he'd been examining.

Wilson folded up on the couch, his legs now shaking as if he'd run a marathon.

Rachel moved closer, their knees nearly touching. She stretched out both hands and took his own in hers. "*All* addictions?"

He nodded, convinced she'd put him under some mild hypnosis. "Actually, it's a fungus that I discovered about ten years ago—we'd known about it in its asexual state, but I found it in the sexual state, feeding on a beetle grub in the woods of upstate New York, and that opened up all kinds of possibilities."

The president's restless hands fluttered, first to secure a tendril of white hair, then to yank the sleeves of her blouse up a quarter of an inch, and finally to settle, tight-fisted, in her lap. "Can you explain in a bit more detail?"

"What alcohol, tobacco, cocaine, and heroin do is elevate the level of dopamine in the brain." He checked whether she was truly interested, and found those gray eyes of hers trained on his. "Dopamine is a neurotransmitter, a molecule that carries messages around in the brain, from one neuron to another. Levels of dopamine can rise simply from a hug, a kiss, or a compliment—"

"So when I interrupt you now, to say that your work is utterly extraordinary, then the dopamine in your brain just went ka-pooey?" Her knobby, fascinating thumb, straightened and pointed to the ceiling.

Wilson grinned. "Yup."

"What does this drug of yours do?"

"It disables the dopamine gene, and at the same time, creates a sort of pseudo-effect, a mimicking of dopamine's activities but without the residual left-overs, like addiction."

"Having your cake, eating it, too . . . and not getting fat."

"Precisely." Wilson looked at the president's knees, which were chastely covered by translucent black silk stockings.

"It seems like a dream come true," she said. Her head dropped forward and she stared at her white hands. The nails were bitten all the way down so that the rounded tips of her fingers looked like balls of white bread dough.

"Seems?"

"Do you think it is?"

"It's a miracle."

"The medical profession tends to simply make discoveries and worry about their impact later." She pushed the wheelchair backward.

"Like this sheep they've cloned. God knows how much money's been spent on cloning a sheep and now the President's making official statements about how unethical human cloning would be," she said.

"Jesus Christ!" Wilson's voice rose.

Her gray eyes opened wider and she actually smiled again.

"This is a drug that'll end all addictions for the human race. There's nothing remotely unethical about that!"

"But people need to hide from themselves, their weaknesses—" she paused, "and their pain."

"I'd forgotten, your field is psychology."

"Yes, it is."

"But you don't *really* see anything wrong in controlling the addictive impulse, do you?"

"It's far more complicated that you've realized. What if people *abuse* the existence of your drug by choosing to become addicted to, say, cocaine, and then expect their family physician to write them a prescription that'll stop the craving? Where does that leave us?"

Wilson stood up and jammed both hands into his pants pockets. He felt the loose coins in one and the mass of keys in the other, and he jangled them deliberately.

President Sebastian pushed her wheelchair back several feet, whirled, and headed for her desk. "For now, I think we should schedule a task force to discuss how to handle the announcement and the probable publicity."

"Fine." Wilson walked toward the office door, then turned back for a moment.

Her long, elegant face was somber, but her eyes winked with fun. "It's a marvelous discovery. I'm terribly proud that you're here at Columbia with us."

He stared at her.

"I didn't mean to take away from the momentousness of this—not at all—my training means I think in a certain way, just as your training means *you* think in a certain way."

Wilson smiled slightly. "I know. And thanks." He was at the door when she spoke again.

"Have you named the drug?"

"No, not yet, just a number, the WS-100."

"You can do better than that, surely."

"I'm waiting for inspiration to strike."

"Ah, but you understand the futility of that."

His hand rose slowly and scratched at his hair. "I guess I do."

Wilson left the office without saying good-bye. But then, she hadn't said it, either.

ngela pushed the children in an enormous double stroller with wheels of inflated tires and an effortless brake system. Though a four-year-old was too old to be pushed in a stroller, Emily's tiny body and feather weight allowed Angela to spoil her with rides. They were a pretty sight, the late October sun catching in Angie's hair and the brisk air putting apples in the children's cheeks. She stopped at the Korean fruit and vegetable stand at the corner of Broadway and Eighty-fifth to buy four yellow pears and one ripe banana for Jimmy.

She couldn't get enough of the imported fruit available in New York City, or of having the Streatfields' money with which to buy. She glanced down at the carriage, proud that "her" children were so beautiful.

"You're lucky children, you know that?"

"You always say that," Emily said. Her skinny legs swung forward, bam, bam, bam.

"'Cause it's true."

Was her baby so lucky?

Angie forced herself to walk toward Riverside Park quickly. Her early rising often caused her to slow down right about this time in the morning, and she still had that extra weight to lose, from the baby.

Angie turned into the park and aimed the stroller in the direction of a particular bench that was close to the baby swings. She nodded at other nannies, but deliberately didn't speak. She'd made no friends during the months here, and she intended to keep it that way. She was lucky that the Streatfields had hired her, especially now with the way immigration laws were changing, and she'd no intention of getting them in trouble, not to mention herself.

She set the children up in swings next to each other and started pushing, first one, then the other. Her mind drifted back.

They were kissing behind a gravestone in the village cemetery. It was April and rain fell in a thin curtain. Her hair curled and clung to her cheeks, and puffs of warm air hung about their mouths when they stopped to breathe.

"I love you." Patrick swallowed and bent to kiss her again.

Her body flushed with the words and she pushed into him. She wanted to say the same back, but she was so shy she didn't know if she could. Angie wore an old oilskin jacket that creaked as her arms moved to hold him. Suddenly she buried her face in his neck, breathing in his smell of cigarettes and sweat. His sweat was sweet, like the work of the world wasn't too hard for him.

His fingers found their way beneath her heavy braid and tickled like flower petals. Her breathing surprised her, coming so fast. She pressed even harder against him and turned her head up to him, mouth so ready.

She felt like a baby bird in its nest, eager for a feeding.

Angela began to sing an Irish tune, the one she always sang first when they were at the swings, and Emily's voice piped in with the chorus. As Angela sang the second verse, she heard a man singing along. She looked to the left, so surprised by the Irish brogue that she forgot to appear indifferent.

A young man stood where a leg of the swing set was anchored by cement. He wore khaki pants and a soft, deep green shirt. Black hair curled in small, tight loops. He grabbed the steel leg high above his head and then slowly started to pull himself up by letting go of one hand at a time, reaching and grabbing higher. Up and up and up he went, all the while singing. His legs dangled, and Angie could see that his laced shoes were old and from Ireland.

Tears stood in her eyes as she laughed at him, hanging like a shirt on the laundry line. "Get on down. You'll break something," she shouted.

"Who, me?" he yelled back.

Suddenly Angela realized her own foolishness. What she didn't need was another charming Irish boy.

She turned away from him and began speaking to Emily. "Are you ready for the sandbox then, darling?"

"Yeth." Emily struggled to lift the bar holding her in the swing.

"Okay, let's get you down."

Quickly Angie plopped Jimmy into the stroller and hustled across the park. She wasn't surprised when he appeared, but this time she was ready.

He sat down on the log that framed the sandbox. She saw his hand, thick and strong, begin to dig wee holes. She waited for the usual, *where are you from, how long have you been here, when are you going back.* But there was nothing. She found herself wanting to hear that lilting Irish voice again. Oh, how she missed the sounds, like music, of her people talking. She was bent over Jimmy, her hands hovering to stop him from eating sand, and she just couldn't help herself.

She peeked.

And, oh my Lord, there were his blessed damn blue eyes peeking back at her.

Emily dug in the sand so deep that it turned cold and nasty. She glanced up at the man talking to her Angie. His blue eyes danced like a toy that's been turned on, and he was very good at digging.

She smoothed the sand back into her hole, trailing her fingers so that they made lines. She liked the lines, and she started making more of them. They looked like what you see in the book of songs Angie used for singing to them.

Emily carefully drew in notes, as best she could remember, placing them all over the lines. She hummed. The man talking to Angie was nice, the sun was hot, Jimmy wasn't crying, and she remembered the pear Angie bought at the fruit market. So yellow and sweet.

Klein ran both hands through his graying blond hair and abruptly leaned forward. His green eyes were bloodshot and he hadn't shaved that day. He reached into the breast pocket of his camel-hair jacket and pulled out a Mont Blanc pen.

Julia briefly closed her eyes, horrified by the image of that pen filling all those pages, hundreds of pages, with words and sentences and paragraphs. Every word of his new book had been fake, with the main character so self-conscious and pompous that you couldn't help loathing him.

Now he pulled out a little leather-bound notebook and flipped it open to a blank page, balancing it on his knee. With pen poised, he spoke. "What's wrong with the book?"

"Put away the note-taking devices."

He looked shocked, but he recapped the pen and closed the notebook.

"What I'm going to say will be difficult for you to

hear." Julia crossed her legs and wrapped her ankles into a tight, discreet knot.

Klein looked like he was about to pass out.

"I think you should put this book aside." She deliberately didn't use the book's title, as a further suggestion that the book didn't really exist. "Let it be on the back burner, simmering, while you work on something new."

He turned completely white, his stubble of beard black and coarse.

"Write *another* book?" Klein whispered.

"You know, sometimes one book, though in itself not entirely successful, is really like the *prelude*. And the book that follows this prelude, if you will, practically writes itself."

She hoped he wouldn't toss his cookies right in her office. She wasn't conning him. In fact, she believed the next novel would be great, and that he'd write it fast. She felt that way not merely because he was a handsome devil, though it never hurt to be handsome when it came to selling books to a recalcitrant public. Look at John Irving.

He stared at her. To her surprise, she saw his eyes change from an ominous green to a deeper color, almost black. It happened to her all the time, men's eyes shifting from sun to shadow, interest to desire. All the time, that is, except at home.

She'd learned how to deflect the attention, but Julia still felt a trickle of sweat between her breasts.

"I was thinking maybe I should try nonfiction." Klein's eyes had shifted again into a disinterested, professional expression.

"Do you have something in mind, you know, an idea? With nonfiction, all I need to get a decent advance is an outline."

"Aren't memoirs big right now?"

"Were. I think trends like that are to be avoided. Now, if you've had an abusive childhood, or your sister was kidnapped, or something, then okay, we can talk about it."

"How's this for a title? *A Perfectly Ordinary Life.*" He grinned at her.

One-book writers were scattered everywhere these days, weedy seeds blown over inhospitable ground, but Julia took pride in never yet having lost a client to the one-book garden.

"I did have an idea last night—when I couldn't sleep," Jacob said, "a sort of reversal of the movie *The Graduate,* where a young man just graduating from college returns home and begins a typical affair with a woman his own age. Then he meets her mother, who's divorced, and falls madly in love."

"What a great idea!"

"Do you really think so?"

"Get to work. We could call it *The Graduate, Part Two.*"

Klein's handsome face split into a grin. "I've never gotten an idea from the right side of my brain, to be honest. It's a little nerve-racking."

"You've been writing literary fiction up until now. But maybe you're ready to try something different." Julia hoped she'd made the idea of writing commercial fiction *more* of a challenge than literary fiction. Suddenly she saw him as a popular writer.

"It's appealing," he said.

"I want a ten-page outline and fifty pages, we'll go from there."

He reared back, grinning more widely. "Jesus."

After he'd been sent on his way, Margaret handed her a stack of pink slips. "He was here a half hour," she scolded Julia.

"And he came up with a terrific, commercial idea," Julia muttered as she skipped through the messages.

She put on the headset of her phone, ready to make calls for several hours, but she paused before dialing the first number. Her eyes stared at the business office across from hers in the building next door. A man in a white shirt and tie was pacing back and forth, holding a dictating gadget close to his mouth. He looked like he was kissing the darn thing, and then she wondered why she was thinking about kissing at all. Wilson hadn't kissed her in a long time.

CHAPTER 5

"Are you legal?" George said, soft as fresh butter.

She kept her head bent over the baby, the long braid slipping across her left shoulder. Pretty hair.

She'll try to run, he thought, watching her scoop up the baby.

"Emmy, let's go, time for lunch," she said.

The baby wailed as she rubbed the sand off his hands.

"No!" the child, Emmy, said.

"I'm not meaning any harm," George said.

Still she didn't answer.

He had three days. But she might not come to the

park tomorrow or the day after, to avoid him.

"Maybe you'd like to *be* legal," he said.

She shot him a look and her movements slowed.

"I can't make any promises, but it's a possibility." George stood and stamped his shoes free of sand. He smelled something burning, leaves maybe, and he looked around for smoke.

Fast, she got both kids into the stroller.

"Your name's Angela Byrne, you've had an illegitimate baby which you put up for adoption eight months ago, and you're an illegal immigrant. I wouldn't go running away if I were you." George watched her startled face turn toward him, mouth open in a small circle.

"Leave me alone. I'm doing no harm." Angela whispered the words.

"We need a little cooperation, a little help with an important project, that's all."

"What kind of project?"

"Let's call it a research project." George looked around carefully, checking to see if they could be overheard.

The kids stuck in the stroller began to fuss and carry on, irritating him. He glared at them.

Angela knelt down and rummaged in the large canvas bag hanging off the back of the stroller. She pulled out a pear and gave it to Emily, then peeled a banana, breaking off bits in her fingers and pressing them into the baby's mouth. The baby smacked his lips, happy.

Still kneeling, she stared up at him.

"Your boss, Dr. Streatfield, has some papers of interest to us. That's all," George said.

"I don't know about his work."

"We want the papers. You don't have to know anything. You don't matter. Remember playing Whisper Down the Lane? You're just playing the game, passing the message."

Slowly Angela rose from where she'd been kneeling next to the baby.

The index finger of her right hand stroked her right eyebrow, obsessively smoothing the already smooth brow of pale red hair. It arched slightly, giving her a pleasant expression. But when she finally stopped the gesture, her brow seemed to deflate and flatten, and he realized that her finger had been forcing the brow up.

"You mean like spying on him?" she said.

He shrugged, bored by her reluctance. She was stupid, that was clear. "You got a pear for me?"

She gaped at him for just a moment. Then she bent over, fished around in the bag, and brought out a pear. The sun shone on the pear she offered him in the palm of her outstretched hand. A yellow jacket circled, then darted down to the little girl's pear. He grabbed the pear from her hand as Angela turned to wave the bee away from the children.

George took a big juicy bite. His left hand slipped into his pants pocket and he felt there the key to his own apartment. His fingers fiddled, memorizing the key's shape.

He wanted to walk through the apartment wearing only his boxers and drinking a tumbler of good whiskey, the thick carpet soft under his bare feet. He planned to make a call back home to his granny. He'd left Dublin suddenly, and he hadn't said good-bye to her. He could've written, but somehow writing after all these months didn't have any punch.

George looked down where Angela was again kneeling, feeding banana to the baby and shooing at the bees.

She tilted her head back to look up at him, squinting in the sun. "I won't do it."

"You have to."

"I'll leave them."

"Sweetheart," he said, "we'll find you and that'll be that."

"So I get deported."

"Do they deport dead bodies?"

She ducked her head. He gazed around the park, waiting.

"He brings home a briefcase every night, but that's all. He doesn't have a study in the apartment," Angie said.

"That'll be a start. Then we'll see."

She frowned. "But if I take something, he's going to miss it the very next day."

Now George knelt next to her, pear juice dripping off his chin. He swiped at the juice with his shirt sleeve and was pleased to see discomfort cross Angie's face. She didn't like him messing up his shirt. "You get 'em to me, I make copies, give 'em back, and then you leave 'em somewhere that *he* might have left 'em."

Angie looked relieved.

"One problem," George said. "The papers we want might be at his lab. Maybe they're too secret for him to be carrying home."

"I can't get papers out of his lab!"

George opened his eyes wide with mock surprise. "Yes, you can."

"I'm all sticky," Emily complained, holding up her hands for Angela to see.

"Don't worry yourself," Angie said, "we'll clean you up." She pulled out a predampened tissue, the kind you use on a baby's bottom, and scrubbed at Emily's hands.

Emily slid down in the stroller, thrusting her legs and feet straight out and then kicking. A high-pitched whine escaped.

Suddenly Angie stood up, leaving George still kneeling below her. She ignored Emily's obvious complaints. "They have all this security. I went there once, with the children, and you've got to sign in and all sorts of things." Her voice trembled and he could see her hands shaking.

George stood and stretched nonchalantly. The bones in his back popped, which felt so good that he dropped the half-eaten pear and loudly cracked the knuckles of both hands.

Angela looked down at the children in the stroller. She had those sandy pale eyelashes, common to redheads. He reached over and placed his thumbs gently over the half-closed eyelids. Then he pressed.

"It's a little problem you're going to have to

solve." He pressed harder and he felt the tension in her body as she stood still. Her eyeballs felt like the marbles he played with in the streets of Dublin as a boy. He hadn't really liked the way those marbles rolled and scattered all over the place. He always felt like the marbles had it in for him, little George McDuff who didn't have a mother or father. Like the marbles were the eyes of the world upon him, laughing eyes, jeering eyes, crying eyes.

George snatched away his thumbs and she immediately opened her wet eyes to look at him.

They were full of terror.

"I'll see you tomorrow," George said. "Ten o'clock at Jack's Printing, corner of Broadway and Ninety-fifth." He stared hard at her, confirming the appointment and his power.

Then he turned and walked slowly away. As he passed an empty seesaw, he grabbed the seat high up in the air and viciously yanked it down, sending the opposite seat sailing high and hitting its full length with a jolt.

Angela fed the children their lunch and got them down for naps. The major cleaning of the apartment was done weekly by a team of three Jamaican women, so she usually spent their nap time on any number of household chores, like folding the laundry, ironing, doing preliminary dinner preparation, or attacking a set of cupboards that needed tidying.

But that day she went to her room. She stood still and alone in the center of the blue and white rug and then she turned in a slow, methodical circle, trying to figure out why she'd come in there and what she wanted to do.

What she wanted to do was lie down on the bed, but at the same time, she didn't want to mess up the neat bedspread. If she lay down and the bedspread wrinkled under her body, which of course it would have to no matter how careful she was, then she felt as if the wrinkles would work their way into her body, creating cracks like mud that dries and then splits.

She went into the small bathroom attached to her room and washed her hands. She scrubbed and scrubbed, checking her fingernails repeatedly. Lost in the activity, her head rose, and she caught sight of her face in the mirror. She was pure white in color, with dots of red high on her thin cheeks. She'd been pretty, back home.

Probably her mother, Father James, and Sister Brigid all blamed her downfall on that. Sure, they never blamed anyone else. The men couldn't help themselves, like animals they were, and it was up to the young ladies to keep life moral. She touched her eyebrow with a slightly damp finger, stroking.

She knew it wasn't because she was pretty, because how could prettiness have brought this new trouble on her? And trouble was following her, that was clear now. She would turn in one direction and start that way, trying to be good and hardworking, just like she'd been taught, just like she believed in, and then she'd run into a wall.

So she'd take a deep breath, the kind of breath

that filled your lungs with cold, fresh, morning air, and she'd turn again, marching down a new road. Granted, she might not know her way, and granted, she moved slowly. But she tried. She kept trying.

This Irish boy meant every word he said. If she didn't cooperate, she'd be dead. But then, dead was maybe where she belonged. She didn't think she'd go to hell. Angela turned off the water still rushing into the sink. She dried her hands, refolded the hand towel into thirds, and hung the towel on the brass ring.

She headed down the hall to the laundry room. Though this room had no window and was, after all, merely a small space where you did the laundry and ironing, Angela adored it. The walls were painted bright white, and the floor was tiled with tiny squares of black, green, white, and blue, made into a larger design. The washer and dryer were white and clean, and she kept the laundry sink scoured white.

Angela took out the dry clothes and put them into a white woven plastic basket, then carefully transferred the wet clean clothes from the washer into the dryer. When the dryer began its busy, rhythmical thrumming, she started to fold the dry clothes.

She never failed to think of her mother when she worked in the laundry room, and she would, in her mind, lord it over her, her mother who had to wash the clothes by hand and hang them out on the line to dry. She'd smooth the sheets and towels, match corners to corners, so precise and careful, and she'd feel like she was telling her mother, *See. I've done all right by myself. You were wrong.*

But not today. Today she tried to think what to do. If she ran away in the middle of the night, how could they find her? And why would they bother? They needed Dr. Streatfield's papers. And if she no longer worked for the Streatfields, then she'd be of no use.

Only, she didn't think she could leave. Emily and Jimmy meant so much to her, and she'd done so much leaving in the last year. If that had been her mistake, always leaving, if that was why trouble chased her, then she'd have to stay. She'd have to turn toward the trouble, face it, and not budge.

CHAPTER 6

S he'd rattled him, no question about it. In the elevator going down to the street, Wilson's mind tumbled with the troubling questions President Sebastian had raised. The elevator doors slid open and he stepped slowly across the entrance hall. It had been renovated at some point in the past five years, since the last time Wilson had been in the building—he didn't usually have much call for private appointments with Columbia's president—and the space now soared with an arched ceiling and concealed lighting. Tall ficus trees and comfortable seating areas were scattered about, making it seem almost hotel-like.

He paused in the center of the hall to check the

time on his wristwatch. One o'clock, past lunchtime, and he hadn't eaten since early that morning. Usually he ate in the lab's lunchroom, or his own small office, sometimes alone but more often with colleagues. They invariably talked about work. It was really all they wanted to talk about, Wilson included. But now the idea of going back to the lab was stultifying. He thought of going home, except that home would be bursting with children, sunlight, dust, and strong smells like dirty diapers, tomato soup, and clean laundry. Home was not appealing.

Then he remembered it was Wednesday. Quickly his mind surveyed what had been the afternoon's schedule: utterly administrative in nature and utterly forgettable, especially when he realized that he hadn't taken an afternoon off—not even for illness—in ten years.

Checking his watch again, he rushed through the enormous double doors and into the street, where he hailed cabs for ten fruitless minutes. It was the lunch hour, after all, but he'd forgotten how many people actually hit the streets and went out to lunch. It made him vaguely uneasy, the notion that so many people were wasting time like this. How did anything get accomplished?

Finally a taxi pulled over. He leapt in and slammed the door too hard.

"The Metropolitan Opera House, at Lincoln Center." Wilson spoke fast, leaning forward so that his mouth was close to the cabbie's ear.

Now that he'd decided what he wanted to do with

the afternoon, he worried that he wouldn't get there in time. He was quiet for twenty blocks, fretting.

"I need to make the two o'clock matinee," he said finally.

The cabbie didn't reply, and Wilson realized that so far he'd not said a word. He glanced at the man's ID displayed on the car's dashboard. Squinting, he tried to make out the name, but it was something profoundly foreign.

"You know where we're going, right?" he said.

"*Fidelio,* at two o'clock, sure, I know," the cabbie said.

Wilson thought he sounded Russian.

"Is that's what on?"

"You don't know what's on?" The cabbie shot him a disbelieving look. "You got a ticket?"

"No, I figured I could grab a single seat."

The cabbie shrugged, not answering.

"You don't think I can?"

"I'm not Ticketmaster!"

The taxi careened along and Wilson was quiet for a few moments. "Are you Russian?"

"Yes, sir."

"Do you, ummm, know opera?"

The cabbie opened his mouth and in a thunderous voice began to sing the bass part of the opera's first quartet, *Mir ist so wunderbar* ("How wondrous the emotion.")

Suddenly his mouth snapped shut. The End.

Wilson clapped his hands and shouted, "Bravo, bravo!"

Again there was an awkward silence, and it occurred to Wilson that he might invite this man to join him at the opera. He was obviously cultured and undoubtedly well educated. But you didn't invite New York City cabbies to attend the opera with you, and anyway, Wilson wanted to go alone.

He hated to listen to music with anyone he knew sitting next to him. This fetish of his had become a bit of a sore point between Julia and himself, since they'd discovered each other at a Met performance of Puccini's *Turandot*.

Twelve years before, Wilson had elbowed his way to the front of the crowd around the bar and demanded the bartender's attention quickly just by virtue of his height, then surprised himself by ordering a martini instead of white wine. He waited, drumming long fingers on the marble, until he became aware of someone's attention. He glanced to the left without moving his head. He had a shy man's gift for peripheral vision. A woman with short, white-blond hair glared at him. She didn't just give him a look and then turn away. Her entire upper body and head were turned sideways, facing him, and her green eyes drilled into him.

He tried sending her a small smile and then went back to waiting for his drink.

"I was ahead of you, in case you're interested."

There was no question that the blond woman had spoken.

Wilson flushed, truly embarrassed. "I'm sorry, I didn't know—"

"What do you mean you didn't know? I was standing right here with my hand raised to get the bartender's attention."

"I didn't see you, I'm so sorry."

His drink arrived and he immediately spoke. "I seem to have ordered out of turn. Could you please take her order?"

The bartender's eyes were amused. "What can I get you?" the bartender said to the blond woman.

"I'd like a double scotch on the rocks, please." She grinned at the bartender.

Wilson sipped his martini. "I guess it's true that tall people get faster service."

"Men, too."

"Do you think so?"

"I don't *think* so, I know so."

Her green eyes shone, and her short blond hair begged for his hand to reach out and stroke it, then to cup the back of her head in his large hand, and finally, to scratch her scalp. He'd never felt such an absurd desire toward anyone else, except himself. Scratching his own head was a favorite gesture.

Her drink arrived and she plunked down a twenty dollar bill.

She sipped her drink, and then he knew she was looking at him. This time, only her eyes moved.

"I bet you're a scientist," she said.

His left hand rose to his head and scratched vigorously. "How did you know that?"

"You have that distracted look."

"I've never understood why it's called *distracted*.

If anything, a scientist has to be focused and alert."

"You're distracted from the rest of the world, and the rest of the world is what interests most people."

Wilson sipped his martini again, thinking. He liked this kind of conversation, somehow vaguely personal and vaguely impersonal at the same time. "Are you interested in the rest of the world?"

Now her head joined her eyes in their swivel toward him. "Oh yes, completely."

Their eyes met.

He swallowed, wanting to keep talking but needing to beat down the fear from what he'd seen in her eyes. "And, ummm, what do you do?"

"I just hung up my shingle as a literary agent." Her voice was proud and a little nervous.

What on earth was a literary agent, he wondered. He gulped the martini.

"Do you know what a literary agent does?" she asked.

"Well, I'm not really certain, but that's because I've been so *distracted*." He smiled and turned his body so that he faced her.

"I'm the middle man—person—between the writer of a book and the publisher."

He nodded, suddenly realizing he'd heard of this because of a textbook one of his colleagues wrote. The man had used an agent, which wasn't a common occurrence in the scientific community. The agent sold the book to a large publishing company and they'd all been amazed by the size of the advance.

"I bet you're good," he said.

She turned toward him, but her eyes were still sharp when she spoke. "What makes you say that?"

"You're obviously smart and you scare the pants off me."

"The pants, huh?"

He felt the flush of deep red spreading up his neck and then into his face. Sweat broke out at his hairline and across his upper lip.

Wilson stared at her without speaking.

She stared back. Then her eyes softened, as if she'd washed the dazzling green with a pot of white paint, her cheeks flushed pale pink in the ivory skin of her face, and her gentle pale lips turned down.

At first Wilson thought she was frowning and he prepared himself for more snappy words. But then he saw that she was trying to keep from laughing.

It was no use. Her head tipped back and her white throat winked at him. Laughter exploded. When her head bounced forward again, so that he could see her face, she spoke. "Would you like to go out to dinner tonight?"

The cabbie swung expertly to the curb in front of the Met. "Enjoy," he said after Wilson paid him and left a large tip.

"Thanks, I will."

He ran to the box office, managed to get a ticket for sixth row, center, at a discount, and then tore up the wide, red-carpeted stairs.

"Can I make a run to the men's room?" he asked the usher.

"No problem."

When Wilson settled in his seat, he still had five minutes until curtain. He thought again about President Sebastian. He was no longer rattled by her comments. He'd discovered something marvelous, and he was proud of the accomplishment.

For himself, he was worried that the twin side effects of fame and fortune would be, well, *distracting*. He'd initially started researching the fungus as an antidepressant. He'd had no notion of its other possibilities, and the actual discovery had been entirely by accident, or not really an accident, more like he was fooling around. How could he keep fooling around if people were clamoring to talk to him?

Maybe Julia would help. She could step in front and be his spokesperson. It was what she did best, and he didn't think she'd mind the new role. He sighed, pleased by this idea. When he thought of their marriage, the kind of thought that was extremely rare for him, he imagined it as a marriage of silence. They connected, their children made that obvious, but it was a connection profoundly quiet and inarticulate. It made him happy, though not complete. Wilson knew, and he believed Julia understood, that he was a man who stood alone.

The theater darkened and the maestro entered from the left. The audience clapped and Wilson felt his excitement bubbling up. God, he loved the opera.

He didn't need to read the program to remind himself that *Fidelio* told the story of Leonora's disguise as a man to rescue her imprisoned husband.

Sing out in love:
Florestan is mine again!
I succeeded through love
In freeing you from chains.

The curtain rose and Wilson disappeared into the music and story. Only here and in the lab could he lose himself. Nothing else, including sex, ever claimed him so completely.

When he left the Met nearly three hours later, he knew he wanted to stop on the way home to buy a bottle of champagne. It was time to tell Julia about WS-100, and he'd make an occasion out of it, just the way Julia did when she sold a book for six figures.

CHAPTER 7

Angela peered into the large iron pot of Irish stew, stirring gently. Carrots, potatoes, onions, and hunks of lamb tumbled in the rich brown sauce, and the most heavenly smell in the world wafted into her face. She swallowed, sickened with fear.

It seemed too much of a coincidence that Dr. Streatfield would come home early for the first time in the six months she'd lived with them, toting a bottle of champagne. He'd asked her to set the table for dinner in the dining room, and he'd been delighted that she'd made the stew.

"Can I watch TV?" Emily asked.

When Angie turned away from the pot to look at

her, she could see that Emmy was tired, despite her long nap. It was five o'clock in the evening, the time when good little Irish children had had their tea, baths, and were ready for one fairy tale before going to bed. Here in America, where so many parents worked, children stayed up until all hours. Angela disapproved.

But Julia disapproved of television. She periodically threatened to get rid of their one set in the library. Angie was thinking of splurging a little of her own savings on a black and white, used television, just for her room. She thought Julia would say it was all right. Only, she liked Julia to think well of her. Perhaps it wasn't worth risking the disapproval.

"How about if I read you a story instead?"

Emily's face shone. She loved books every bit as much as television, but you needed a grown-up's help for a book.

"Go pick out one of the new library books, and bring it here so I can keep an eye on the stew."

As she sat at the kitchen table reading aloud, she was conscious, in a way she wasn't when she just talked, of her Irish accent. She pretended to the Streatfields that her voice was embarrassing to her, but she knew it was actually charming. As long as she lived in America, even after becoming a citizen, she would keep her Irish voice.

The story's language had rhythm, and Angela found herself seduced into the reading, briefly forgetting that her life, her very life, was threatened.

● ● ●

"Hi." Wilson stood framed in the library entrance, still dressed in a good suit and wearing a strange expression on his face. He held a tall glass packed with ice and a dark liquid.

"What a surprise. You're home early." Julia walked forward and kissed him hard on the cheek. He'd remembered, she was sure of it.

"It was a good day. I wanted to celebrate."

To kiss Wilson on the lips, she had to rise up on her toes slightly. If he expected the kiss, he usually bent over to meet her. Tonight he bent so far over that her high heels took care of the difference. He kissed her lightly on the lips.

"I thought we'd save the champagne for dinner, okay?" Wilson said.

"Mommy, Mommy!" Emily's cries preceded her appearance from the kitchen.

"You've been discovered," Wilson said.

"Where's my sweetie girl?"

"I'm here!" Emily clutched Julia around the legs.

Julia knelt and lifted Emily into her arms. She smelled clean and wonderful. "Mmm," she said, nuzzling her, "you've had your bath."

"Yup," Emily said.

"And what else did you do today?"

"Went to the park and now Angie's reading me a story."

The sweep of gratitude for Angela's appearance in their lives happened at least several times a day to Julia. Her advertisement for a live-in nanny, after Jimmy was born, had brought a deluge of calls, but

Julia ended up interviewing only three candidates. Angela had claimed to have her green card. Julia knew she ought to have asked to see the card, but she'd been so charmed by this lovely Irish girl that she'd just plain forgotten about it. Her instincts were good.

"Sounds great." She put Emily down. "Where's my baby boy?"

"He's been keeping me company in the library," Wilson said.

Julia walked into the library and found Jimmy lying on a blanket in the middle of the floor, his arms and legs waving like crazy. Small hooting noises came out of his puckered mouth. Borderline crying. She crouched next to him, cooing her hellos. His face changed in a second, split into a big smile. Julia sat him up and then rose slowly, careful in her high heels, cuddling him against her.

The mahogany paneling sucked the library's subdued light and color into its thirsty wood so that the room seemed to beam and pulsate with warmth. Though Julia disapproved of fake fires, she'd allowed one in this room, and tonight it glowed.

"You'll get spit-up all over your suit." Wilson collapsed into a far corner of the couch.

"I don't mind," she said, more to Jimmy than Wilson.

She looked over Jimmy's head. "I'm amazed that my *distracted* husband remembered."

"Remembered what?" He glanced at the newspaper and not up at her face.

She sat down next to him on the couch. A sick feeling swept through her body, centering on her chest. "Our tenth wedding anniversary."

There was a long, unnatural silence. Well, why else would he have gotten champagne? Julia stood again, balancing Jimmy on her hip, and walked over to the partner's desk which filled one small wall of the room. She slid open a bottom drawer and bent to take out a white card. Then she walked back across the room and handed Wilson the card.

He'd forgotten, of course.

Wilson took the card, his face reddening only a bit. He ripped it open and gave it a cursory reading, then he looked at her. "I'm sorry, I did forget."

"What's the champagne for then?"

"Some exciting news I have."

Julia turned away from him, bouncing Jimmy more than necessary.

"Angela made an Irish stew—can't you smell it?—and we'll be eating in the dining room." He dropped his voice to a whisper. "I invited her to join us. She's so great that I hated—"

"Of course she should eat with us."

"I thought we could wait until Jimmy goes to sleep at seven o'clock."

"Now, there's a good idea." Julia spoke mockingly into Jimmy's face, who gave a great crow of delight. She kissed his cheek over and over again.

Julia crossed the room to the couch and sat down in the opposite corner with Jimmy settled comfortably in her lap. Emily appeared in the doorway, a white ruffled apron tied around her waist, carrying a small white pad of paper and a red crayon.

She minced across the room. "May I take your drink order?" she asked.

"Oh my, how elegant," Julia said. "Yes, please, may I have a scotch on the rocks?"

Emily bent nearly double over the pad, trying to write in great sweeping strokes with the red crayon. "A—scotch—on—the—rocks," she muttered to herself.

"That's right, madam."

Emily turned and ran from the room, the apron tangling between her legs. "A scotch on the rocks," she yelled at the top of her lungs.

They could hear Angela laughing in the kitchen.

"This certainly is a celebration."

"Oh, come on, you know I'm a wipeout when it comes to the romantic stuff."

Julia didn't answer.

Emily reappeared in the doorway, the apron even more mangled between her legs and her entire being concentrated on carrying the glass of scotch without spilling. It looked unlikely that she'd succeed.

"Can I help you with that?" Wilson leaned forward and placed his own drink on the small cherry coffee table.

"No!" she screamed.

Emily inched across the room. The liquid rocked dangerously, splashing against the glass.

Julia handed Jimmy to Wilson. Then she sat forward, all the way to the edge of the couch, and held out her hand for the drink. "Thank you, madam."

Her hand closed around the drink, but something about the tangle of apron between Emily's legs caused her to make a sudden lurch. Half the drink reared up and spilled over Julia's hand.

Emily turned away, not noticing this small failure, and ran back out of the library.

"Thanks, Angela!" Julia called out.

"Not at all," she sang from the kitchen.

Julia shook her hand several times, her expression amused.

"Should I get a paper towel?" he said.

"No, it's okay." She leaned back, took a gulp of scotch, and screwed up her face. "A little strong."

"Lucky you."

Wilson carried Jimmy back over to the blanket and settled him stomach-down, then moved several toys to within reach.

"Oh, before I forget, your mom called."

"Do I have to call back tonight?"

"Tomorrow will be fine, since she told me what she was calling about." Wilson settled back in the couch and picked up his drink, a dark rum and tonic.

"Do I want to hear this?"

He grinned. "Not really."

He thought she'd forgiven him.

"Will this ruin your announcement later?"

"Nothing's going to ruin that."

Julia had her doubts.

"Just tell me."

"They're coming for Thanksgiving."

"Please, no."

"Your mother's bringing the cranberry sauce."

"All the way from California? Jesus, I don't want her damn cranberry sauce."

"Watch your language." Wilson pointed with his chin to where Jimmy lay, contented and mouthing a rattle.

"I don't think Jimmy's old enough to know the difference between damn and dog."

Wilson just looked at her.

"Double damn dog." She was furious that her parents had invited themselves for Thanksgiving.

"Julia, come on, don't get all worked up. They're only staying four days. We can manage."

"They're not your parents."

"I know."

She could feel the bad mood sweep over her. Thanksgiving with Mom and Dad. Double damn dog. Thanksgiving was three weeks away. Pretend it's a year away, she thought. Just pretend.

"So make my bad mood better," Julia said. "Tell me your exciting news."

Wilson wagged a finger.

He was actually *teasing* her.

She carefully put her drink down on the table, then leapt across the couch so that she crushed him. "You forgot our tenth wedding anniversary, so the least you can do is tell me something exciting." She pounded his chest with both fists.

Suddenly Jimmy began to howl.

"Now look what you've done." Wilson's hands

hovered protectively about his waist and chest. "The baby's upset."

Julia stood up and slid her hands seductively down her hips, straightening her skirt. "I'll get you."

Then she turned and went to pick up Jimmy. Holding him close, she flounced out of the room.

"Where're you going?" Wilson said.

"Diaper duty calls."

The dining room was Julia's failure at decorating, though she wasn't sure what had gone wrong. The room was too large and without focus. She'd thought her parents' double pedestal mahogany table would fill it up, and the walls were glazed a deep red, but it still echoed with a coldness that only a large group of people could dispel.

"I would like to propose a toast." Wilson held the tall, thin glass high.

Julia and Angela raised their glasses to meet Wilson's.

"To my discovery." Wilson leaned over and clinked his glass first against Julia's and then Angela's.

"*What* discovery?" Julia exclaimed. She sipped at her champagne even while she waited impatiently.

Wilson sat down, his efforts at being dramatic already exhausted. "I've developed a drug that cures all addictive cravings."

Now Julia felt the flush creeping up her neck. It might have been the champagne, but she didn't think so. She was turning bright red because something in

Wilson's words, in the simplicity of his statement, had provided a clue.

This was winning the lottery.

"You mean like *drug* addictions?" Angela said in her pure voice.

"Drugs, yes, cocaine, heroin, and so forth."

"But how did you do this?" Julia's voice trembled.

"Remember that fungus I thought might have potential as an antidepressant?"

"Of course I remember—"

"It never worked as an antidepressant," Wilson interrupted, "or not as well as some of the subsequent drugs we've found, but it seemed to have other properties that I found interesting. I got funding first from the government and then Dickson Pharmaceuticals, and I've been working on it ever since. The clinical trials have begun, and the FDA will start human trials very soon. We're still several years away from the drug's release. But I have no doubts that it'll be approved."

"You didn't say anything."

"You didn't ask." Wilson put on a mock peeved expression before raising his glass and draining his champagne.

Angela came into the dining room, though Julia hadn't noticed her leave the room, carrying a bowl of Irish stew. She placed it carefully in front of Julia.

"No, serve Wilson first," Julia said.

She'd never even asked. True, but he never asked

much about her work either. Sometimes she told him things when she was excited and couldn't keep her mouth shut, but his response was always quiet. *That's great, dear. Sounds wonderful, sweetie.*

Angela returned with bowls of stew for both Julia and herself.

Julia picked up a small piece of lamb and put it in her mouth. She held it there, savoring the flavor. "This is delicious."

Angela blushed, that pure white skin of hers becoming an uncomfortable red color.

"I met with President Sebastian this morning—she's excited about what it'll mean to Columbia."

"I can't believe it." Julia chewed and swallowed a large spoonful of stew.

"Actually, the whole thing's making me nervous."

They heard a plaintive wail from somewhere in the kids' bedrooms. Emily was supposed to be sitting up in bed and looking at picture books, while Jimmy slept.

Angela leapt to her feet.

"No, Angie, I'll take care of it. You've been with them all day." Julia stood up and tossed down her linen napkin.

Angela whirled around, nearly to the kitchen. "Please, I want to help, please stay with Dr. Streatfield and enjoy your dinner."

Her face was so white and drawn that Julia immediately sat down again. "Thanks, Angie."

"You're so welcome," she whispered.

Julia waited a few seconds, then leaned forward

and peered into the kitchen. "Do you think something's wrong?"

"She's fine." Wilson picked up his champagne glass and drained it, then knocked the glass gently against Julia's. "You gotta keep up with me."

Julia lifted her glass and drank quickly. Bubbles shot up her nose and she sneezed. "Tell me what this is going to mean. I have an idea, but—"

"It means a lot of money, to begin with," Wilson interrupted, "and it means I'll be somewhat, well, famous." He filled his spoon with stew and slurped it up.

"How much money?"

"I don't know exactly." Wilson's face flushed. "Millions, probably."

Julia stood up, walked around the table, and embraced him. "I'm so proud of you."

His head dropped forward, unsuccessfully trying to hide his grin. "Thanks."

She returned to her seat and picked up her soup spoon. "When will all this go public?"

"About six months before it's approved."

"Can I tell people?"

"Selectively. We've got the patent, and I'm working on an article for *The New England Journal,* but Columbia wants to do a press conference for the public announcement."

She tapped her knife against the stem of the champagne glass, ping, ping, ping. "You know, this could make an interesting book."

"Do you think so?" His head cocked to the side, watching her.

"Yeah, I do. *The Cure: A Story of Discovery*."

"I've been thrashing around, trying to decide what to focus on next."

"So write me a book."

"I don't think I write well enough to do it."

"We'll use a book doctor to clean it up. You just do a draft and we go from there." She picked up her champagne glass and again drained it. "In fact, if you write up a proposal, I bet I can get a contract and significant advance up front."

"Okay." Wilson poured them both more champagne. "We're going to be blotto."

"I love it when you're drunk."

When Wilson got slightly drunk, really only high, he became more talkative. Once he'd even said she was beautiful. He wasn't a romantic man, but then, she wasn't a romantic woman. Julia approved of their relationship, since it seemed the sort of coupling one should expect between clever, ambitious, cultured people. Still, even believing that, she sometimes felt an odd yearning for more. To be beautiful in his eyes, for example.

S ince it was their tenth wedding anniversary, Angela insisted on cleaning up the kitchen alone. Wilson was in Emily's bedroom, reading her a story. With all the stories that child had read to her, Julia figured she'd have to become a writer. She smiled at the silly thought of conducting an auction for her daughter's first novel, let's see, at about age fourteen. She'd be precocious, given Wilson's genes. Julia wandered to the library and dropped into a corner of the couch. Her head spun from the champagne. She picked up the remote control for the television, aimed, and then didn't fire. CNN couldn't match the excitement of Wilson's news.

A sheaf of typed pages were rubber-banded together, plunked in the middle of the coffee table. She picked the bundle up, guessing it was a draft of an article discussing the drug, and started to read.

IN THE RECORD-BREAKING HEAT OF JULY, 1989, I WENT SEARCHING FOR UNUSUAL FUNGI IN THE FORESTS OF UPSTATE NEW YORK.

Hey, Wilson wasn't a bad writer. Not at all. This had real style and narrative intensity. She felt her stomach flip-flop the way it always did when she found a book worth reading and, therefore, selling.

AS SCIENCE HAS PROVED OVER AND OVER AGAIN, IT'S WHEN YOU LEAST EXPECT IT THAT A MAJOR DISCOVERY OCCURS. I WAS CRAWLING ON MY BELLY WHEN I SAW A BEETLE SCOOT UNDER A BUNCH OF DRIED LEAVES. IN THAT INSTANT, I'D ALSO SEEN SOME KIND OF BULGING GROWTH EXTRUDING FROM THE TOP OF THE BEETLE'S HEAD. I GRABBED THE BEETLE . . .

Oh my God.

Julia dropped the papers, feeling their heavy weight in the deep of her lap. She folded her hands neatly on top of them. She tried to keep them calm and steady, but she found herself utterly unable to control the way her hands tightened together, gripped hard in a fist of anger.

Wilson strolled into the library. "I slurred some

words in *Good-Night, Moon,*" he said. "Do you think I'll go to hell for such sacrilege?"

When she looked at him, he knew that she was angry. And, strangely, she exuded a wonderful beauty. The red silk skirt of her suit framed the draft of the article in her lap, and her hands were gripped on top of the papers. The champagne had flushed her cheeks bright pink, and a dangerous glitter shone from green eyes. Blond hair, always spiky, stood up as if electrified.

"What's the matter?" he said.

"I read the first paragraph." Her voice was intense but quiet.

"I guess I was trying to be too arty, huh?"

"It's very well written."

Though he still knew something was wrong, he couldn't help the sense of pleasure her compliment gave him. "Thanks." He smiled.

Julia stood up slowly.

She dropped the article to the coffee table. Without the rubber band, the papers splayed across the top. She walked to the window and yanked on the velvet curtains. The brass rings tingled as she drew them.

"Very well written for a lie," she said.

"What?"

She turned and faced him, the fury she'd been controlling now beamed across the room at him. "I understand it's not important, it doesn't, in the grand scheme of things, matter a hoot *who* actually found the beetle—"

"What on earth—" he interrupted.

"Let me finish, if you don't mind." Her small hand rose to make a stop sign.

"Jesus." He shoved his hands into the pockets of his pants.

"But we're a couple, we're married ten years tonight," her voice rose to a yell, "and I'd have thought you'd want to give me that small bit of credit."

Wilson was so perplexed that he simply thrust his hands straight from the pockets up into the air, waggling them helplessly. She was insane.

He spoke in a whisper. "*What* credit?"

Julia knew then that he didn't remember. His face was so long and slack. Angry, sure, but not defiant. And defeated by trying to understand her.

The muscles in the back of her neck relaxed and she took a long, hopeless breath.

Before speaking, she let that breath out and took another. "Wilson, I found the beetle and the fungus growing out of its head." She spoke as if to Emily, or even Jimmy, as if he were a baby.

"I'm sorry?"

Wilson had been raised an only child, by a mother who believed in the value of good manners. When he was reaching for complete control, he lapsed into the old-fashioned phraseology of his mother's teaching. His question, *I'm sorry?* was the clue that he'd almost lost it.

"*You* didn't find the beetle," Julia said. "I did."

"Are you crazy?"

She turned back to the full-length drapes and fingered the tassels decorating the edges where they came together. Once, when she was pregnant with

Emily and heavy with sleepiness, she'd left the office early and come home. The afternoon had floated in dull, gray November weather and in a fit of inspiration she'd drifted around the apartment, drawing all the drapes and switching on small lamps here and there. Julia spoke with her back to Wilson. "Then tell me exactly what happened. How you saw the beetle, how you caught it, what happened next, and next, and next."

"Jesus Christ."

She heard him jerk out the desk chair and sit down. She slid her eyes to the left and peeked at him. His head of thick black hair dropped forward as he stared at the desk pad. "I caught sight of it just as it disappeared under a log."

She whirled around and pointed a finger at him. "In the article you said *a pile of dried leaves.* So which is it?"

"It went under a log, and the log was partially covered by dried autumn leaves."

"Autumn leaves in July?"

"There was no landscape service to clean up." Wilson's tone was dry.

"Would you like to hear my version of events?"

He blinked. Then he stood up, his long body unfolding like a sheet of paper with bad news. "Take two aspirin and go to bed," he said. "The champagne on top of that strong scotch has gone to your head."

And, yes, it was true that her head had begun to crack with the pain of knowing her husband didn't deserve her.

• • •

At three o'clock in the morning, the apartment was quiet. Angela eased open her door and peered out into the hall. She listened. A slight snore came from the left, where Emmy's door was ajar and her night-light shone its pale whiteness into the dark hall. Angela left her room and closed the bedroom door behind her. She moved away from Emmy's room, down the hall to the right.

The white kitchen gleamed from city lights reflecting into the room, but the dining and living rooms were quite dark, and the library was like a tomb. She groped her way to the window and raised the shade so that some light spilled in. Turning, she saw Dr. Streatfield's briefcase propped against the desk.

Her heart pumped and she felt her knees quiver. It was almost like when you were in love, this fear.

Papers were strewn messily across the coffee table. She picked some up and held them slanted toward the window, just making out densely written paragraphs. Other sheets of paper held columns of numbers, and strange symbols. She stared, unsure. Then, decided, she whirled and plopped down on the desk chair, her fingers quickly feeling for the computer's switch. She clicked it on and the screen glowed. Now she did the same with the printer. Thank the Lord she'd been enrolled in secretarial classes for secondary school.

But now, when she tried to look at the paper's numbers again, she was blinded by the computer's bright light. She would have to turn on a light. If someone came, it'd be all over, no way to hide what she was doing. Either someone would come or not. No use worrying. Still, her heart raced again when she switched on the desk lamp.

Quickly she began typing. She was able to work fast, but there were fifteen pages, and after an hour she was still far from finished. For a moment, she stopped working and sat quietly, listening and catching her breath. She peered at page seven, and then, nervous and hurrying, turned to the last two pages. Angela typed madly, her fingers flying. In fifteen minutes, the new document was being sent to the printer. Angie turned off the light and immediately, though illogically, felt safer. As the printer clicked, and the paper slowly fed out, she returned the original pages to the coffee table. She stared at them for a minute, disturbed by how neatly they were stacked, and then reached down to mess them up, even crushing the corner of the top page.

Now, desperate to be out of there, Angie grabbed the newly typed papers, turned off the computer and printer, and trotted back through the apartment to her own bedroom. She folded the papers in half and carefully put them away in her top bureau drawer.

She climbed into bed and stretched, pushing her bare feet against the sheet's coolness. The apartment was always overheated, and though Angie usually enjoyed the warmth, tonight her nerves had made her sweat. She was sticky, unclean, and she'd have liked to take a bath. But she didn't dare to even flush the toilet for fear of causing a disturbance.

For fear.

Julia shot awake and glared at the digital clock. Four-ten. *Shit.* She turned over, away from the clock. Wilson's back was to her and she glared at him. You'd think he'd wake up just from the power of her anger. But why should he worry? He thought she was crazy, simple explanation. Julia rolled onto her back and stared with wide-open eyes at the ceiling. Lights from traffic and the apartment building across the avenue crisscrossed up there, moving in vague and watery patterns.

She'd never doubted Wilson was the man for her. Was that wrong? Is a healthy dose of doubt desirable? If she thought about it now, pretended she was talking to a psychiatrist and making her case for why she'd married Wilson, she could begin to see the strangeness of his appeal.

I'd always been popular. Really, too popular. I was the girl in the third grade who was literally hit in the head by all the love notes sailing through the air. They'd land on the floor, the desktop, perched on a shoulder. And all I'd do was duck my head with shyness, modesty, confusion. I didn't ask for all the attention. I was just there, and they chose me, all the boys chose me.

What?

Yes, I guess I was beautiful. A beautiful little girl. Of course I enjoy being beautiful—it's clearly an asset and makes life a lot easier. I won't dispute that. It'd be ungrateful of me to say that being beautiful was a hardship.

So, you know, back to Wilson. It wasn't as if I was inexperienced and grabbed the first man who loved me. I'd been loved by boys and men for years before Wilson.

What?

Yes, I'd say Wilson is handsome, handsome like you are, Doctor, with that intellectual look. He's tall, thin, distinguished.

Why Wilson?

I can tell you that exactly. I loved him because of what he loved about me. It wasn't my beauty or my body. Wilson loved this (tapping my head). He thought I was clever.

Sure, I think I'm clever. I guess. Not a lot, actually. You know how in families, each kid has a label? My brother was brilliant and capable, my sister was a genius, and I was beautiful. That was my calling, and then Wilson came along, the first man to notice something else entirely about me.

Julia flung herself away from Wilson and closed her eyes. She didn't like where this "discussion" was going. It sounded as if she'd married the right man after all. Her body still didn't want to sleep, but the anger was seeping away.

Squiggles of light danced wildly in the darkness behind her closed eyelids. She transformed the squiggles into bodies of people swaying and cavorting. She loved to dance and was good at it, but she didn't get many opportunities because Wilson loathed dancing. She thought, It wouldn't kill him to dance with me at a wedding. But he never did.

She fell asleep, rocked by fresh rage

CHAPTER 9

G ran? It's me, George!"

"Georgie?" Her voice quavered, filled with tears in an instant.

"Granny, yes, it's Georgie calling from America."

"I thought you were dead."

"Oh, jasus, I'm sorry, Gran. I got the opportunity to work on a ship coming to America, and I just had to grab the chance. I didn't have time to call, Gran, or I would of."

"You staying out of trouble, Georgie?"

He gazed around the apartment. Though it was four-thirty in the morning, all the lights were blazing like it was day. Truth be told, he was a wee bit drunk.

"I wish you could see my apartment—thick carpet, clean white walls, and so warm, Gran. Maybe I'll send you a ticket and you'll come visit."

She let out a girlish laugh and George threw back his head with a loud guffaw.

"Are you drinking?" she asked.

"Just a sip or two."

"That's medicinal, we know that. Keeps the germs away and eases the bones."

"I'll send you money, Gran, in a couple of days."

"Moynihan's got a Kawasaki for sale."

"Aren't you going to stop riding cycles?"

"Not yet, Georgie."

"So what do you hear about Noelle?"

"Still thinking of that sorry girl?"

"Just asking." He picked up his glass and gently tilted first one way, then the other. The whiskey slid seductively up the glass, clinging a bit to the slippery surface, then falling back level.

"You be a good boy—don't keep getting in trouble all your life, Georgie, and send me some money for that cycle."

"I will, Gran. I'll talk to you again real soon."

He replaced the telephone receiver but kept his fingers resting there, staring at the white nails that needed trimming. It was Sister Mary when he was seven years old who'd told him that when he got angry about something, he ought to stare at some part of his body, with wide open eyes and no blinking, stare until the eyes filled with tears. And he was to think only good thoughts about his body. So now he thought how his hands were strong and his nails healthy. A picture came into his mind, a picture of a bucket full of frothy milk. And that was Georgie, fresh and good-tasting, like milk.

He slumped into a soft armchair and raised the glass of whiskey to his lips. The ice was nearly melted, thin and pathetic, floating in the whiskey.

The telephone shrilled and he jumped.

"'Lo?" George said in a whisper.

"We need a couple of girls." Mr. Wong's voice was soft and nonchalant.

"When?"

"Right away."

"Yes, sir."

George leapt up, reaching for his pants. He'd done this kind of job for Mr. Wong a couple of times and he'd learned that he wasn't very particular. Black, white, Asian, Indian. Thin, fat, pretty, ugly. Just female. It took the challenge away, but George wouldn't complain. He was looking to the day when he had some young boy doing the same for him, even though, if he'd faced it square, whores made him queasy. He swallowed the rest of the whiskey before bolting out the door.

He told the taxi where to go, then ordered him to pull over at the corner of Forty-second and Seventh, and wait. George stepped out of the cab, buttoning his thin jacket against the crisp autumn night. The street was bright as day and jammed with people.

He smiled, two dimples popping into each cheek. The sexual depravity that went on here, just inside the doors of the peep shows and bookstores, should have been sordid to him. But much as he'd looked forward to that fine apartment, he was just as glad to be out of it. Sure, it was warm, but its lonely heart was cold for sure.

Now here, on the streets, you found the red blood pumping, practically steaming it was, and he bounced up on his toes, in no particular hurry to find Mr. Wong's girls.

But the whores trailed after him, sensing his mission, pestering him. He shooed them away, even flapping his arms like they were chickens in the barnyard.

He strolled about half a block, his warm breath puffing out of his mouth and clouding his vision. Then he saw the fattest hooker he ever could've imagined.

Women on the streets weren't often attractive, but they were usually, if anything, too skinny. She leaned against a building, staring out with a mean look, daring a man to approach her. She wore a massive, ratty fur coat draped over her shoulders, her gigantic breasts barely contained by a white dress hanging on slender straps. She was quite the sight, and somehow George knew Mr. Wong would find her magnificent.

"A hundred for two hours if you've got a friend," George said. He looked her right in the eyes, though it was difficult to find them in the folds of painted flesh.

Her upper lip curled.

"What do you say?"

"Three-fifty." Her voice was disconcertingly high and thin.

"Three-fifty for two?"

"Four hundred for two."

George dropped his head, shaking it in mock disgust. He found it incredible that this woman was negotiating. Still, there was something about her. He looked again.

Just then she hiked up one corner of the fur coat, making her breasts jiggle.

"Okay—where's the friend?"

"Two blocks up, on Fifty-second Street."

George turned and waved for the taxi. "We'll pick her up on the way."

He got into the cab first. When she was all settled, heaving her body this way and that, he finally spoke. "Can you tell the cabbie where to go?"

She leaned forward and directed the cab driver, still in a high-pitched voice.

"So what's your name? I'll need to introduce you."

"Sherry."

"And your friend?"

"Cherry."

George tried to hide his smile. But every time he imagined Luke Wong's partner, Mr. Mao, pronouncing Cherry and Sherry, the giggles floated up out of his chest like little soap bubbles.

If only there was someone to tell.

Wilson turned and found Julia's small body. She always slept naked. He'd tried to do the same when they first married, but nudity was not comfortable for him. Julia never complained, and in fact she was always cuddling up to his pajamas, almost wrapping herself in them.

He never made overtures in bed to Julia, waiting,

instead, for her to be ready. He was convinced that she tired of men desiring her, that his only attraction was that he never pushed her. And so, this night, he held her gently. One hand grazed her breast, by mistake, but he kept it there.

Somehow he thought she just might be awake. After ten years of marriage, things like that could be sensed. Not only when the other was awake, but also when the other was awake and pretending to be asleep.

He lay still, hardly breathing, hoping she would turn and reach for him. It had been a celebration tonight, and he'd known Julia was impressed. That'd been wonderful, seeing her surprise and amazement.

And then the big fight. His eyes opened wide as he thought of her strange statement. He could remember like it was yesterday, his hand reaching out and snatching that beetle grub. *I mean, it didn't make sense that Julia would find it. How would she know it was important?* The hand touching her breast opened and he felt the beetle as it clung to his palm and the sweat from a July heat wave and the smell of earth, so rich and heady that he'd almost fainted.

He remembered.

"You awake?" Wilson's voice was only an exhale of air, barely existing.

Her breathing deepened.

He wanted her, and he allowed his hand to open again on her breast.

She grunted, almost a snore, and wrenched her body away, to the edge of the bed.

Sometimes she did that in her sleep, hauling herself here and there as if in her dreams she was on the move. Places to go while she slept.

Carefully he slid to the opposite side of the bed and then swung his feet to the floor. He sat still, letting his eyes adjust to the dark. Like a turtle, he inched across the room. On a straight chair to the right of the door, he found his robe. Though he knew it was unlikely he'd run into Angela, he was always careful where she was concerned.

He headed down the hall, first past Jimmy's room and then Emily's, on through the entrance hall and living room, and into the library. He eased the door shut behind him and turned on the desk lamp. A small circle of yellow light fell in pretty patterns on the mahogany wood. At the built-in bookcases, he picked up earphones and plugged them into the stereo system. He flipped through the CDs quickly until he found *Fidelio*. He settled on the couch, head comfortably supported by a small velvet pillow, earphones in place, closed his eyes, and offered himself up to the music.

CHAPTER 10

Angela dreamt that she was having a baby. Her stomach clenched into a tight fist ready to fight, and she moaned with the pain. Then her belly relaxed, slack again.

She heard a quiet tap-tap at her door. Her eyes flew open in confusion and she discovered herself lying on her back, legs folded up and knees pointed to the ceiling, her hands resting protectively across her stomach.

"What is it?" Angela called out.

"Are you all right?" Dr. Streatfield spoke in a low voice.

"I'm sorry to be bothering you, Doctor, I must've had a nightmare."

"As long as you don't need anything."

"Nothing at all, thank you."

She heard his soft footsteps go down the hall toward the kitchen. The room was light, though only just so. Angie straightened up and felt the warm dampness between her legs.

"Mother of God!" She leapt out of bed and pulled back the covers. Two bright red stains of blood, the size of shillings, dotted the white sheets. Angie cleaned herself up first and then the sheet. She hung the sheet over the shower curtain rod, sure that the bathroom was so warm it would dry soon.

Her stomach cramped hard and fast all through the early morning, and she blamed that for the way everyone seemed out of sorts. Julia and the Doctor were hardly speaking to each other, and the Doctor left for his lab by 7:15. She worried for a moment that he knew she'd copied the papers, but then she talked herself into believing that he *couldn't* know.

Julia left a half hour after the Doctor, early for her. She was decked out in a tight black silk suit and black patent heels, but her face was white, pinched like tight shoes.

"Is the leftover stew all right for dinner tonight, then?" Angie asked.

"Fine." Julia glanced at her suddenly. "Are you feeling okay?"

"I've just got my friend and I'm a little peaked."

Julia looked confused, but when she saw Angela's hands rubbing at her belly, she seemed to understand.

Angie knew that Americans called their friend something else, but those words were too hard and obvious for her.

"For heaven's sake, Ange, can you *please* take it easy today?" Julia smiled a mother's smile.

"I'll take a rest when the children go down," Angela said.

Julia headed for the apartment's door.

"Julia?"

She swiveled neatly around on the heels, her slim legs gleaming in the silky hose. "Ummm?"

"You look so beautiful today."

Julia almost frowned.

Now, why was that? Wouldn't she smile at a compliment?

"Thank you, Angela." Then she was out the door.

Angie immediately headed back to the master bathroom and rummaged in the medicine cabinet until she found the codeine. In the kitchen she took two with a glass of milk.

Jimmy sat in his infant seat, bouncing and mouthing a toy while Emily was at the kitchen table, dreamily eating a bowl of oatmeal.

Angie sat down opposite her, wanting to keep still until the pills worked. She watched Emily's eating method, a dipping of the tip of the spoon into the bowl, the careful lifting of spoon to mouth, the flicking pink tongue licking off the oatmeal, and all the while, eyes trained on the windows. Angie blinked three times to Emily's one.

"I bet you had a nice dream last night," Angie said.

"Yeah."

The spoon dipped again.

Dreams were private, even for four-year-old girls, so Angie wasn't sure about prying into Emily's. Angie stared around the kitchen, a little weary at all the work there was to do.

But Emmy's eyes were now twinkling at her above the spoon and licking tongue.

"What, you devil?" Angie laughed.

"You were in my dream!" Right away, as if knowing that she could get away with it, Emmy pulled over the small glass bowl of brown sugar. She liberally sprinkled brown sugar on the oatmeal, coating the top.

"And what was I doing then, missy?" Angie leaned back in the chair. The codeine was starting to work and the release from pain was a gorgeous thing.

"You were getting married—you looked so pretty."

"Did I now?"

Emily scooped up an enormous spoonful of oatmeal and brown sugar and shoved it into her mouth. Then, mouth full and still working mightily to chew and swallow all that hot cereal, she spoke. "I was your little flower girl and I wore a long white dress."

"I thought the bride was to wear the long white dress." Angie felt herself sucked in, placated by the dream.

Suddenly Jimmy let out a shriek. Both Emily and Angela jumped and stared at him. He grinned, still chomping on his toy, a plastic replica of Piglet.

"And was Jimmy the ring bearer?" Angela asked.

Emily looked blank. She swallowed the last of the oatmeal and pushed the bowl away. "Jimmy wasn't even there." She hopped down from the chair and disappeared out the swinging kitchen door.

"She killed you off, Jimmy my boy," Angie said.

He looked right at her. Then he whined, kicked his legs, and waved his arms.

She stood slowly, moved around the table, and unsnapped the safety belt that held him in place. She could smell his dirty nappy, but it didn't bother her. She cuddled him to her. His body relaxed and melted into hers.

"Jimmy my boy," she whispered and smoothed his hair with her cheek, over and over again.

George stood opposite the Streatfields' apartment building on West End Avenue. He wore a new Harris tweed sport coat, but the drizzly autumn day was cold enough for a raincoat, hat, and maybe even a thin pair of brown leather gloves. Clothes were something George loved and he wasn't ashamed to admit it. His gran had a passion for motorcycles, and who would've expected such a thing in an old woman? So he had a weakness for clothes.

He'd window-shopped early that morning, after paying the hookers and sending them off in a taxi. He particularly liked Barney's, though at the same time, he found their windows frustratingly bare and simple. He wished they'd pack the windows full, though not like the shops in Chinatown, where such a variety of cheap stuff warred with each other and him.

He liked the Ralph Lauren advertisements, whole rooms decorated in his design and style. He'd do windows like that, with each type of clothing suggesting a different room. Like that morning he'd seen a suit by Todd Oldham. So the room would've been sleek and modern, not his taste maybe, but all kind of connected.

George sighed, wondering what he was doing here anyway. He was due to meet her at ten o'clock at the copy place. The truth was, he was feeling a little bored. Mr. Wong seemed to be under the faulty impression that getting Angela to steal the papers would be very nearly a full-time job. That meant they could call on him for night duties, but his days were supposed to be devoted to Angela.

His eyes watered from the cold wind, and he cocked up the collar of his jacket. Then he saw her coming out of the building, the doorman holding open both doors so she could fit through with that huge pram. Its roof was on, covering the kids, but he could see their little mittened hands.

"Ta," he heard her voice sing out. She tilted her head back to smile at the doorman.

She could use a little fashion help. She wore the most ridiculous rain hat made of bright red shiny plastic with enormous, flapping sides and front. Lord, with that tangle of red hair clashing against it. Her coat was brown, old and shapeless, and her feet were encased by those terrible American running shoes, oversized and a dirty white color. You could have the daintiest feet in the world and never know it wearing those clodhoppers.

She started off down the street, her attention focused straight ahead—sure, she didn't know he was watching her. He let her get nearly to the end of the block before he pushed off in the opposite direction.

He checked his watch. Time to have a cup of tea somewhere first. He'd had two cups at Mr. Wong's, waiting in the kitchen of the mansion. But Mr. Wong's household served only black Chinese tea, bitter and strange-tasting to him. He'd been alone in the kitchen, watching the digital clock in the face of the oven click off the minutes. He must've dumped three spoons of sugar in each mug of tea. Like medicine, it was.

George ducked into a coffee shop and sat down at the counter. A blond waitress, frazzled and overweight, sighed in disgust when he ordered only tea. But he didn't care. His thoughts were on Angela. Something about the cold rain, her ridiculous outfit, the whole situation, was making him anxious. What if the Doctor hadn't brought home any papers? George had played tough with her about getting into the lab, but he knew he'd have to help if it came to that, and he knew it'd be tricky.

He picked up the spoon and dandied it off his fingers. It gently hit the countertop, bam, bam, bam.

"Do you mind?" the waitress said. The place was nearly empty and she was leaning against the counter about halfway down, filing her nails.

He dropped the spoon with a clatter, pleased

when he saw her frown of annoyance. Quickly he dug in his pocket, pulled out a wrinkled dollar bill, and tucked it under the saucer.

When he left, George checked his watch again. Twenty minutes to go, and it would only take him ten minutes to get there. The rain was a little heavier and he realized he needed an umbrella. It had never occurred to him that he'd need an umbrella in America. Two blocks down, walking fast with his head tucked in, he came to a street vendor selling them. He bought a green umbrella for six dollars. When it was open and shielding him from the rain, he danced his shoulders around, trying to fling off the wet.

And now, finally, it was time to meet Angela.

CHAPTER 11

A ngela was five minutes early and as soon as the pram stopped moving, Jimmy began to fuss. She dug in the diaper bag and pulled out a hard piece of pretzel. "There's my good boy," she murmured.

Then Angie found a book for Emily, such a favorite that she'd memorized all the words. Angie was sure she'd be reading to herself soon.

"Good day to you."

His voice was unexpected because she'd been leaning under the roof of the pram. She straightened up fast. Without looking at him, she reached into the pocket of her coat and pulled out the papers.

Holding them out to him, she allowed her eyes to

reach his chin. She wouldn't look at him straight. A fellow Irishman betraying her. So what else was new?

"I'll just be a moment," George said.

"You don't have to make copies."

"What do you mean?"

His voice was so sharp and mean, like little needles sticking into her.

"I copied them myself, retyped them on the computer and printed them out."

"You dumb fuck."

Shocked, her eyes met his. "This way there's less risk. He won't suspect anything."

"And what if you made an error? How many mistakes do most people make when they're typing?"

"I was careful," she whispered.

George viciously crumpled the papers in one hand. "So now we start all over again. Tonight you take the papers and you bring them to me at ten o'clock. Right here." He tossed the papers into the stroller.

Angie heard Jimmy's crow of delight and then the sounds of ripping paper.

"Look, Dr. Streatfield told us about what he's done," Angie said. "It's real important—I don't think I'll be able to take the papers 'cause he's going to check his briefcase before he leaves for the lab in the morning."

George's small, muscular hand, the skin rough and dry, closed around her chin, tilting it up. His eyes, boring into hers, were blue as a bright autumn sky. "You're just the nanny. You don't know anything.

He'll think he left them at the lab and got confused.
For one day, he's not going to suspect you."

She knew Dr. Streatfield would discover any
missing papers, and she knew she was the logical cul-
prit. Her eyes shifted away from George, unsettled by
nerves and the sense that there was something else in
his eyes—not lust, common in men when they looked
at her—but more like hurt. He reminded her of a baby
boy, as wee as Jimmy in the pram, who needed a
good, long cuddle.

But she'd done with such nonsense.

His fingers squeezed into her cheekbones. What a
mean bastard. Her eyes shot open and pinned him
one.

She had green eyes, and not just browny-green like
most of the population. They were sharp and clever.
He'd called her dumb, but she wasn't. George figured
she'd planned it this way, knowing her typed pages
would be unacceptable and buying her another day.

So what'd she want with that extra day? To run
away despite the threats? Had she told Dr. Streatfield
and they'd informed the police? And where the hell
did that leave him—should *he* tell Mr. Wong? He
wasn't sure, but he thought it possible he'd be killed
for screwing up.

"Let's go to the lab," he said suddenly.

Her eyes opened wide with the shock and surprise. Good. Pull the rug out from under those bright
eyes.

Suddenly Jimmy began to cry, and not just a little

whimpering cry, but the full-blasted kind, the *I can't stand another minute of this pram on this cold rainy and going nowhere morning* kind of bellowing cry.

Both Angela and George reacted viscerally, their bodies becoming taut with anxiety.

"What's he want?" George demanded.

"He wants to move, to get going."

"So let's start walking and see if that shuts him up." He stepped back several feet and waited for Angie to maneuver the pram toward the center of the sidewalk.

They moved along, and sure enough, Jimmy stopped crying.

"Discuss how we're going to do this," George said.

"I guess I can get inside, with the children, but why am I stopping there all of a sudden?"

"What if you say one of the kids is sick and you were worried? You were out for your usual morning stroll, and the baby vomited. You were close by the lab, so you thought you'd stop in and have the Doctor check him over."

"Where's the vomit?"

George placed a hand on the pram, stilling it. He knelt down and peered under the roof. Carefully he pried open the baby's mouth, feeling its soft and damp gums, and then he touched the very back of the baby's throat with his index finger. He pulled out fast, but not fast enough.

Angela, above him, cried out when she heard the baby's retching sounds. "You're terrible, terrible," she murmured, pushing him out of the way and starting to mop up the mess with a cloth nappy.

"Don't get it too cleaned up," he warned. He pulled out a nice white handkerchief, brand new, shook it out, and wiped off his hand.

In a moment, they began walking again. Both children were quiet.

"I've got to get in with you," George said.

She sighed, exasperated and frightened both. "There's no way."

"I'm your boyfriend."

"I've never gotten so much as a phone call the whole time I've been there. And I haven't gone out in the evenings. So where did you come from?"

For a second, George thought about how sad and lonely her life must be, all the time with the kids, never seeing people her own age and never going anywhere.

"I just got off the boat."

"I can't believe this is happening to me." Her head was bowed and shaking back and forth. Or, to be more exact, as he liked to be, the terrible red rain hat was shaking back and forth.

Suddenly remembering the rain, George paused and opened his umbrella. In order to still walk fairly close to her, he had to hold the umbrella halfway over her.

"Getting wet is the least of my worries," she said.

"So you're thrilled to pieces that I've arrived and you invited me for a walk because I don't even have a place to stay yet and you wouldn't presume to invite me up to their apartment when they're not even home, and then the baby got sick, and you thought you'd better stop."

"You're a good storyteller," she said, wry.

"That's what my gran always said. Told me I should be a writer." The words came out without his thinking.

"A mean boy like you's got a gran?"

"A mean gran."

He saw the corners of her mouth start to turn up into a smile, and he waited to see the smile, waited like it was all that mattered. That's when he realized he was enjoying himself, which somehow didn't seem like the proper thing to be feeling. Anyway, he waited in vain. No smile. Not today and not for him.

"Maybe that much works. But then what?"

"Are we heading in the right direction?"

"Ten blocks from here."

"Good—okay, we're up in the lab and while the Doctor is checking out the baby, you know, probably taking his temperature and pulse and so forth, you excuse yourself to go to the ladies'. That leaves me standing there. I start wandering around, hands in me pockets, all nonchalant like, peering at this and that. The Doctor's caught up with the baby and—"

"His name's Jimmy," she interrupted.

"I'm going to call him Dr. Streatfield, not Jimmy," George said, disgusted.

"The baby's name is Jimmy."

Who cares? He shrugged, trying to get back on track. "Where was I?"

"I'm in the ladies' loo and you're whistling 'round the place."

"Right. So I spy his desk, probably got his name on it, and then you come back from the ladies' and you stand between him and me, blocking his vision, if you see what I mean."

"I see," Angela said quietly.

George glanced at her, disturbed by her voice. He was bloody well rising to the challenge here, and truth to tell, liking it, and suddenly he didn't trust her again. Maybe she'd go to the loo and alert the authorities. He grabbed her arm and twisted her around to face him.

"Don't," she said.

"Maybe you don't realize we know your Da? You fuck me over with this, and he's dead. Not a sweet death, neither, but a bad one."

Her eyes filled with water. She was being stupid again. Did she really think they'd go all the way to Ireland, find her father, and kill him? Funny how she bounced back and forth between smart and stupid, smart and stupid. Right at this moment, he needed her smart. Smart for fooling the Doctor, and scared to death of him.

Even through her woolen coat, his hand could feel the thin and wiry upper part of her arm. He tightened his grip in increments, watching her face as he did. When the tears spilled out and ran down her cheeks, he let go.

"To finish up," he whispered, "I grab papers from the desk and then we get the hell out of there."

She nodded, not daring to speak.

"I'll push the pram," George said. "You hold up the umbrella."

"I'm fine pushing the children."

But he took it away from her and felt strangely peaceful, strolling along the streets of New York City, steering around the holes in the sidewalk, an umbrella held over his head by a pretty Irish girl.

Emily was now in the backseat of the stroller. She leaned forward and whispered in his ear. "Jim-Jim, it's me, Emmy. You don't need to cry because we're going to see Daddy." He stopped and listened to her.

She reached with both hands and tickled his cheeks. "Dad-day, Dad-day," she sang over and over. When she could tell he wouldn't cry again, she leaned back.

It was boring in the backseat. She found the book Angie'd brought along, *Blueberries for Sal,* and opened it to the beginning. She couldn't read, but she knew the story. She stared at the picture of Sal going clam hunting with her father.

The picture showed the sea splashing up on the rocks, and gulls dipping in the sky overhead. Emily could smell the sea and feel the cold of the rock under her bare feet. It was a little scary, the sharp tang of salt in the air and knowing Sal's tooth was about to fall out, but Sal's daddy was with her and Emily knew everything, in the end, would be all right.

CHAPTER 12

Wilson sat at his desk, strangely lethargic. First on his long list of projects was to review and revise the draft press release the public relations office had hand-delivered that morning. He'd read it and been disturbed by a number of inaccuracies. There were also dozens of letters to answer, questions from other scientists, where he might make an important difference to their research. He yawned and quickly clamped a hand over his mouth.

He hadn't been this tired in years. His computer was on, its glow reminding him that the last time he checked his e-mail, there'd been at least thirty messages waiting for him to read and reply to. Though he'd already had three cups of coffee this morning, one more than his usual, he stood and picked up his mug. He had to do something. Soon he'd start dozing at the desk.

The coffeepot was in the room with all the secretaries, or, as he tried to remember to call them, the administrative assistants. In fact, one of the two was a young man. The other, Joan, was speaking on the phone in her calm, measured way. She was not a flashy young woman, and he'd always liked her for that. Dark brown hair cut in a straight line at the level of her chin, small tortoiseshell glasses, and a heart-shaped face. Joan had been working here for six years or so, but if Wilson had been asked the color of her eyes he couldn't have said. And he didn't have any idea whether she was married. Suddenly curious, he looked at her left hand.

No wedding band. He picked up the coffee carafe and poured a full mug. Then, surprising himself, he added two spoonfuls of sugar to the hot coffee. When he turned around, he looked at Joan again.

She was looking back at him. Another surprise. Joan didn't often look at anyone. Now that he thought about it, he realized he didn't know the color of her eyes because she so seldom allowed her eyes to be seen. He walked several steps and deliberately stared into her eyes.

Brown, just like her hair. Nothing very extraordinary about them, but certainly pleasant.

His own eyes dropped, unexpectedly, to her bosom. She wore a white blouse with a high neck and small, plain buttons down the front. She seemed to have a healthy bust. When his eyes returned to her face, he saw that she was bright red.

There was a long, long moment of silence.

He coughed. "Everything okay?"

"Yes, Dr. Streatfield," Joan said. She swung around in her desk chair to face the computer, her back to him.

He saw the faint line of her bra strap.

Just as he was about to turn into his own office, a young research assistant who worked in a lab farther down the hall leaned around an open doorway.

"Got a minute?" she asked.

For you, definitely.

"Sure." Wilson ambled down the hall, taking a sip of hot coffee as he went. He'd watched Susan since she started doing her post-doc research with them three months earlier, not only because she was a stunning woman of Asian descent, but also because she was bright, a bit of a flirt, and available. Or so office gossip indicated.

They talked briefly about some data she was running, but he wasn't engaged by the discussion. She wore perfume, a gentle scent that seemed to be released by her skin and hair. He knew perfume came from a small, odd-shaped bottle, but the impression was of a floating cloud wrapped around her slight, elegant body. He felt himself intoxicated, like he was drunk on champagne again, and he leaned closer.

Susan's long black hair had been twisted into a knot at the base of her neck. His fingers literally twitched with the desire to reach up and undo the knot of hair. She glanced at him and her eyes were amused.

She knew her power, and he thought, suddenly, that she'd intended it.

They were alone in a small, windowless office.

His right hand rose quickly, yanked, and the hair tumbled down her back. He leaned close, his body towering above hers. "Would you like to have lunch?"

Her eyelids opened wider and then closed for a brief second. "How about tomorrow? I've got an appointment today."

Wilson felt a flare of annoyance, but he tapped it down. "Great. Say one o'clock?"

She moved away from him, one step and then two. Both arms reached behind her head and she began to stroke and wrap her hair. Zip, zip, the knot of hair was back in place. "I don't think we should leave the office together," she said.

"Right." He thought for a moment. "I'll get reservations at DaVinci's and see you there, okay?"

"Perfect." She turned her back to him and walked several feet toward the computer, sat down, and began typing.

Wilson stared at her profile, drinking it in, astonished at what had just happened. He'd made an assignation.

My God.

The phone was ringing when he got back to his office, and he snatched it up on the fifth ring.

"Dr. Streatfield?"

"Yes." He shouldn't have answered. It was probably yet another invitation to lecture.

"This is President Sebastian's office. Can you make a lunch meeting today with Jed Peterson?"

The head of PR for Columbia. Wilson had met him once, a dapper little guy who wore bow ties.

He glanced at his watch, but really didn't notice the time. "Uh, sure, what time?"

"About one o'clock?"

"I'll be there." The receiver was on its way to the cradle when he heard the voice continuing to speak. Quickly he returned the receiver to his ear. "I'm sorry, I didn't hear you."

"Could you be sure and take a look at the draft press release you got this morning, and bring it with you?"

"Yes, of course."

He waited a moment this time, before daring to hang up. He plopped into his desk chair and stared down at himself. Old khakis and a flannel shirt wasn't lunch-with-the-president attire. He'd have to rush home and change.

Wilson called the apartment from his office to warn Angela that he was coming home for a few minutes to change his clothes. But no one answered, and he remembered that she religiously took the children to the park every morning.

CHAPTER 13

Angela and George were half a block away from the entrance to Dr. Streatfield's building at Columbia when Angela saw the Doctor himself rush out the door and into the rain, without so much as a coat or hat, and hail a cab. She felt her body start with fright, but George didn't seem to notice.

What should she do now?

And then she knew: nothing at all. This was the best thing that could happen. They'd be told Dr. Streatfield was out and they'd be sent away.

Angela tried to hold the two doors open for George to push the pram through, while she struggled with the umbrella. George finally propped the left door open with the toe of his fine leather shoe, stained by the rain, and managed to steer inside the building.

The pitted and dirt-streaked tile floor covered a space of only about nine by twelve. An old gray steel desk blocked access to an elevator. A guard, also old and gray, was sipping a soda through a straw. He kind of straightened up at the sight of them. The double stroller often had that effect, Angela had noticed.

"I work for Dr. Streatfield," Angela said, her voice shaking. "These are his children and I was wondering whether we could go up and see him?"

The guard, though he was looking at her with a benign expression, still sipped at his drink. His eyes were bloodshot, and Angela recognized the look of a drunk. She ought to. Angie would bet he was sucking up vodka. She glanced at George and saw that he knew, too. That worried her. What might he think of, knowing the guard was as good as drunk?

"He went out."

Now George was surprised. "But it's not even the lunch hour."

The guard shrugged. "You're out, ain't ya?"

"Well, thank you very much. Sorry to trouble you." Angela began to maneuver the pram backward.

"Couldn't we go up?" Suddenly George leaned under the pram's hood and scooped up the sleeping baby.

Jimmy began to howl in outrage.

"See, the baby was sick all over the place, and we gotta walk them home 'cause cabs won't take this big pram, and it'd be great just to use his office to clean the poor kid up."

"Sure, go on. You know the floor and office number?"

"I've been there before, but if you could just remind me?" Angela said.

"Lessee," he ran his finger down a ratty piece of paper. "Here goes. Seventh floor, Room 719. I'll just call up and tell Joan you're on the way."

Angela couldn't believe it. This stupid guard was letting them waltz on up there. Lord almighty, he didn't even have proof that these kids were related to Dr. Streatfield.

She grabbed Jimmy from George's arms, and let George steer the pram around the guard's desk and over to the elevator. Jimmy buried his face in her shoulder, burrowing there for comfort.

"Are we going to see Daddy?" Emily asked, the first words Angela had heard her speak in a long time. Usually she was a bit of a chatterbox.

"No, darling. We're going to stop in his office to get Jimmy cleaned up."

The codeine was wearing off and she was starting to feel sick to her stomach. It was one thing to copy papers. What difference did it make? Who would it hurt? But this was different, with the kids so involved. And poor Jimmy, vomiting all over himself. The smell rose like thin smoke from his hot body.

George whistled between his teeth as the elevator creaked its way up to the seventh floor. The tune was Irish, but she didn't know it.

She could just see him on the playing fields when he was a small boy. He was the one with patched pants and a sweater a size too large, red chapped cheeks and hands from practically living outdoors, and a merry, mean way about him. He didn't pick fights and knock the little kids down. No, he fairly danced about, making fights happen like play. Fights were fun, didn't you know?

"I'll hang back when the doors open," George said.

Angela pushed off the elevator with the large pram in front. "Hallo," she said to Joan.

"Hello," Joan said.

Angela could tell George kept the elevator doors open by holding in a button.

"I've got Dr. Streatfield's children, and the baby's messed himself. Could I use the Doctor's office and the ladies' for a quick clean?"

Her head under the rain hat was hot and itchy, and she was worried that the cramps coming so hard and fast might mean she was leaking.

"Sure. If you keep going down the hall from 719, the ladies' room is on the right-hand side."

"Thanks," Angela whispered.

"I was just going on break. Is there anything else you'll need?" She stood and tucked in her blouse, straightening herself up.

"Nothing at all," Angela said.

The elevator doors started to close and for a wild second Angela thought George would simply disappear. But just as the doors nearly came together she saw his hand slip between them. Joan stepped away from the desk and walked down a long corridor in the opposite direction. The elevator doors parted, George stepped out, and then hustled them down the hall to Dr. Streatfield's open office door.

"Take the baby and kid to the ladies'," he said.

Angela helped Emily out of the stroller and then firmly took her hand and led her back into the hall, where they turned left. She didn't think about what he'd do, or how he'd do it. She'd just take care of herself and the children. That was the best and only choice.

George didn't waste any time. He lifted the bag that hung from the back of the pram, unzipped the top, and placed it on the floor, mouth gaping. He could see that the papers on top of the desk were correspondence, and he doubted that would be useful. He opened a lower left drawer. His right hand dug under the files and his left hand grabbed the tops, scooping out at least a dozen of them, which he carefully placed in the bag. He figured he could squeeze in another dozen, but, nervous, he thought better of it.

Just after he'd zipped up the bag and flung it over his shoulder, Angela returned with the kids.

"Here I am!" Emily squealed. She climbed up onto the desk chair and pointed at the framed photo of her.

Angela peered at the picture. "That must've been before I knew you."

Good time for his exit, George thought. He

ducked out of the office and headed down the hall. He passed the elevator and found a door to the stairs around the corner. His feet flew down the seven flights, like little elves' feet they were, and he watched them in admiration. When he went through the entrance hall, he chose to ignore the guard. Just act like he was one of the workers leaving on his lunch hour.

"See ya," the guard called out.

George waved one hand in the air and then quickly pushed open the door. He'd left the umbrella.

Angela turned, Jimmy in her arms, and she knew immediately that George was gone. For good, or so she hoped. Suddenly she felt much lighter.

Jimmy was in a fresh nappy, and he was all cleaned up. She gave him a kiss on his scrubbed check and then strapped him into the pram.

"Come on, Emmy," she cooed, "we need to get home for lunch."

"I want to see Daddy."

"'Course you do, sweetheart, but he's out to a meeting, probably an important one with important people." She picked up Emily and lowered her into the front seat. "Did you know your Da's made a big, important discovery? So you see, he has to be out and about, meeting with everyone."

"What's for lunch?" Emily asked.

Angela deftly guided the pram through the office door and down the hall. "I think we need a big, warm lunch, don't you?"

"Yes."

"What about eggs and sausage and buttered toast?"

"And hot chocolate?"

"And hot chocolate, of course."

"Can we make cookies after Quiet Time?"

"Well, there's only one difficulty with that plan."

"What?" Emily's voice was worried.

"How will we decide what *kind* of cookies?"

"I think chocolate chip."

Angela pushed the elevator button, and they waited. The receptionist was still on her break. "What about oatmeal?"

"I had oatmeal for breakfast."

"You're so smart, that's true, you did."

The elevator opened with a creaky squeal. Angie quickly swiveled the pram around, then backed into the elevator so that Emily faced front.

"And Jimmy likes chocolate chip best."

"Did he tell you that?"

Emily giggled. "Uh-huh."

When the elevator doors opened on the ground floor, and Angie pushed the pram around the guard's desk, she looked sideways, checking whether the same man was on. The guard would notice that they were coming out alone, without George, wouldn't he? But he appeared to be asleep, while sitting straight up, and Angie was through the entrance and out the door without waking him.

The rain poured down and Emily screamed with excitement. Angie paused to tie the red rain hat firmly under her chin. "Okay, here we go!" She began to run down the sidewalk, pushing the pram as fast as she could.

The kids' yells of delight could hardly be heard over the rush of rain and lunchtime traffic.

She felt a terrible cramp in her belly, and then a surge of warmth between her legs. Well, not to worry, they'd be home soon.

Julia sat very still, her hands folded together on top of the desk. Her nails were, predictably, a mess. She'd bitten them until she graduated from college and started her first job as a secretary at the enormous literary and talent agency in Los Angeles, ICM. Though the job was a high-stress one, and she yearned to gnaw on her nails, her job also kept her jumping, placing and taking telephone calls, typing correspondence and contracts, stroking the egos of successful writers, obsessed producers and directors, and uncertain yet egocentric actors. On the Saturday after her first week on the job, she'd been soaking in a deep, hot bath and suddenly discovered the glorious rim of white nail circling the tips of each finger. She'd been determined to learn how to do her own nails, or if that failed, to get a weekly manicure at a beauty parlor.

Obviously it wasn't meant to be. She still didn't bite her nails, but because she forgot to file them they grew thin and straggly, then broke off so that she had to trim them with her front teeth, like a rabbit nibbling on a carrot. Today they were not only ragged, but also dirty. She and Wilson weren't speaking, and somehow the prospect of taking a shower while he shaved had been too much. She skipped the shower, dressed in black, and left the apartment as quickly as possible.

The morning crawled.

She just couldn't work. To seem busy for Margaret, she kept flipping the pages of a manuscript, but she wondered whether Margaret was fooled.

Julia didn't think she'd ever felt quite like this. She tried to distill it down to one word. Oh, yes, she knew.

Fear.

She was terrified that Wilson was going to leave her.

When she'd asked him to dinner twelve years earlier, standing at the Met's mezzanine bar, she'd been certain he'd say no, not because she wasn't attractive, some might say beautiful, but because of his grace and insular nature, so obvious as he sipped his martini, he did not seem the sort to need a woman. In the second after she'd blurted out the dinner invitation, she'd thought he might be gay and she'd been mortified at having put them both in an awkward spot.

She could remember sitting in the dark during Act Three, watching the figures on stage move like small children, and aware of the music as only idle background noise. She could remember falling in love and feeling discombobulated as she did so, as if she'd jumped from the window of her eighth-floor studio apartment window with the serious intention of reaching the street fast. She'd been in love many times before, so she was clear about what was happening, but never with a man she'd had to work at charming, and never with a man who appeared to be oblivious to her as a woman.

She figured it out later: Wilson Streatfield needed no one, neither lover nor friend. He was alone. And the appeal to her had been enormous, knowing that he would never really need her, and that she would never really have to give.

Now, in her office years later, she sat for a few more minutes, her fingers stretching out of the hands' clasp, then rushing back because they needed the gentle touch. Panic rose into her chest and beat furious wings. She reached for the telephone, snatched up the receiver, and pushed Direct Dial number five. Her best friend, Lauren.

"It's me," Julia said.

"What's the matter?"

"Are you in the middle of something?"

Lauren was a corporate lawyer, where she was usually too busy to talk much on the phone.

"I've got an eleven A.M. deadline for this brief— can we talk after that?"

"How about lunch?"

"Sure. Noon at Le Bistro."

Julia breathed better when she hung up the phone, relieved that Lauren would listen and understand every nuance of the previous evening with Wilson.

CHAPTER 14

I t was peculiar for Wilson to enter the empty apartment. His footsteps seemed to echo and he suddenly wondered if he'd ever been alone there before. Yes, once, the morning after Julia had given birth to Emily. He'd been bone-tired after twenty-four hours of Julia's labor. He remembered brewing some coffee and the quiet drip-drip as it filled the carafe. It didn't feel lonely then, and it didn't feel lonely this morning. Only odd.

He sometimes wondered what would've happened if Julia hadn't come after him with such persistence. He believed now more than ever that solitude was his most natural state. It was true that in his research he spent quantities of time alone, though also quantities of time directing his lab assistants, arranging funding, and dealing with office politics. But he was alone in his head all the time.

Family life had been a kind of blessing, pulling him out of himself a little bit, and he was usually grateful. But not always. He remembered what it used to be like and there was a craving deep inside him for singleness. Some men left their families from time to time, to go on hunting or golfing excursions with other men, a community of masculine life. That wasn't appealing to Wilson. But he liked to hike along the Appalachian trail, alone.

Back in their bedroom, he kicked off his shoes and dropped the wrinkled khakis to the floor. Flipping through his closet, he found a pair of dark gray wool slacks Julia had bought him the year before, after she'd successfully auctioned a big book about, of all things, God as a woman.

He remembered that she'd matched the pants to a sweater. Wilson stood on tiptoe, rummaging around on the shelf above the hanging clothes, until he found the gray and white patterned V-neck sweater. He wore a freshly laundered, white, button-down-collar shirt with a red, gray, and yellow tie.

He brushed his hair with Julia's brush because he couldn't find his own, and he noticed how his long black hairs mingled with her short blond ones. She'd be annoyed if he didn't clean the brush out, but he just didn't feel like cleaning Julia's hairbrush. Or maybe the idea of her annoyance was appealing.

Staring into the mirror, he tilted his face this way and that, looking for dirty spots. He certainly looked for nothing else. He knew he was handsome, but being handsome never meant anything to him. He supposed he squandered it, this face of his.

Wilson checked his watch. It would take the cab twenty minutes.

He left the building and discovered that the slight rain had developed into a downpour. He borrowed an umbrella from the doorman and hailed a cab. In the taxi, he rolled up the window so his hair wouldn't blow, and he touched the knot of his tie.

Le Bistro was jammed. Though Julia didn't have a reservation, they made room for her by squeezing in a small folding table, hidden under a long, white, starched tablecloth.

Julia arrived before Lauren.

Mark, her favorite waiter, smiled down at her. "Are we drinking today?"

"Darling, have I ever *not* had a drink?"

His thin brown hair was skinned back into a ponytail the size of a thumb, and his long pale fingers were laced together across a stomach that actually folded inward. "When you were pregnant."

"That's right."

"I was proud of you."

"Why, thank you," she said. "I was proud of me, too."

Lauren arrived and gave Mark a peck on both cheeks before sliding into her chair. She wore a typical lawyer's dark blue pantsuit, but the effect was more dramatic than numbing by the addition of a white silk blouse with a jabon knotted at the neck. Four pearl necklaces of varying lengths spilled in and out of the silk. Her thick black hair was tucked behind her ears and fell in a neat swoop all the way to the middle of her back.

"I'll have a glass of Chablis," Lauren said to Mark.

"And I'll take an old-fashioned."

"My, aren't we Jane Austen." Mark swiveled and was gone.

"You look happy." Julia smiled at Lauren's bright eyes.

"Bill and I have a lead on a baby."

Lauren was Chinese-American and Bill, her husband, came from blue-blood Waspdom. They'd met as undergraduates at Yale, and their marriage was just plain fun to watch, the way Bill's blond curly hair and pale skin contrasted with Lauren, while their twin natures pulled them together. Bill was a partner in the same firm as Lauren, and they'd been trying to have a baby for five years.

When Mark delivered the drinks, he opened their menus and jabbed with his finger. "Busy today, let's get those orders in."

"Actually, I do have a meeting at two-thirty," Lauren said. "I'm going to have the Caesar salad with grilled chicken."

"I haven't even thought about what to have."

"How about the French onion soup?" Mark said. "You love that."

"Yeah, okay, and then I get dessert," Julia said.

When Mark whisked away, she turned back to Lauren. "You didn't tell me Bill agreed to adopt."

"Isn't it wonderful?" Lauren shook her head and smoothed her long hair.

Julia sometimes wondered whether she loved Lauren so much because she was like a live, aesthetically beautiful, and satisfying experience whenever you were with her. But it made her uncomfortable to believe love could be so shallow and she knew, really, that their friendship flowed from how they each filled the empty places in the other.

"Should you have had lunch in the office to prepare for your two-thirty meeting?" Julia asked.

"I'm all set, and you sounded urgent."

Julia smiled at Lauren, an unspoken thank-you.

Mark flew up to the table and deposited the salad in front of Lauren and the soup for Julia. She picked up her spoon and tapped at the melted cheese on top of the soup, finally breaking through and reaching into the dark beef broth to scoop out onions. "I'm going to smell lousy this afternoon."

"Margaret's used to your smelliness."

"Thanks a bunch."

Lauren's eyes rested on Julia for a moment. "What's the matter?"

"Wilson entirely forgot our tenth wedding anniversary."

"Jesus, that guy—"

"There's more," Julia interrupted, "but I have to back up and tell you about other stuff first for you to understand."

Lauren stabbed a large lettuce leaf and piece of chicken, then crammed the whole business into her mouth. Somehow she still managed to chew like a lady.

Julia told Lauren about the camping trip in upstate New York ten years earlier, when she'd found the beetle grub with the fungus growing out of its head.

"You're an English major, how'd you know it was important?"

"I didn't say it *was* important."

"It's obviously important, you can tell from the story."

"Lauren, shut up and let me finish."

Lauren drained her wine and looked over her shoulder for Mark.

"Are you listening to me?" Julia said.

"I just need another glass of wine, hold on a second."

Julia bent over her bowl of soup and quickly ate three dripping spoonfuls of cheese and onion while Lauren ordered more wine.

She'd noticed in the last several months that Lauren seemed to be drinking a lot; even a few years ago, Lauren would have ordered an iced tea at lunch. To Julia, it was further proof that the infertility Lauren and Bill were dealing with had become a problem that needed to be resolved. She hoped they'd get lucky and find a baby fast.

"Wilson explained to me how funguses grow wherever they're eating, that's their nourishment,"

Julia said. "And there's this business about the sexual and asexual state of the fungus—"

"This actually sounds fascinating."

"You cannot pretend to me at this late date that you're interested in sex."

"I've *always* been interested in sex, it isn't a subject I talk about with you, that's all."

Julia grabbed her napkin and wiped up the broth and onions dribbling out of her mouth. She could get the onions neither in nor out. Finally, desperate, she sucked them in with a loud, disgusting sound.

"Lovely," Lauren said.

Julia grinned. "I'm jealous, who do you talk about sex with?"

"Bill." Though Lauren still held a fork in her right hand, she'd stopped eating.

"No one talks about sex with their *husband*. That's ridiculous."

"We tell each other stories, fantasies."

Julia reached for a roll and ripped it in two. She offered half to Lauren, who shook her head. "But isn't it embarrassing to tell Bill sexual fantasies that don't involve him?"

"Who says he's not involved?"

"Give me a break." Julia broke off a chunk of cheese and ate it. The taste was rich and musty, almost, in a peculiar way, sexual.

"He's always there, a voyeur."

Julia felt the blush spread across her cheeks.

"See why I don't talk about sex with you?" Lauren pointed her empty fork at Julia's face.

"I'm pathetic." Julia dipped the corner of her napkin into ice water and then dabbed at her cheeks, trying to avoid the images of Lauren that had crept into her head.

"Back to the fungus."

"Okay, so this beetle grub I found turned out to have an important fungus growing on it, and by finding it *on* its food source, they were able to replicate it in the sexual state, which is quite unusual and essential for any future studies."

Lauren nodded.

Julia wasn't certain how much she should reveal about the drug's purpose, so she kept the explanation general, saying merely that Wilson believed his research was major, a potentially prominent discovery.

"And Wilson's taking credit for finding the beetle—"

"You don't get it," Julia interrupted. "He really thinks he did find it."

Mark descended and cleared plates. "Dessert?"

"I'll have the crème brûlée," Julia said.

"And I want that chocolate cake, the one made with sour cream," Lauren said.

Lauren finished her second glass of wine and fiddled with her hair, tucking and retucking strands behind each ear. "You're in complete denial."

"*I'm* in denial?"

"You don't just forget something so important."

"Wilson doesn't believe he forgot."

"The point is, *we* know he's chosen to forget."

Their desserts arrived.

"Coffee, sweetums?" Mark said.

"I'm not your sweetums," Julia said.

"I just like to see you smile," he said.

Julia smiled grimly, all teeth.

"Not quite what I meant." Mark's tone was gentle.

"No coffee for me." Lauren's fork was in the air, poised for action as soon as Mark left them. "I'd love another glass of wine, but I'll go to sleep in the middle of an important meeting if I do."

"A regular coffee," Julia said.

"Okeydokey." Mark whirled around.

Lauren's face was bright. She ate a bite of chocolate cake, eyes laughing at Julia.

"So we had this huge fight," Julia said. "We're not speaking at all." She slid half a spoonful of crème brûlée into her mouth and left the spoon thrusting straight out of her lips like she was sucking on a popsicle. The sweetness of the cream jolted into the taste of burnt sugar.

"You have to make him remember who found the beetle grub."

"But it's *bigger* than that."

"Is it?"

"*Why* doesn't he remember, Lauren, why?" Tears filled her eyes.

Lauren chewed the last piece of cake—which she'd demolished in five bites—eyes wide and thoughtful.

"You're the one who spent five years in analysis,"

Julia said. "What does it mean that he's done this?"

"I know what it means." Lauren sipped her ice water and then aimed the fork still covered with thick chocolate right at Julia. "So do you."

CHAPTER 15

The president's boardroom table was spread with a white cloth and five places were set. The plates of cold poached salmon shone with a sheen of gelatinous goo.

"President Sebastian will be with you shortly," the secretary said.

Wilson, the first to arrive, was alone in the room.

"Thanks." He walked over to the windows and looked out at an uninspiring view.

His stomach felt odd. Wilson had always found living in New York City a strain. It was too loud and hammering for him. He didn't necessarily hanker after nature and trees, but a little peace and quiet was appealing. Also, fewer people.

"Dr. Streatfield, congratulations!"

Wilson turned and saw Jed Peterson. Pink bow tie today.

The men shook hands.

"Thanks."

"This is such exciting news—I just hope you can explain what you've done in terms I can understand." Jed grinned, small white teeth gleaming.

"I'll try."

President Sebastian wheeled in, her calm face broken by a large smile. "Jed, Wilson, why don't you take a seat?" She settled herself at the head of the table.

Wilson pulled out the chair two down from her, his back to the window, and Jed sat right next to her, across the table. Typical, Wilson thought.

"We're expecting Joe Ritten from development, and Jeffrey Tannenbaum." She looked at Wilson. "You've met Jeffrey, haven't you?"

The provost. Good grief.

"Yes, at some point or other."

The two other men arrived at that moment. Words of congratulation flowed around him. It wasn't that Wilson didn't feel as excited as they, but he was nervous. Lunch in a president's boardroom. Cold salmon. This was not where he belonged.

President Sebastian picked up her fork, signaling them that they could begin eating as well.

Wilson broke off a small piece of salmon, lifted it halfway to his mouth, and then just stared at it. No one seemed to notice.

"We're going to form a task force to coordinate all the publicity and development associated with the drug's announcement," the president said, "so I need you all to come up with those people you think might serve."

A task force?

"Wilson, your chair, Dr. Elliasen, ought to be on the committee, right?"

"Yes, that would be appropriate."

"I actually feel we might want to appoint a representative from the board of directors," Joe said. "I know it's unusual, but this is such a special circumstance, we simply must make use of every opportunity . . ."

"Who were you thinking of?" Jeffrey said. He was a rather obese man, squeezed into his wool suit like a sausage in its casing. His forehead shone with perspiration. He skillfully bit off a large portion of salmon from his fork.

"Patrick Kennedy, is who I was thinking."

"Brilliant!" President Sebastian said, pointing her fork at Joe.

"I guess I don't understand why you'd need a board member on the task force," Wilson said. He felt his face reddening just with the effort of speaking.

"Because we want to get the word out in the community," Joe said, "even before the FDA approval comes through and *that* translates into dollars."

"It does?"

"Nothing feeds success like success." Jeffrey tore a sourdough roll in half and smeared it with butter.

Saliva flooded Wilson's mouth and he wondered whether he was about to be sick. His belly grumbled and cramped.

"The main thing is that we want to be sure and get a jump on the pharmaceutical company—J. Dickson wasn't it?—who'll be producing this masterpiece," Joe said.

"Actually, I think there's something specific in the agreement with them about that . . ." Wilson started to say.

"You signed something without checking with us?" Jeffrey said.

"It was the initial agreement, five years ago," Wilson said, "before I really knew what I had, and after all, they funded all the research."

"I better give them a call."

"And let me know if you think I should talk to them," the president said.

Wilson ate a small piece of salmon. He drank some Perrier water and cut off a larger chunk. His head tipped to the plate and he lost track of the conversation as he ate. It was clear that he had nothing to offer, anyway. He supposed he'd have to attend the meetings, but they'd expect little from him. Suddenly he remembered the book idea.

"I'm thinking of writing a book," Wilson said. He'd interrupted the president in the middle of a comment.

She paused and gave him an indulgent smile. "What a fabulous idea—when can you finish it?"

"I haven't even started."

"It's the perfect vehicle for the entire launch," Joe said. His small hands fluttered around his bow tie.

"I've got to write it, and then see if we can find a publisher," Wilson said. "My wife's a literary agent and she thinks that with just a proposal, she might—"

"I didn't know your wife was an agent. What's her name, who's she with?" Jeffrey said.

Wilson turned to look at him. "She's got her own firm, Julia Fleming Literary Agency. She's small, but she represents good people, people you'd have heard of."

"So fiction and nonfiction?" Jeffrey said.

"Yes."

"Do you happen to have her card? I've written something that I'd love—" he paused, reddening, "well, I'll give you a call."

"All right, we're on track," said the president. "We'll have meetings about every other week or so, until six months before expected approval, when we'll go weekly."

Wilson sat quietly for the rest of the meeting, eating the delicious lunch, his mind moving backward.

When he was six years old, Wilson had dreaded the start of first grade. His mother walked him to school that morning through the woods surrounding their community of houses in Vermont. The morning was warm, air just touched with the suggestion of autumn and the sun spiking through leafy tree branches. Wilson wanted to be on his way to play Pooh Sticks in the creek.

His mother led him inside the school building and he basked in the cool and shade of its halls. They paused outside a classroom door, his mother checking a piece of paper. The door stood open and children scrambled about inside.

She left him at a desk and he stared out the window, watching for her until he saw her leave the building, cross the playground, climb the small hill, and disappear into the woods.

Later in the morning, the teacher taught them about the little boys' and little girls' rooms, and how you had to raise your hand to ask to go. He raised his hand immediately.

"Yes, Wilson?" The teacher looked puzzled.

"May I please be excused to go?"

She smiled. "Of course, here's the pass you should carry at all times." She handed him a big block of wood painted blue.

He took the pass.

"Do you know where the boys' room is?"

He nodded and left the classroom.

The door to the playground was propped open, letting in fresh air. He propped the blue bathroom pass against the door, walked outside, and headed for home. His mother didn't make him go back until the next day, and she took him to the creek for a picnic lunch and Pooh Sticks.

CHAPTER 16

It took George fifteen minutes to walk back to the apartment. The rain, falling hard and serious like the hand of God the priests warned them about, had soaked through his wool jacket. He rode the lift up to the tenth floor. Why the hell hadn't he taken a taxi, he wondered suddenly. It was like he couldn't believe he had money in his pocket and the right not to get wet.

In the dining alcove he quickly removed the files from Angela's bag and spread them out on the table. Damp clung to them, and the smell of wet paper mixed with wet wool made him feel achy and sick. Weather like this could get you down. He wanted a good cup of tea, like his gran made in the pot, pouring it through a strainer into his mug.

In the kitchen he found the bottle of scotch and made himself a neat finger in a juice glass. He held it up to the light, staring through the pretty amber-colored liquid, wondering what the bloody hell he was doing. Suddenly he was bone tired of everything, including this fucking job. He turned and headed back to the dining room table, sinking into a chair.

He opened one of the files and stared at the first paper. The type was minuscule and jet black, with paragraphs long and dense, broken only by a column of numbers. He turned the page. Next he found a drawing of something unrecognizable. Objects were connected and each succeeding object was bigger. The words strung together like crazy loops of wire. It was beyond him.

George closed the file. He'd been told to leave the papers here for pickup. But this was a far bigger catch then they'd expected. They thought this part of the operation would take two or three weeks. So maybe he should call and report?

He rose and crossed to the window. Rain pattered and streamed in rushing rivulets against the glass. He leaned his forehead on the cold windowpane and stared across the avenue to the Streatfields' apartment. The rain and daylight made actually seeing into the apartment impossible, but he could tell a light was on in the kitchen.

He decided to take a hot shower and then call his boss. He dumped the remaining scotch down the kitchen sink, kicked off his shoes in the living room, and whistling between his teeth, headed toward the bedroom and bath. He wouldn't stay down for long, not George McDuff, not him.

Emily and Jimmy were wet and bedraggled by the time they got home, and once their tummies were packed with warm food, they'd been eager for their naps.

Angela shut Jimmy's door and fairly tiptoed down the hall, turning at the end and going directly into her room. She ran a bath, letting the water get good and hot, and stripped off her clothes. Once soaking in the bath, her stomach stopped clenching with cramps and she lay back with relief, closing her eyes.

She wasn't supposed to see her baby because they said that would make it easier. But she'd started bleeding heavily just after the birth. The doctor had left already, and she knew the nurse was busy behind the screen, washing the baby. She'd called out about all the blood and she could remember the nurse peeking around the screen, thinking she was being a trouble-maker, and then her face all astonished and frightened at the sight of the blood dripping onto the floor.

The nurse had run from the room and Angie heard the baby, *her* baby, start to cry, so she knew the baby had been left alone. She'd sat up immediately and fairly slid off the table. Blood poured down her legs, wetting her feet and making the business of walking treacherous. Her baby cried and cried, like its little heart was broken.

She rounded the screen and saw its fists waving in the air. It was in a little bathtub, but no water had been added yet. Angie heard the nurse and doctor come through the door, their voices raised in worry about where she was. The baby was a girl and she'd had only a moment to press her lips to the child's forehead.

Angela opened her eyes and kicked at the bathwater slightly. She saw that her belly was no longer round and pushed out. She did not look like she'd had a baby. It was over.

Quickly she sat up and washed. Then she was out of the tub, drying herself roughly, and getting dressed in fresh clothes, from top to bottom. She carried her small pile of clothes worn that morning to the laundry room and started the washer.

They promised her that the baby was adopted by a wealthy, professional couple. She imagined her daughter asleep at this very moment, in a fancy crib, nearly lost beneath the warm down comforter trimmed in white lace.

And she just knew that her baby's Irish nanny sat in a rocking chair singing lullabies. She just knew.

The taxicab inched through post-lunch traffic toward Julia's office building. Rain pummeled the cab's windows like small fists banging to be let in. Though it was early afternoon, headlights glittered in the dark day and there rose in Julia an unusual nostalgia for her childhood in Los Angeles.

Her sport in high school and later at Yale had been swimming, and she remembered all those years as if they had been lived entirely underwater, the sensation of cool, smooth water caressing and embracing her, and the way her mind dove deeper than the depth of the water allowed her body to go. Julia gazed out at the drenched streets of New York City and imagined plunging into the rain as it fell, swimming ruggedly through the water-laden air a few feet above the sidewalks.

When she came into the office, Margaret was also just back from lunch.

"Guess we gotta get to work," she said. She picked up the phone and quickly jotted down messages.

"You know what I have to do right away?" Julia kicked off her high heels and walked flat-footed into her own office.

"The Elinor call?" Margaret whispered.

"Yes."

"I'll get the M&M's."

"You are such a dear."

Elinor Schaeffer, her most successful author, wrote literary fiction that actually, and confoundedly, sold well. When she won the National Book Award the year before, her reputation had soared.

Julia called her at least once a week.

Margaret scurried in just as Julia greeted Elinor in her syrupy *you're my most successful and valuable client* voice. She plunked down a wooden bowl brimming with M&M's and gave Julia a conspiratorial grin.

Julia nodded. She was using the headset so that her hands were free. She selected an orange candy, popped it into her mouth, and listened to Elinor.

"I had the worst diarrhea this morning, I mean I almost didn't make it to the bathroom for God's sake, so I took some Imodium A-D, and it's a little better and I only *just* got to work. I've written maybe a paragraph."

Elinor's voice, high and nasal, was one of her most unattractive qualities. This was particularly unfortunate, since *All Things Considered* had told Julia flat out that they simply couldn't bear to interview her again; listeners had flooded the wires, begging that they get her off the air. Television coverage, for the same reason, was getting more and more difficult to arrange, and even speaking engagements had dwindled to only a few a year.

"Elinor, I know you'll hit your stride later today. And if you don't, it's not the end of the world. No one's got a stopwatch running. You can start fresh tomorrow morning."

"I was just trying to tell myself that. Julia, you are so wise."

"We haven't had lunch in ages." Julia popped a brown M&M in her mouth. "Let's go to Elaine's tomorrow, what do you think? It's Friday—we could drink martinis."

Elinor drank religiously.

"Oh, that would be marvelous."

"And I have an idea to discuss with you."

The time had come to broach the issue of a voice coach. It'd be tricky to convince Elinor without delivering a punch to her self-esteem, but Julia had to be ruthless about certain issues. Sales would start to slip.

Elinor needed to be out and about, but no one could stand to listen to her.

Triumphant, she hung up the phone. "Mission accomplished!"

She scooted in her chair to the doorway between the offices. Her black patent heels, returned to her feet, went tap-tap, tap-tap. "I've got a great idea."

Margaret stared at her with a calm expression. Julia knew that when she got hyper, Margaret exuded peace and tranquillity in an effort to bring her down.

"We could dub your voice for Elinor's!"

Despite herself, Margaret laughed out loud. "You're nuts."

"You *sound* like a writer," Julia said. Then she stared at Margaret with narrowed eyes, as if she'd never really seen her before. "You look like one, too."

"Maybe I am one, secretively." She smiled enigmatically.

"I get first dibs."

The phone rang and Margaret turned to answer.

CHAPTER 17

Wilson walked by Joan's desk without a greeting. His shirt collar had been soaked with rain just from dashing between the taxi and the front door of the building. He wanted to sit in his office and not move for at least fifteen minutes. His collar would dry a little, and he could catch up on some thinking that needed doing.

His door stood open about two inches, an amount of space that said neither open nor closed, but instead implied hurry. He remembered that he'd rushed out to get home and change his clothes before lunch with the president. He pushed the door open wider, slammed it shut behind him, and collapsed in his old, creaking chair. His eyes closed briefly and then peeked at the desk with dread. All his chores were boring, answering e-mails, accepting or rejecting speaking invitations, writing speeches, outlining a book, preparing to teach a course in the graduate department. Oh God, he groaned inwardly. I need to start a new research project. I don't want to do these other things.

Then Wilson noticed his left file drawer, yanked out, hanging open, and at least half the files missing. He jerked forward and rummaged through the remaining files, trying to think of the others that had been there. A dozen or so files were gone. He jumped up, threw open his door, and ran down the hall to where the implacable Joan sat with a ramrod-straight back, typing into the computer terminal.

"Joan, did someone go into my office while I was out?"

She twirled around on the chair so that she faced him, her hands still on the keyboard. "Your kids stopped by."

"My *kids*?"

"With their nanny. The baby had vomited or something and she needed to clean him up. I thought you wouldn't mind."

"Of course I don't mind about that, but I'm missing at least a dozen files from my desk."

"But why would she—"

"I'm sure our nanny didn't take them," Wilson interrupted. He ran both hands through his hair. "I think we better call security."

"Right away, Dr. Streatfield."

Wilson went back to his office, stared at his desk, and remembered how odd the door had looked, open a mere two inches. Back in the hall, he headed down to Dr. Goldfarb's office, where he stuck his head around the door. "Ronny, I'm missing some files from my desk. Security's on their way up, but I wondered if you were here over the couple of hours at lunchtime."

Ronny raised his small bald head and blinked at Wilson. Finally he spoke. "I got a sandwich at Junior's, didn't notice a thing." He blinked again. "Important stuff?"

"I'm trying to remember."

"I know what you mean." Ronny looked at his own office, where files, papers, and books were heaped everywhere. "Frankly, I'm impressed you even noticed."

The whole department knew of Wilson's work, and an element of jealousy had been apparent for more than a year now, since it became clearer that his discovery could actually do what he'd theorized.

"I don't suppose it matters, really. Aren't the clinical trials just gearing up?" Ronny said.

"I know, but it's still weird. You should be concerned about your studies."

Dr. Ronny Goldfarb blinked for the third and last time. They both knew his research on another fungus had been disappointing. He turned back to the papers spread over his desk, removed his glasses, and peered at a page covered in columns of numbers.

"Thanks, Ron," Wilson said.

On the way back down the corridor, he ran into

the security man, who wore a blue uniform, and to
Wilson's surprise actually carried a gun in his hip hol-
ster. He had a round face and shiny dark skin. "Dr.
Streatfield?" he asked in the musical lilt of the
Islands.

Wilson held out his hand. "And you are?"

"Armand Jones." His hand, firm and dry, suggested competence.

"Right in here, Mr. Jones." Wilson led the way
into his office and pointed at the file drawer still jut-
ting out. "My best guess is, I'm missing about a dozen
files."

Armand Jones squatted next to the drawer and
balanced there with wide thighs bulging. His large
head peered carefully into the drawer. He rose slowly
to his feet while his gaze searched the room.
"Anything else moved or missing?"

"I didn't notice anything else." Wilson shoved his
hands into his pockets and stared at the top of his
desk. "But I didn't really *look*, if you know what I
mean."

"Best do so."

"Of course." Wilson stepped closer to the desk
and then picked up a pile of correspondence in order
to look beneath it.

"Doctor, you might want to look first, without
moving any objects." Mr. Jones stood by the window,
glancing outside as if genuinely curious about the
view.

Wilson replaced the papers and let his eye travel
the desktop. He noticed a small path, where objects

had been shunted aside. He followed the path to where it stopped at the framed photos of Julia and his children, and he saw that Emily's picture had been turned sideways so that if he were sitting at the desk he wouldn't have a full view of her. "The photo of my daughter's been moved, but our receptionist, Joan, said the baby-sitter brought my kids in—needed to use the bathroom or something." Wilson turned and looked at Armand Jones.

"What do you know about the baby-sitter?"

"Angela's a lovely Irish girl. She lives with us, there's no way she'd take files from my office."

"May I sit down, Doctor?" Jones placed a thick hand on the back of the only chair other than Wilson's desk chair.

"Of course, I'm sorry."

Both men sat, and Wilson stared at Armand Jones's black clodhopper shoes, polished to a sheen, the laces tight and straight.

"Those shoes don't look too comfortable," Wilson said.

Armand's face froze in a mask of professionalism for a momentary tick. Then the wide mouth widened even farther and opened to the kind of grin only good men gave. "I grew up going barefoot and I don't find any kind of shoes a decent fit."

"I spent summers barefoot, too."

Now the men's eyes shifted back to the window and a mutual longing clung to them like the clouds hanging around the tall New York buildings. To be a barefoot boy again. Each exhaled softly, not hearing the other.

"Why would someone want your files, Dr. Streatfield?" Armand said.

"I've made a discovery." Wilson felt himself on uncertain ground here. He doubted that the luncheon group with whom he'd just met in the president's boardroom would approve of announcing his discovery to the building's security force. It wouldn't do much for the publicity campaign.

"Top secret?" Armand's eyes twinkled.

Wilson grinned. "Somewhat. But the crazy thing is, it's not *really* top secret. The clinical trials have already started, so plenty of people know about it." His hands rubbed together and then just the two index fingers, as if he were out in the woods and scraping two sticks together for a fire. "I sure as hell can't think of anything that could be done with my files."

Armand leaned over with a grunt. His strong fingers delicately untied the shoelaces of first one shoe, then the other. A small groan escaped as he loosened the tongue of the shoes. He straightened up. "So, an important drug, a big deal?"

"Yes," Wilson said. "One of the most important ever."

"In that case, I think we've got to take this seriously. Call in the city police and let them loose."

"But there's nothing—"

"Look, I'm sure you're right," Armand interrupted, "but some dumb cluck isn't going to know that. You could be in danger."

"Oh Christ." Wilson stood up and grabbed the back of his chair, bouncing it on old hinges.

"Don't touch anything. They'll probably try for fingerprints."

Wilson yanked his hands away from the chair, which continued its lonely bounce for a few seconds.

"I'll use the receptionist's phone." Armand leaned over again, quickly retied his shoes, and stood up. "Hands off," he warned again as he left the office.

Wilson shoved both hands into his pockets and walked over to the window. The rain had stopped as he and Armand talked, but drops now pinged against the glass. He didn't think of the missing files. He knew they were unimportant and he now wished he'd never reported them gone.

No, he thought of his luncheon date the next day. Excitement gathered in the center of his chest, tremulous and slightly sickening, but not to be denied. His toes stretched inside his cotton socks and touched the leather walls of his shoes. He wiggled them as hard and violently as he could.

Since Mr. Wong wanted the files and papers immediately, he sent the limo over for George. They barreled down Park Avenue, running a couple of yellow and red lights, and George felt the breath start to come short and spurting. He ricocheted between being convinced he'd done a great job and having somehow jeopardized the entire operation.

The limo entered the underground garage, hidden beneath Mr. Wong's mansion, and let George out right by the elevator before parking.

"Go to Mr. Wong's office," the driver instructed.

The elevator was small, accommodating only two small men at the most. He hit the button for the second floor and watched as the elevator's steel doors slid shut. His heart fluttered and he felt light-headed. The whole endeavor had turned real, much more real than procuring hookers and tailing a homesick Irish girl. Suddenly he knew he could die.

The elevator opened into a small antechamber that was entirely carpeted, floor, walls, and ceiling, in a heavy black carpet. On previous visits, he'd thought it was an interesting effect. Now he could imagine the screams and blood it would disguise. He pressed the bell to the right of the only door. After a pause, the door swung open.

In the office where he'd gotten the original assignment, Mr. Wong was seated behind his massive desk. He snapped his fingers by way of greeting, then tapped the top of the desk with one small, manicured finger.

George always wanted to clasp his hands together at the chest and bow deeply, in the Chinese way, but he'd so far managed to stifle the urge. Mr. Wong was actually very American, and George doubted that he'd appreciate an Irishman using Chinese customs.

George placed all the files on top of the desk and then took a giant step backward. Abruptly he made a decision. If he got out of here alive, he'd disappear. Enough of this shit. He'd rather do anything, including the damn fish market, anything other than this.

"Return to the kitchen and wait for your orders,"

Mr. Wong said. His voice, as always, was low and without inflection.

"I'm not feeling too hot—"

"Ask cook for something to eat."

"Yes, sir."

Mr. Wong nodded, dismissing him.

George walked toward the door through which he'd entered the room.

"No, use the stairs," Mr. Wong said.

George turned right and glanced back toward the desk out of the corners of his eyes. Mr. Wong had already opened several files, scattering the contents across the smooth mahogany. One sheet of paper was lifted and in his hands, raised for him to read. His thin, tense body curved like a question mark over the desk and files.

George came out into a hall with walls that were done in a deep maroon and ornately scrolled wallpaper, turned right, and passing several closed doors, ended up at the large, gracious landing. Two wing chairs were balanced on either side of a spindly table that held a Chinese vase exploding with white roses. The scent of the roses wrapped strong fingers around his throat. He coughed and hurried down the stairs, one hand gliding along the smooth banister. The black and white marble floor in the entrance undulated dizzily below him, and his mind swirled with confusion.

He'd always been the tough guy, a little scrapper even at three years old. He'd had to be, of course, but he'd thought he liked it, he'd thought it was who he was. He collapsed at the long kitchen table and dropped his head forward, panting a bit.

"George, you okay?" the cook said.

He had a terrible feeling that all hell was about break loose. And it'd be his fault. Maybe he'd just go home. "Can you make me a cup of tea?" he asked.

The Chinese cook, a tiny, shriveled old man, stared at him. He picked up a green enameled teapot that was sitting on a burner of the stove and poured a small amount into a tiny teacup, then carefully placed it in front of George.

The tea was black as George's heart, black and bitter and broken.

The kitchen intercom buzzed and the cook answered with a gruff noise in Chinese. He released the intercom button and spoke to George. "Boss wants you."

He should have run when he had the chance instead of sitting here sipping this black business. He stood, unsteady, and the fear settled on him. Once, back in Ireland, when he'd been drinking and caused a little uproar, he'd gone running out of town and suddenly been lost in the trees' shrieking shadows. A drink would be good right about now.

"Better hurry," the cook said.

George strode out of the kitchen, through the murky dining room, and into the entrance hall. The overcast, rainy afternoon swelled through every room in the house. He took the stairs two at a time, running now. If this was it, he'd get it over with. He could have tried the front door, the kitchen door, the deeply buried garage, but they were all guarded, and even if he'd been lucky, he had no faith in hiding from Mr. Wong, whose reach was so tenacious and stretched to such lengths. Better to get it over with.

The office door was open, which was surprising. Two men, also Chinese, stood on either side of the door, their faces calm. They didn't *look* like they were about to kill him. Mr. Wong was seated behind the desk. There were no signs of the papers and files George had so recently delivered.

"Please sit down," Mr. Wong invited.

George, puzzled by the sense of gaiety in the room, sat and stared at Mr. Wong, who smiled. He looked very weird, smiling.

"I'm delighted," Mr. Wong said.

That was when George thought that he might pee in his pants. Relief rushed through him like a whiskey on a bitter cold Christmas Eve. Just like that, he forgot his promise to get out when he could.

Mr. Wong took the biggest gold ball that was sitting regally on his desk and rolled it toward George. "Keep it," he said.

George wrapped the ball in his hand and turned it hurriedly, pressing and stroking like it was a woman needing his attention.

"Most delighted," Mr. Wong said. "You have a couple of days off—enjoy yourself—stop back in for work then. A good boy like you, I'm sure we'll have plenty of opportunities."

George stood up because Mr. Wong did. "Yes, sir." He headed back toward the door.

"Use the elevator, George, the limo will take you anyplace you need."

George swerved and changed direction. When he entered the black carpeted room, the elevator was waiting, doors wide as if with open arms. He stepped in and pushed the button marked BG. His hand still clutched the gold ball. What the bloody hell was he supposed to do with that, he wondered. Melt it down?

The limo was waiting just outside the elevator, engine idling. He climbed in, busy thinking about what to do with his days off.

Nothing came immediately to mind.

CHAPTER 18

When Julia got home at five-thirty, the apartment was so quiet that at first she thought Angela and the kids were out. Small discreet lights suggested the path to follow: a lamp in the entrance, two dimmed sconces in the living room, and finally the glimmer of light spilling from the door to the library. Julia walked on tiptoe. It was every mother's dream to glimpse the life of her children without revealing herself.

Angie sat in the center of the couch, Jimmy cuddled in her lap, tight in the crook of her right arm, while Emily crushed into her left arm. She held the picture book low so that the children could see, and her voice danced deeply, with a measured cadence.

Jimmy's eyes were half-lidded from sleepiness, his head tucked into her breast, but his attention trained on the book. Emily's head was erect, even alert, and it seemed as if her entire body was engaged in listening to the story, looking at the pictures, smelling the pages of the book, touching the cover with one finger. She had entered the book.

A rush of emotion filled Julia.

Was it gratitude? In part.

Was it relief? Certainly.

But why did her hands tremble and her knees weaken? Why did her eyes fill and her heart pound?

Love.

Not for her children, though of course love was always there for them.

Love for a young Irish woman named Angela Byrne. Julia loved her. She felt as if she would give her life for Angie, as if she now possessed an older daughter, whom she'd discovered only recently. And beneath this joyful love sounded a different rhythm, something sad, crushed, and broken.

Angela looked up first, aware of Julia's silent shadow and presence in the open doorway, perhaps feeling this enormous emotion directed toward her. She smiled at Julia.

"Angela, you're magnificent," Julia said.

"Mommy!" Emily leapt off the couch.

A blush rushed across Angie's pale cheeks.

"Hi, darling." Julia picked up Emily, who clutched her around the middle with strong legs.

Angela still held the book open and Jimmy

pointed a knobby, baby finger at the page, jabbing in a smooth motion.

"Take the night off," Julia said impulsively. "Go see a movie or something—you deserve a break."

"Oh no, I couldn't." Angela, flustered, closed the book and put it on the coffee table. Then she pulled Jimmy more securely onto her lap. "How's your diaper?" she whispered to him.

Julia, still carrying Emily, walked across the library and sat down on the couch next to Angela. She leaned sideways and gently touched her shoulder to Angela's. "It would really make me happy if you went out. You're not supposed to be working all day and the evenings, too."

Now Emily tumbled off Julia, on top of both Jimmy and Angela.

"Oh Mother Mary!" Angela laughed.

Jimmy's feet moved like the wheels of his toy truck, around and around. Kick, kick, kick.

"Are you sure you can handle things?" Angela glanced with smiling eyes at Julia.

"I can do it, Angie, promise," she said. "Now, get out of here." Julia picked Emily up under her arms, sailed her over the coffee table, and plunked her down on the floor. Then she swiveled back around and grabbed Jimmy. "Go on!"

"I'll just change, then." Angie ran out of the library with Emily chasing after her.

"Come back here this minute," Julia yelled.

Emily stopped at the library door to turn and give her mother a mischievous look.

"Emily Streatfield," Julia warned.

She bounced back into the room.

"Will you help me with Jimmy so I can get out of my good suit?" Julia asked Emily.

"Okay."

"Pick out a book for him, and two toys, and I'll meet you back in my bedroom."

Julia got into a pair of black sweats and thick red socks, shooed Angela out of the apartment, and headed for the kitchen. Six o'clock, time for the kids' dinner. She was surprised that Wilson hadn't come home yet. After she put Jimmy in his high chair, with a bagel crust to gnaw on, she took out the leftover stew, spooned it into a saucepan, and heated it over a low flame.

Emily appeared with paper and crayons, which she efficiently set up on the kitchen table. Julia gazed at her, feeling the usual sense of awe at her daughter's confidence, focus, and pleasure at working alone. They were qualities she'd inherited from Wilson, Julia knew well enough. She herself had been the kind of kid who tore around the neighborhood on a bike too large for her, dashing from group to group, welcomed by all, exuberant because of the existence of so many people in the world, source of endless talk and touch.

Now she listened to Jimmy's gobbledygook mutterings and hoped he might take after her. He watched her watching him, and in his delight waved the bagel crust in half circles above his head, crowing.

They all heard the key in the lock and then the apartment door swinging open.

"Hello," Wilson said.

Emily dashed out of the kitchen.

Julia had planned to forget their disagreement. He believed what he believed, and no amount of talking was going to change his mind. But his voice tonight as he said hello was furry and damp, like the wet ground where mushrooms grew. So, she knew, they were not yet finished. Her stomach tightened, and the discomfort rose up into her chest.

She stood in the kitchen doorway and watched as Wilson hung up his raincoat and then gathered Emily into his arms.

"Hi, sweetie," Julia said.

"I *said* hello." He looked through her.

"I was returning your greeting," she said. "I gave Angela the night off, by the way."

He stepped toward her. "Why?"

"She's supposed to get evenings off."

"Since when?"

"It's the *law*." Julia turned and headed back to the stove, where she picked up the large wooden spoon and stirred the thick stew. She opened the refrigerator, found an opened bottle of red wine, uncorked it, and added about a cup of wine to the stew. She stirred again.

"Wow, great drawing," Wilson said to Emily. "Jimmy, how're you doing?"

Beneath his obvious irritation with her, there was an unusual sense of merriment. He walked to a cabinet and took out a wine glass, which he filled with the last bit of red wine.

No, please, you have it.

Julia entered the dark dining room, switched on the recessed lights, which she loathed, and peered at the bottles clustered on the sideboard, searching for the Chivas. Holding the scotch firmly, she marched back to the kitchen and made herself a stiff drink.

"So, I hear you guys were at my office today." Wilson sat at the kitchen table, opposite Emily, sipping his wine.

"What?" Julia said.

"I saw my picture on your desk," Emily said. From when I was just a *baby*."

"You were at Daddy's office?" Julia said. "Why was that, Emily?"

"Jimmy was sick and it rained'ed so much."

"Did you see anyone else there?" Wilson's back was to Julia.

"Lots." Emily was concentrating on her picture, the crayon moving like a machine.

"I mean in my office."

Julia walked around the table so that she could look at Wilson's face. "Where were you?"

His expression shifted and then closed to her. "Lunch with the president." He spoke with such pride that Julia felt like a toy cap gun had been fired inside her head. Pop, pop, gotcha.

"Why're you asking Emily if there was anyone else around?"

He shrugged, eyes still avoiding hers. "No big deal."

Julia took a gulp of Chivas and held the scotch in

her mouth for a long moment before finally swallowing. She stared at him and tried to imagine why she'd ever fallen in love with him, married him, and had his children.

It was unfathomable.

"Are we eating soon?" Wilson asked.

"I'm just heating up the stew. About another five minutes."

He jumped out of his chair. "I want to get into jeans—I'll be right back."

That's when Julia noticed he was wearing the slacks and sweater she'd bought him a year ago. He must have come home to change, since she could remember he'd had on old khakis and a flannel shirt that morning. Uneasiness swept through her and she suddenly turned back to the stew. Though only moments before, she'd been wondering why she loved this man enough to have had his children, now she was terrified that he was going to leave her. He'd always thrown her off-balance.

Always.

After the Met's performance of *Turandot,* so many years ago, Wilson walked Julia three blocks north to his favorite eating place, DaVinci's. The Italian restaurant was tiny, even by New York City standards of minuscule space, and when Julia looked at Wilson Streatfield's face, she could see the pores on the skin of his nose. He was the color of honey, but the open pores gleamed white. When she blinked, they disappeared and his face blended together, the distinguished nose, liquid brown eyes, thick black lashes, carved cheekbones, dimples. My God, she thought, this man is gorgeous.

His eyes roamed around the room, then peered down at his empty place setting. Though he looked like a seducer, he didn't behave like one. Julia remembered he was a research physician, and she thought that, in her cleverness, she saw him as he was: an absentminded scientist who slept in his socks, wore his hair long because he never went to the barber, and was essentially, if not exactly, a virgin. She could have this man so easily, and in knowing that, she decided she wanted him.

At that very moment, his putatively shy eyes rose to hers and he spoke. "You look like you're good in bed," he said, "but I must tell you I don't say that because you're attractive. We theorize it has something to do with pheromones. Probably most men want to get you into bed—am I right?"

Their drinks had been delivered only seconds before this remarkable series of sentences. Julia felt like she was having one of those nightmares about academic failure, where you've no idea an exam has been scheduled for a particular time and place, and you're utterly unprepared. She gulped at her gin and tonic, noting that the restaurant made a weak drink.

Julia stared at him. She knew just how to hold her gaze, position her chin, deliver with wide eyes. "Yes," she said.

He was puzzled. "Yes what?"

"Yes, all men want to go to bed with me." Her

eyes deliberately wandered the room. She saw nothing, but she knew he believed she saw everything.

Score: one to one.

"Umm," he murmured, not in a suggestive, sexy way, but more bored, as if she really didn't count for much.

No matter how fast she was, no matter how smart, she could never stay ahead. Wilson always won. When she realized that this quality of his was so central, she simply gave up. It was his game. She didn't want to play. Let him think what he liked. *She* wasn't keeping score.

Now, twelve years later, she saw the incredible dilemma she'd created. They were adversaries in the marriage game and Wilson had been winning for a very long time.

CHAPTER 19

E linor Schaeffer was always late, but Julia took no chances. She arrived five minutes early and ordered them both martinis, and then, since she couldn't sit in Elaine's and stare off into space as if she were unemployed, she took out her organizer and began flipping through it. Two weeks and there was Thanksgiving glaring at her. She scribbled Y-U-C-K across the four-day weekend, a letter on each day. Seeing that marvelously descriptive word yawning across her calendar felt good.

She wished her parents would stay at a hotel instead of the pullout couch bed in their library. Before Angela moved in, they'd stayed in that extra room. Maybe the library's bed would be too uncomfortable to bear.

I wish.

Julia glanced up and saw Elinor at the coat check. Quickly she closed the organizer, recapped her pen, and crammed everything back into her bag. She stood and waited while Elinor meandered through the dining room. She wore plaid wool slacks in a navy and red color scheme with a matching navy turtleneck. Her dark brown hair was pulled straight back from a plain face to fall in a braid down the middle of her back. She looked like something out of a Wellesley yearbook, circa 1962.

"Hi." The nasal whine again.

Deep breath, Julia.

"Elinor, how lovely of you to join me." Julia gave her a peck on the cheek.

"You're my agent, of course I'll have lunch with you." Elinor sat down in the chair being held by the waiter. With both hands clutching its seat, she jumped it forward.

"You can bring the martinis now," Julia said to the waiter.

"Yes, ma'am."

"How did the writing go this morning?"

Elinor opened her eyes wide, as if surprised by such a question, though it seemed like a logical one to Julia.

"Terrible." Two plump fingers plucked at the edge of the tablecloth.

"Where are you?"

"About midway, I *think*." She gave Julia a significant look.

"We know about midway."

"Do we?"

"Remember in your last one," Julia said, horrified to realize that she'd momentarily blocked on the name of Elinor's previous novel. "Right at the midway point you got bogged down."

"Now I do remember that. Thank goodness I have you."

To Julia's dismay, her eyes seemed to be swimming with tears.

The drinks arrived and Julia held up her glass as if to make a toast. Elinor's arm slinked out from her lap and picked up her martini. They gently touched glasses with a tiny ringing noise, barely audible in the crowded restaurant.

They sipped and smiled at each other. Suddenly Julia liked Elinor again, the way she honestly had when she'd first read a short story by her, called her up, and urged her to write a novel.

"What else is bothering you?" Julia leaned forward and across the table.

Their waiter loomed over them, offering menus. "Ready to take a look?"

"I'll just have your linguine in clam sauce," Elinor said without even taking the menu.

Lord, she was always lunching with women who knew what they wanted. It would be complimentary to Elinor if she ordered the same thing, but she loathed clam sauce. She grabbed the menu and scanned the specials.

"I'll have the grilled tuna."

"Very good," the waiter said.

"How do you always know when something's bothering me?" Elinor said.

"Because you have such an honest face."

Elinor giggled. "I hope not *too* honest, since I'm having an extramarital affair."

"Elinor! How exciting."

"Yes, isn't it?"

She'd flushed crimson and her eyes were wet again.

No way she'd finish the book by the new year, not if she was having an affair.

"Do you disapprove terribly?" Elinor said.

"I don't disapprove at all."

"Oh, thank God." She collapsed backward against her chair, clutching the martini with both thick hands. Her nails were bitten raw.

Who on earth would want to sleep with Elinor Schaeffer?

"He's someone I met when I was at Barnes and Noble." She smiled. "He was buying my book and I just couldn't resist introducing myself, and can you believe it, he's an attorney but he wants to write novels. Not literary, of course, more like Scott Turow material, but I'm advising him."

"Have you read his work?"

Who knows, maybe the guy would be a find.

"Not yet. He's too shy, but I'm going to insist soon."

"Allen doesn't suspect anything?"

"I don't think so. But it's all so—" she waved her hands helplessly, "exciting."

"Of course it is." Julia sipped her martini. "I only hope this won't threaten your marriage."

"I love Allen completely and utterly." Elinor drained her martini and then stared into the empty glass. "This affair is such an upper, you know, it just inspires me."

"I'm all for inspiration." Julia signaled to their waiter for two refills on their martinis.

"You're so good to talk to, Julia."

"Have you told your shrink?"

"Oh, absolutely. He thinks I'm working out some important issues."

"Uh-huh."

Their lunch arrived and they both began eating as if they'd been on a two-day fast.

"There is something of a professional nature I needed to discuss with you, in preparation for the book tour and publicity that'll be part of the next novel." Affair or not, they had to do something about Elinor's voice.

"But I'm only halfway done."

"Trust me, you'll finish and it'll be marvelous."

Elinor's face flushed, and now Julia could see why a man would find her attractive.

"I wanted to suggest that you get some one-on-one media coaching."

"What's that?" Her green eyes were amused. "Is this the new look of publishing? You know, marketing one's books?"

"I confess, it is."

Julia pulled a sheepish expression, hoping to make Elinor laugh.

Elinor laughed.

"So what would this *media coach* teach me?"

"How to handle yourself on camera, how to pitch your voice, how to dress, all that."

"But I am who I am, Julia. My writing sounds just like I look and people seem to love my books just as they are."

"I know, but . . ."

"I'm not going to get into the same boat that's sinking poor old Hillary."

"You mean Hillary Rodham Clinton?"

"She's been so busy doing her hair and worrying about her image, she's lost herself in the hustle and bustle."

Julia peered down at her plate and carved off another piece of excellent tuna. One more attempt wouldn't hurt. "But you do need to sell books, while Hillary needs to sell nothing."

They ate quietly, neither speaking.

"Okay, forget it. Just write your book and enjoy your affair," Julia said.

"Have the coach call me—I'll try one meeting and see what I think."

Yup, Julia couldn't help but like her, despite the plaid pants.

The rain had stopped, but the sky still hung low with dark clouds, and Wilson imagined the interior of

DaVinci's, its cozy wood paneling and the intense odors of tomato sauce, oregano, basil, garlic, and pasta. He realized suddenly that he'd taken Julia to this restaurant when they first met. Guilt surprised him, flashing to the front of his brain like the neon signs over Times Square. He'd never been unfaithful to Julia, though he figured that had more to do with his virtual love affair with WS-100 than with any moral scruples. Fidelity wasn't something one could regulate by philosophy or religion. It was, he thought, both deeper and more shallow than that. He didn't truly believe infidelity mattered, as long as a man didn't hurt his wife. He wouldn't hurt Julia since this lunch—and whatever else it became—had nothing to do with her.

Susan sat with perfect poise at their table, a glass of white wine in one thin hand. Her nails were shaped and smooth, covered with a pale, pearly polish. She didn't smile, which pushed him off-balance.

"I hope you don't mind that I went ahead." She held up the wine.

"Of course not."

Wilson ordered a martini for himself.

"If you're having a martini—" she said.

He ordered two martinis.

"What's happening with the drug?" Susan asked.

He looked into her beautiful face and felt his erection begin. God, this woman. "President Sebastian has appointed a task force to deal with the PR." He shrugged, modest. "Not my kind of thing."

"No, you're just a brilliant scientist," she said, grinning.

The martinis arrived, and Wilson held his glass up. "To Susan—may she, too, find a scientist's good luck."

She flushed. "That's so sweet."

They touched glasses delicately.

"But it's not just luck, you know that," Susan said.

The martini's warmth filled his stomach and swept into his chest. "Right." He opened his menu and began to study the choices.

They both decided on a penne with sausage, and placed their orders. Wilson looked at his watch. "At this rate, we'll be out of here in just an hour."

"Do you have any meetings this afternoon?"

"No, not a thing but piles of correspondence."

He didn't want to mention an appointment with Armand later because he'd been told to keep his counsel about the missing files.

"I thought we might have coffee back at my place," Susan said. "It's not far."

Wilson picked up the martini and gazed at her over the rim of the glass. The only question, as far as he was concerned, was why they had to bother with food.

The kitchen in Julia and Wilson's apartment was beautiful that night. White cabinets washed by dim lights, the black granite countertops shining, maple floor swept and gleaming, the heavy black Dutch oven on the stove, bubbling with potato and ham soup.

Julia was trying hard not to show her surprise that Wilson wasn't home yet. She hadn't said anything to the kids or Angela about actually expecting him, so that when they finally sat down to dinner, she acted as if it were not strange.

But it was. He hadn't even called to tell her when he'd be home. Where could he be? Was he all right? She'd telephoned his office in the late afternoon, and Joan said that Dr. Streatfield hadn't mentioned he'd be away, but that he *was* away.

Julia and Angela both drank glasses of red burgundy. A false calm hovered so steadfastly that even Jimmy, in his high chair, was quietly gnawing on a piece of toast. His jaws moved rhythmically, mashing and mashing. Julia thought the sound might drive her mad, so she turned on the radio. Something classical, with French horns, plaintively filled the lovely room.

She and Angela got the kids bathed and into bed by eight o'clock. Then Julia told Angie that she had a manuscript to read and she was going to climb into bed and do the reading there. Angela, unassuming as always, had seemed a bit relieved.

Julia did have a manuscript to read, the first that Margaret had ever passed along. She unhooked her pleated, black wool skirt, stepped out of it, and carefully hung it up. Then she yanked off the stockings, grateful to be stripping off these confining clothes. Though she usually slept naked with Wilson, tonight she chose her oldest flannel nightgown, so worn that she wore it only when she really needed to.

Julia settled on her side of the bed and angled the reading light to shine directly on the pages. Clipped to the front of the novel was the original query letter sent to her, asking whether she'd like to read the book. She saw her own "yes" written on the letter, and then Margaret's brief note asking that the writer send the manuscript to them if she could guarantee an exclusive interest for a period of two months. Julia checked the date of when the manuscript came in. Only two weeks ago, so she didn't actually need to read it tonight.

She sighed and looked up. They had no television in their bedroom, and usually Julia didn't want it. But mindless TV would have been comforting. She could hear faint traffic noises from the street nineteen floors below, a car alarm blasting over and over again, horns beeping, and then, sweeping through it all, the sound of a strong wind that had begun blowing late in the afternoon.

Now she turned and looked at the telephone. She picked up the phone and punched in Wilson's office number. As she knew it would, the phone rang and rang. Not there. Then she punched in Lauren's code.

Lauren answered immediately. "Hi, what's up?" They didn't usually talk to each other in the evenings.

"Wilson's not home, and I'm worried," Julia said.

"Maybe he has something happening with the big news you mentioned to me."

"But he'd have told me he'd be late."

"You mean you haven't talked to him?"

"I haven't heard from him since he left for the office this morning."

"That's strange."

Julia kicked at the covers, restless. "What should I do?"

"You left messages at his office?"

"Yeah, it's just so odd. He's never done anything like this."

"What happened last night? Did you make up?"

"I wanted to, and I tried to be nice, but—"

"Still pissed, huh?" Lauren interrupted.

"It was like he was annoyed with me, but also happy."

There was a long pause. "Julia, have you ever suspected that he might be having an affair?"

"Christ, no." Her heart pounded and a sick feeling swam in her stomach. She swallowed against the pool of saliva that suddenly flooded her mouth.

"Wherever he is, he obviously doesn't want you to know about it, or he would've called."

"I'd have had some idea if he was sleeping with another woman."

"Not necessarily." Lauren's voice was more determined than Julia liked to hear.

"What if he doesn't come home tonight?" Saying those words made Julia feel crazy.

"He'll come home," Lauren said. "Do you have anything to help you sleep?"

"I think there's stuff in our medicine cabinet."

"Take two of whatever there is, knock yourself out, and when you wake up tomorrow morning he'll be snoring next to you."

"Okay."

"I'll call you in the morning."

Julia stared down and slowly unclipped the cover material from the manuscript sitting so heavily in her lap. Then she removed the rubber band that held the pages together. She played her usual guessing game: how many pages? Lifting the book in both hands, up to eye level, she stared at it knowingly, then she gently bounced it in the air. Her guess was three hundred and eighty-nine pages.

Julia let the book drop into her lap and turned to the last page. Three hundred and ninety-four. Close, but not close enough. Sighing again, she left the bulk of the book in her lap and lifted the first page closer. She suspected reading glasses were in her future.

She read the first sentence, a rather long first sentence, especially for her, especially tonight. She stifled a yawn. And she kept reading.

CHAPTER 20

Angela sat in the dark kitchen, sipping a cup of tea. She'd raised the window blinds so that she could gaze out at the lights of the city. She felt an enormous lump in her throat. It kept swelling and swelling, and no matter how many times she swallowed, the lump grew.

Her arms twitched, aching for her baby girl.

She was staring out the windows, unseeing, the lights opposite a twinkling glitter shining through the dark, like stars in a country sky. But now she blinked, focusing on the apartment where she'd seen that man just a couple of days ago. The lights were on bold and bright across the way and she saw a man's figure moving about.

Angie crossed to the window and peered out, eyes wide. She knew that because the kitchen was dark, he wouldn't see her. Now she cupped her hands around her eyes, pressed against the cold glass of the window. The wind was blowing something fierce, moaning around the building.

It was George, she was sure of it, and he was tossing something like a ball into the air, catching it, and tossing it up again. He marched around the room with a steady rhythm, and Angela guessed he had music playing.

She felt so helpless, watching that maniac.

Suddenly he stopped, pocketed the ball, or whatever it was, and reached with both hands to swiftly remove his shirt. He swung it over his head twice, then let it fly. Now he strolled over to the window and looked straight at her.

She had to remind herself that he couldn't possibly see that she was watching him, but even so she reared back, letting her hands drop to her sides. He cupped his hands around his eyes and pressed against the window, as she'd been doing.

Her eyes filled with tears and she didn't know why. She took a step back. He tilted his head forward, still with hands cupped around his eyes, and she saw that he was looking down at the street far below. The small of her back was damp with anxious sweat.

The kitchen was dead dark. Oh well. He'd have liked to spy on her a bit, maybe even give her another scare.

He wondered about the baby she'd had. The

baby's father was probably married, only not to poor old Angela Byrne. He dropped his cupped hands from the window, grasped them together behind his back and turned them inside out, stretching his arms straight. He ambled toward the center of the living room.

Now that he had some music playing, he didn't mind the apartment quite so much. But it was still lonely. He squinted and looked around. Also too bright. Wouldn't a crackling fire be fine on a cold night like this? He crossed to the kitchen, suddenly inspired to throw open cabinets and drawers. He found twelve white tapers, which he paired with small white china plates and saucers. Dozens of matchbooks, a collection from restaurants all over the city, crowded half a drawer.

He lit matches, held them under each candle until the wax was softened, then stuck the tapers onto plates until the wax cooled and the candles stood upright without support.

In the living room, he placed six candles on the brass and glass coffee table, then distributed the remaining six on odd tables, bookshelves, and the television cabinet. He struck a match and moved around the room, lighting one candle at a time. Finally he turned off all the lights.

George sank into the couch and gazed about him. The room, so empty and forlorn before, now was magical with something—what, he wasn't sure.

He went back to the kitchen, poured himself a large scotch on the rocks, and then returned to the living room couch.

He sipped the drink and let his eyes rest on the candles grouped on the coffee table just in front of him. His eyes swam until he had to blink. He could be out at a nightclub right now, though it was a little early yet, and he wondered at himself staying in this apartment with a bunch of candles keeping him company. It was like a great love scene, only the main object was missing.

God, he was such a fool.

Angela watched George. She couldn't quite believe what she was seeing, and she stepped closer to the window again.

Candles flickered mysteriously, and if she hadn't already seen that he was utterly alone, she would have figured he had a girl. He was the type girls fell all over, a little rough and a little smooth and a good dresser, so he probably had a girl somewhere.

She hoped his apartment would catch on fire and that he'd be burned to toast.

Julia woke at four o'clock in the morning. Her reading light shone down on the half-read manuscript scattered over the sheets and comforter.

Oh God, Wilson hadn't come home.

She scrambled out of bed, anxiously looking about the room at the same time. The bedroom was exactly as it had been. No Wilson. She grabbed her robe from the closet and started down the main hall of the apartment. Opposite Emily's room, she turned right and ended up in the entrance hall.

The apartment was dark, but neither Angela nor Julia had pulled the drapes or let down blinds, so the city lights were just enough to see by. She walked quickly toward the library, but the dread was already rising in her.

The room was empty.

She turned and went back to the entrance hall, where she opened the coat closet. His raincoat was gone, as it had been all day. She turned and retraced her steps to the library and snapped on a desk lamp. She pressed all the buttons for Wilson's computer and waited as the screen shone faintly and then burst into the room with color and light.

Julia knew Wilson's password, only because they'd played a guessing game about it one Friday night when they'd finished a whole bottle of fine red wine, a gift from a grateful writer. Julia had bet Wilson that she could figure it out in three tries, and he'd claimed she couldn't.

Her first choice had been his mother's name, Joyce. He'd laughed at her and turned a little pink. Her second choice had been her own name. He'd merely shook his head at her, making her feel quite foolish. And then she'd remembered the opera, *Turandot,* where they'd met. Her final guess had been Puccini. Bingo! He'd been so impressed that she doubted he'd changed it, though for security reasons he ought to have.

In moments, Julia was gazing at his extremely long list of unread e-mails. She saw that he'd last signed on yesterday morning, at 11:00 A.M. She scrolled to the end and opened the last item, a request for a recommendation written in an awestruck tone, from a researcher who'd worked for Wilson two years earlier. She went backward, rapidly checking the last five e-mails. Nothing.

She turned off the computer and stared at the blank screen. Then a thought struck. She turned the computer back on and waited impatiently. She signed on to her own service and checked her e-mail messages. There were five messages, one from Jacob Klein, but nothing from Wilson.

Where was he?

She edged her way through the dim apartment. In their bedroom, she drank a small glass of water. She peeled back the comforter on the bed and climbed in under only the sheet. She lay against the pillow, arms straight at her sides as if she were in her coffin.

Her wide-open eyes watched the pattern of light playing on the white ceiling. She'd been a true insomniac when she was a child, though the family pediatrician would never admit the seriousness of Julia's problem. She was so active, a skinny wink of a girl with heavy blond hair weighing down a small head. Her arms and legs were covered with purple bruises from tree climbing, and when she curled into a corner of the couch reading a book, one leg jiggled.

When she remembered her childhood, it seemed like life had been only those endless hours lying awake, listening to the house cracking its tired bones and letting out sighs of exhaustion.

She no longer had a real problem with sleeping and no longer called herself an insomniac. Sleeping difficulties ended when she cut her hair short. Her head could hit the pillow so cleanly, nestled into its cool embrace without fuss. And sleep, then. Easy, easy sleep.

She slept.

And woke late, having forgotten to set the alarm. The odor of bacon was strong, and even as she shuffled to the bathroom, her stomach rumbled with hunger. She'd eaten little the night before, but would've expected to be unable to swallow this morning.

In the bright kitchen, Jimmy banged his spoon on the high chair tray when he saw her. Julia cupped both hands around his head and then scratched his scalp with her nails. He moaned with the pleasure and like a cat stretching out its neck for more, dropped his head forward.

"Is Daddy still asleep?" Emily's voice was strong and pure with curiosity.

Julia's eyes darted to Angela, who tended the sizzling bacon.

"Daddy's already gone to work this morning," she said.

Angela quickly turned around. So she knew something was up. Julia deliberately caught her eye and passed along the unspoken message, *Protect the kids.*

Angela returned to the bacon, prodding and poking it more than necessary.

"Anybody mind the radio?" Julia switched on the all-classical station, which was unfortunately playing a singularly inappropriate piece by Copland. Spring, my ass, Julia thought as she poured herself a cup of Angie's excellent coffee. She looked out the window and registered briefly that it was raining again. No wonder the kitchen seemed so brilliant.

Suddenly the phone that connected to the doorman buzzed.

"What on earth?" Julia said. But her stomach dropped as if she were on an elevator. She picked up the telephone receiver like it was a bomb.

"Letter just arrived. Looks important, so I thought I should let you know," the doorman said.

"Thanks, I'll be down."

Julia walked quickly back to the bedroom, yanked off her flannel nightgown, and pulled on a red sweat suit. She trotted to the front door of the apartment. "I'll be right back," she called out to Angela.

The doorman handed her a white envelope with her name, Julia Fleming, written on it in Wilson's hand. Julia waited until the elevator doors closed behind her before opening the envelope and removing a single sheet of thick, cream-colored paper.

Dear Julia,

Things haven't been right with us for a while. You know that. I'm afraid I've got to tell you that I've fallen in love with someone else. I will naturally fulfill all my obligations to the children, but right now I just need some time to

*be alone and think. Sometimes I wonder whether
that's really been the problem in our marriage.
You like company and I like solitude. Perhaps, in
the end, we ought to have known how utterly
incompatible we'd be.*

*I'll be in touch sometime after Thanksgiving,
I promise. In the meantime, I'd appreciate your
understanding and, of course, your care for the
kids. I know Angela will be a big help in that
regard. The checking account has this month's
paycheck already on deposit, so you should be
fine financially.*

*I'm sorry to do this in writing, but as you
know, I'm not very good at talking, especially
when it comes to talking about our marriage.*

Wilson Streatfield, M.D.

The flush shot up her neck and across her face.
She felt it pulsating, hot and steaming. Her hands
trembled. Halfway down the hall to their front door,
her body sagged to the right and she caught herself
against the wall.

She spoke quietly as soon as she entered the
apartment. "Angela, please take care of the kids. I've
got something important to do," she called out when
she entered the apartment, her voice surprising her
with its own strength.

She turned left and walked on rubbery legs down
the long hall to her bedroom. Then she ran. She just
made it to the bathroom, where she was violently
sick. She slumped to the cold tile floor and for some

reason thought of only two things: Wilson had signed his letter without the word *love*, and he'd felt it necessary to put "M.D." after his name.

Then she remembered he'd said he was in love with someone else. Her thin arms encircled the base of the toilet and she rested her head against the seat. The frigid clutch of porcelain reached all the way into her soul.

CHAPTER 21

George woke at seven in the morning to find the candles sputtering in pools of melted wax. He groaned, tasted the leftover scotch in his mouth, and felt the dull throbbing in his head.

He moved around the room and with a viciousness that surprised him, he spat on each candle. In a hot shower minutes later, his loneliness grew so big that he felt like he carried a tumor on his back, a tumor of friendlessness. He thought, then, that he might die from the longing.

And then he thought he'd go home.

George ironed a shirt and pair of khaki trousers, dressed, and sat down on the edge of the bed staring at the telephone. He really wanted to just head for the Aer Lingus terminal at Kennedy and sit there until he got on a flight, but he knew that could mean as much as a twenty-four-hour wait. Cleanliness and fresh clothes were so important to him that he couldn't risk it. He pulled out the telephone directory and began to search for the airline's reservation number. A lilting Irish accent put him on hold. He kept hearing the echo of her voice as he stared blankly out the window.

He didn't think he wanted to go home to Ireland after all. There was nothing for him there, and his gran would give him a terrific hard time for being broke, which he just about was.

What he wanted was a good breakfast.

At the corner coffee shop, he sat at the counter and ordered three eggs over easy, sausage, pancakes, and home fries. While he waited, he stared around at the other customers. The place was crowded and you got the feeling that the rain had followed everyone inside. Puddles from drenched umbrellas pooled on the cracked linoleum floor, and the smell of wet wool made George think he definitely didn't need to go back to Ireland—the odors and sights of Dublin were right here.

His waitress was cute, and he gave her a wink when she put down his overflowing plate. She smiled a real smile back at him. When she passed by the next time, he spoke. "When do you get off?"

"Half hour."

"You're kiddin' me. A half hour?"

She dashed up and down. "Where are you from?"

"Ireland."

She looked at him. He could see she was interested. Maybe she'd even come to his apartment when her shift ended. The counter blocked most of the view of her from the chest down, but when she was way at the opposite end, he kind of leaned forward, pretending he needed another napkin, and saw that her lower half was lumpy. She wouldn't do, no, not at all.

After three cups of coffee, it was time to go. He wondered about checking things out at Mr. Wong's, but the place made him nervous. He hit the street and started walking.

At the next corner, George bought another umbrella, this time black, with a huge curved handle meant to resemble ivory. He opened it up and took refuge. He drifted along the streets while people on their way to work rushed by, jostling him, and despite his aimlessness, making him feel like he had somewhere to go.

Angela thought Julia looked like she'd been shot through the heart. She knew it must have something to do with Dr. Streatfield, but she couldn't imagine what. He'd certainly not seemed the philandering type to her. The children were behaving well, thank the Lord, and she managed to keep things moving without stepping in front of Julia. One look had been enough.

She was making Emily's bed when Julia appeared in the doorway, dressed for work.

"Angela, I may be late tonight. Can you handle

things okay?" she said in a soft voice.

When she heard the front door slam behind Julia, she straightened up from Emily's bed and stared out at the rain beating against the windows.

They'd go to a museum, and since Julia wouldn't be home until late, she'd rent a video for them to watch in the late afternoon.

Julia got to work before Margaret. She turned on lights, switched on computers, both hers and Margaret's, then took the coffee carafe down the hall to fill it with water from the ladies' room. She made the coffee and settled behind her own desk.

She signed on to Wilson's system, wondering if he was staying somewhere that would allow him to read his e-mail. She might write to him that way, if he was checking. But no, his e-mails were piling up at an extraordinary rate. She ran through some of the most recent ones, and noticed something from the president's office. Surely he wouldn't remain out of touch for long, not when he was involved with such important things.

Julia heard the door open. "Hi!" she called out to Margaret.

Keep up the pretense. Just keep it up.

"Morning," Margaret said. She stood in the doorway to Julia's office, unbuttoning her wool coat. "Jesus, more rain."

"I know, it's dreadful," Julia said.

Margaret disappeared, hanging her coat up in the closet.

"By the way," Julia called to her, "would you like to join us for Thanksgiving dinner this year?"

"That would be wonderful." She reemerged from the closet. "Hey, thanks for making the coffee."

"It seemed like the kind of morning when coffee would be essential," Julia said. "Has it finished dripping?"

"Yup."

Julia walked into the outer office, picked up a mug, and filled it with fresh coffee. The smell made her want to puke. Her hand holding the mug trembled and the coffee slowly sloshed. Julia cupped the mug with both hands and headed back to her office.

"I saw you took home the novel I recommended," Margaret said. Her expression was light and easy, but Julia knew better.

"Yeah, I fell asleep with it and woke up at four A.M. with a stiff neck."

"Uh-oh."

"No, it's good, but I can't tell yet. It's worth finishing, though, that's for sure."

The phone rang. "I'll get it, I'm expecting Lauren," Julia called out to Margaret.

"Have you heard from him?" Lauren asked immediately.

"Oh yeah."

"That doesn't sound good."

"Believe me, it isn't. But I really can't go into it right now." She made her voice deliberate.

"Margaret's there and you can't talk?"

"Bingo."

"Is it someone else?"

"Bingo."

"Oh Christ, are you okay?"

"Not really," Julia said.

There was a long silence as they both breathed into the telephone receivers. Julia sucked in Lauren's breath, taking comfort.

"Could I invite myself over tonight?" Julia said.

"Of course. You mean without the kids?"

"Definitely without the kids. Angela said she could handle all day and evening. I'm giving her tomorrow off."

"We'll be home by six o'clock."

"I'll be sitting on your doorstep."

"Can you make it through the day?" Lauren said.

"I hope so."

Lauren and Bill had decorated their apartment in secondhand furniture and a heavy reliance on the Pottery Barn catalog. Neither sophisticated nor beautiful, it reminded Julia of a summer home in Maine. The couch was ramshackle and worn, upholstered in a faded plaids, and two slipcovered wing chairs were done in mismatched chintz. A deep green wall-to-wall carpet was always scattered with pieces of paper, lint, and hair, but the effect was of warmth and ease, despite the mess.

The two women settled on the couch facing each other, legs pulled up and tightly tucked under themselves. A six-pack of Guinness stout sat out on the coffee table.

"Where's Bill?" Julia tried not to seem relieved by his absence.

"Working late on a brief." Lauren's eyes were serious. "If you don't tell me this instant—"

Julia took a swig of stout. Then she spoke in a rush, wanting to get the worst out of the way. "Wilson wrote me a letter which I got this morning. Must've been hand-delivered. He says he's fallen in love with someone else."

Lauren's mouth actually dropped open.

"It's unbelievable," Julia said.

"My God." Lauren tipped the bottle and swallowed four times before lowering it.

"Did you bring the letter?"

Julia leaned over and pulled the letter out from a separate compartment of her purse. "Here," she said simply.

Lauren scanned the thick piece of paper, then turned it over to look at the other side. Now she picked up the envelope, examined Julia's name on the front, turned it over, and stared at the other side.

"What are you looking for?" Julia asked.

"Seems strange."

"What?"

"The whole thing." Lauren rose and walked around the room, still holding the letter and glancing at it from time to time.

"Usually a man tells his wife about an extramarital affair because she suspects something and asks him." Lauren paused, twisting her body from side to side as if she were doing workout exercises. "Or they're having a huge fight and he blurts it out unintentionally."

Julia's mouth went dry and she took another swallow of stout. "This was a horrible way to tell me and, you know, Wilson's not *mean*."

Suddenly Lauren tossed the letter at Julia. "Gotta go pee so I can drink more." She trotted down the small hall that led to the bedroom.

Julia found the letter where it had drifted to the floor, folded it carefully, placed it back in the envelope, and tucked the envelope into her purse. Her head was throbbing. She ought to quit drinking this stout. She rummaged around in her purse until she found the tiny pillbox that held four Excedrin tablets. She leaned forward and grabbed her bottle of stout by the neck, then took a long swallow, washing down two of the Excedrin.

Lauren came back in, her blouse left untucked. "You want to order Chinese?"

"I can't eat anything." Julia watched Lauren settle into the opposite corner of the couch. "But if you want—"

"No, I was just being polite." Lauren picked up her bottle of stout and took several gulps.

Julia watched Lauren's white throat move rhythmically as she swallowed and then put the bottle down on the coffee table.

"It's bad enough that I can't reach him in case of an emergency," Julia said. "But this means I can't talk back! It's so unfair."

"There's no good way to handle something like

this, but he's managed to do the worst possible job," Lauren said.

"I keep trying to figure out where he might be, then I'd just go there and demand we discuss everything."

"Do you have any idea who the woman is?" Lauren's voice was low and careful as she brought up the delicate subject.

"I haven't a fucking clue."

"Is there some friend he might've told?"

"Wilson doesn't have friends. You know that."

The words echoed in the cluttered, gracious room. Julia's throat closed and tightened into a hard knot.

"*I* was his friend," she whispered. Her lips trembled, and the trembling undulated in waves down her neck, into her chest, arms, hands, finally reaching her thighs. She was a mass of shaking jelly, like a pudding when you take it out of the refrigerator and the whole business shudders.

Lauren slid across the couch and wrapped both arms around Julia's shoulders.

She needed a hug, Julia knew that, but even in her need she was aware of how strange it felt to be held by Lauren. In fifteen years of friendship, they'd seldom touched.

Awkward, Julia let her head fall forward and rest on Lauren's bony shoulder. Tears poured down her cheeks and wet Lauren's red silk shirt. Her eyes closed briefly and then opened. She straightened slightly and pulled away.

"I'll ruin your blouse." Julia sniffed and swiped at her eyes with one hand. Lauren's arms pulled back and Julia missed their warmth immediately. Lauren's wrists were so tiny and thin, almost brittle.

"Have you lost weight?" Julia said.

Lauren pushed her sleeves up abruptly, as if to dismiss such nonsense.

"You have any tissues?" Julia said.

Lauren hopped up. "I'll get some."

They heard Bill's key in the door and both women began unconsciously adjusting themselves.

"Hi, you guys," Bill called out. He wore a wrinkled raincoat and small, round tortoiseshell glasses perched on a tiny nose. Pale blond hair frizzed out from his head.

"Hi, Bill." Julia sniffed.

He hustled into the room and peered at her. "What's the matter?"

Brutally brief, Julia told him.

"Holy Christ," Bill muttered.

"The truth—did you know?"

"Wilson and I weren't really friends, Julia."

"Are you surprised, then?"

"Completely. He doesn't seem like the type at all."

Lauren returned from the one bathroom in their apartment, her hand clutching a wad of toilet paper, which she thrust at Julia.

"Thanks." Julia held the toilet paper from one end, let it unfurl, then carefully began to fold it. Finally she blew her nose.

"What have you been drinking?" Bill strolled farther into the living room. "Just Guinness?"

"Yeah." Lauren stayed close to him. One of the reasons Julia disliked seeing them together too often was that they seemed to cling to each other.

"She needs something stronger than that," Bill said.

"What would you like?" Lauren asked, turning to her.

"I wouldn't mind a gin and tonic."

Bill gave her an amused look. "It's almost Thanksgiving, Julia, gin and tonic season is long gone."

"I always feel like drinking gin at your apartment. I don't know why."

"Then gin and tonic it is."

They sped into the kitchen together, leaving Julia alone in the living room. She could just hear their low voices over the sounds of ice being retrieved from the freezer and the hiss of the tonic water being opened.

They were feeling sorry for her, of course. Murmuring questions to each other about what should they do and what should they say, all that. Julia didn't mind. It was comforting, in fact. She hoped they'd somehow figure it all out, those lawyer minds of theirs ought to be clever about such things.

"Lime?" Lauren said from the open kitchen doorway.

Julia nodded yes.

Lauren disappeared again. The ice clinked into glasses. Julia thought she could actually smell the lime as Bill cut it into wedges.

When they came back into the room, Bill carried three tall gin and tonics on a tray, while Lauren held a plate of cheese and crackers.

"Try and eat something," Lauren said.

Bill sat next to her on the couch and Lauren dropped gracefully at his feet, curling herself around his lower legs and simultaneously reaching for her drink.

"Are you going to try and find him?" Bill said.

"I keep checking his e-mail, to see if he's signing on from somewhere, but so far he hasn't." She drank some of her gin and tonic, then put down the glass and ran two hands through her short hair. It stood up straight, like the bristles on a pig. "I guess you haven't heard about this big deal happening to him?" Julia looked at him, one eyebrow arched. "Or maybe Lauren told you?"

"I described a little bit, but explained you weren't giving out details because of secrecy issues," Lauren said.

Bill pushed an index finger into his drink and began chasing a thin ice cube. "I know he's been working with that fungus he found upstate, but I thought he wasn't sure what its qualities were."

"That's as much as I knew," Julia said. "I guess he got careful about talking too much because of what he realized it might do—well, *does* do."

"Can you tell us?" Lauren said.

Julia noticed that Lauren's drink was already finished.

"Actually, the clinical trials started about two

weeks ago, so it's not really a secret anymore." She took another gulp from her glass. "But it's an enormous thing."

Bill sat forward. "Jesus, what is it?"

"He's found a drug that will cure all addictions."

"This is *proved*?"

Both Lauren and Bill were staring at her, their mouths open in an identical way.

Julia nodded, trying to find a smile. "I suppose the trials will tell them about any side effects, obviously, but I got the impression that Wilson was confident about it."

Bill fished out his last ice cube, popped it in his mouth, and chewed with loud, crushing noises.

"Do you guys think I should call his office tomorrow?" Julia reached for a cracker, but spoke again before eating it. "It's not very professional to tell his secretary that he's left me for another woman and, gee, did he by any chance give her a forwarding address?"

Bill frowned. Lauren smeared brie on a cracker and held it up to his mouth. He opened, she placed the cracker inside, he closed, and he chewed.

"I think I'd wait another day," Bill said after he'd swallowed.

"Why don't you try sending him an e-mail?" Lauren said.

"He's not reading them."

"You can sometimes log on, read your mail, and mark them as unread."

"That's on AOL."

"You can probably do it on any system."

"It's worth a try," Julia said. "I'll send him one when I get home."

"Better idea." Lauren hopped up. "Let's send him one from here. He won't know that it's from you, so he'll open it for sure."

Julia felt a ridiculous, buoyant hope fill her chest. Just to do *something* was better than sitting around, unable to contact him.

They placed her in the chair in front of the computer, got her signed on, and then started to back away.

"Don't you dare leave me to do this alone," Julia warned.

"But it's private—"

"I need help figuring out what to say." She twisted around in the chair and looked at Bill. "Especially from you. You're a man. You can keep me from saying the wrong thing."

Lauren stepped forward so that she could peer over Julia's head. "Dear Wilson," she said.

Julia's fingers typed.

Dead quiet.

"I got that," Julia said. "Now what?"

Bill's hand roamed through his hair. "I was surprised to receive your letter," he began.

"How about astonished?" Julia said.

"Dear Wilson, I was astonished to receive your letter this morning. Though we've had our ups and downs, like most marriages, I had no idea that the problems, from your point of view, were so severe."

"Good," Julia muttered, her fingers flying.

Now Lauren started dictating. "I would appreciate the opportunity to talk to you in person, and I believe you owe me at least such an opportunity."

"Hey, you guys are a good writing team."

"I also have real concerns," Bill said, pausing long enough for her to type, "that in case of an emergency with the children, I have no way to reach you. I hope to hear from you very soon."

Bill stopped talking, blinked twice, then spoke again. "I love you," he dictated.

For the first time, Julia's fingers stopped moving. "How about just 'Love, Julia'?"

"I think that's better, too," Lauren said firmly.

"You wanted a man's point of view."

"Why should she say she loves him when he's been such a shit?" Lauren said.

"He needs to know that despite having been a bad boy he can come home again. He needs that reassurance."

"Woman's point of view?" Julia said. "Fuck him."

Lauren placed a small hand on her shoulder and squeezed hard. Julia's eyes brimmed with tears and she ducked her head low. The computer hummed in the silence.

Julia lifted her head and mentally tried out various three-word messages. *I adore you? Don't leave me? I love you? I miss you?*

No, none of the above.

She typed three words, the words that came straight from her heart.

"Please come home."

CHAPTER 22

I n the office early the next morning, Julia poured herself half a cup of coffee and added a brimming teaspoonful of sugar.

"Are you okay?" Margaret asked. "You look kind of green."

"Too much to drink last night."

Margaret knew that Julia usually limited herself to one drink an evening during the workweek, and two drinks a night on the weekends. She looked thinner. On Julia a loss of two pounds could show.

The door to their office opened and a large black man entered. He wore a dark blue uniform and a gun was tucked not so discreetly into a holster fastened around the waist.

"Good morning." He spoke in the gorgeous cadences of the Caribbean.

"Good morning," Margaret said. "May I help you?" Somehow she didn't think he was dropping off a manuscript, though she'd been wrong with such predictions before.

"I'm looking for Julia Fleming," he said. "My name's Armand Jones—I work for Columbia University's security force."

Margaret nodded too quickly and rose from behind her desk. "Please take a seat, and I'll just—"

"I'm here," Julia said. She walked into the outer office, looking even taller and thinner than just moments before.

"How do you do?" Julia held out her hand.

Margaret saw the Adam's apple bob conspicuously in the security officer's thick, knotted throat. Julia's usual effect on men.

"Armand Jones, ma'am."

"I overheard you say you're with Columbia's security force?"

"Yes, I was hoping to speak to you, if you have a moment."

Julia closed the door to her office with a soft click.

Margaret pressed the intercom button and held it in.

Julia's heart beat with the fast, loud pulse of an alarm clock ringing. Armand Jones's presence meant bad news.

"Please sit down." She gestured to the love seat.

From long experience, Mr. Jones knew his bulk would about fill the seat, so he settled smack in the middle, letting out a sigh as the down pillow puffed about him. He placed one large hand onto the pillow and patted gently.

Julia pulled her office chair closer and sat down, crossing her legs in as quiet a manner as she could. Nevertheless, she caught him staring for the briefest moment.

"I'm concerned about your husband's where-abouts, and I was hoping you'd have some information to help me out."

"I don't know where Wilson is." Her voice was low and edged with panic.

He didn't respond the way she expected. First, no sympathy. Second, no surprise. Third, no curiosity.

"I had an appointment with him two days ago and he never showed up." Armand heaved a strong leg up and over the other. Again a deep sigh escaped.

"What about?"

"He didn't tell you some of his files were missing?"

Julia glanced down and saw the toe of one high heel. For an absurd moment she admired the shape of her foot and then the polish of the shoe leather. The office was quiet.

"Ma'am?" Armand said.

"I don't think there's anything to worry about— not for you, anyway." Julia rose and walked quickly to where she'd left her purse on top of the desk. She fished out Wilson's letter and handed it to him.

While he read the letter, she stood still in the center of the office and listened to the traffic in the street below, where all had seemed so silent just moments before.

He looked at her. "Did you know anything about this?"

"Not a thing."

"I know it's difficult to say, but would you have considered his actions within the parameters of your husband's character?"

Julia listened to his language and was impressed by the man. Then she thought about the question. "Absolutely and utterly out of character."

Armand Jones held the letter out to her and she stepped closer to take it. Now he signaled to her chair. "I'd like to share some more information with you."

His expression had shifted from a blank one to serious. Julia sat down quickly, no longer worrying about her enticing legs. Her stomach had plunged into a state of nausea. She swallowed.

"A young woman, a research assistant in Dr. Streatfield's lab, has been found in her apartment." Mr. Jones waited, gauging her face to make sure she was ready for the rest. "Murdered."

Why would this have anything to do with Wilson? Mr. Jones seemed to be waiting, expecting a question, but she had no questions.

He finally spoke again. "The police have traced her last hours, which appear to have been spent with Dr. Streatfield."

My husband's name is Wilson, not this strange

moniker, Dr. Streatfield. "What?" she said.

"They had a quick lunch together at DaVinci's and then the young lady's doorman remembers them taking the elevator to her apartment at two o'clock in the afternoon."

He took her to their restaurant, where they'd had their first date. A little crack spread up her back, the fissure a rock develops under pressure.

"The woman is dead?"

Armand Jones nodded.

The merest moment allowed one thought: serves her right for screwing my husband. Then she shoved such ideas away.

"Are you suggesting Wilson—"

"The police are anxious to find him, for obvious reasons." Armand Jones leaned forward, peering at her intently. "I wanted to get to you first and, I must tell you, I don't believe Dr. Streatfield would be capable of murder."

Her mind ricocheted around like a pinball machine that's gone mad. Ping, ping, ping, the ball hits score after score.

"No, he's not capable." Julia stared down at her hands and was surprised to find them loose in her lap.

"My guess is that he saw something, the murderer knows he saw something, and now he's lying low. Even sends you this letter so you're not implicated."

Julia felt her head growing heavier and heavier, and waves of nausea rose up in her throat. She leaned forward in the chair. "I'm sorry, I don't feel too—"

Her body hit the floor with a thud. Armand Jones

immediately rose to his feet, leaned over, and scooped her up in his arms. He deposited her on the love seat, carefully arranging her legs and pulling down her skirt. He yanked out a capsule of ammonium carbonate, broke it open, and shoved it under her nose. She coughed and her eyes opened.

"Should I call a doctor?" he asked.

"Please no, I'll be fine."

The door to the office opened and Margaret rushed in. "Is she okay?"

"I'm all right," Julia said. "Margaret, could you go down and get me a Coke?"

"Right away."

Julia struggled to sit up.

"Just stay lying down for a while." Armand walked with loud steps to her office chair.

She wished he would go. "I don't know what to do. I haven't got any idea of where he might be."

"Are his parents around, brothers and sisters, good friends, anyone you can think of?"

"Only child. And his parents live the hell and gone up in Vermont." Julia swallowed and ran one hand through her hair, making it stand straight up off her forehead. "He might've gone there."

Mr. Jones swiveled the chair around, spotted the cordless phone, and brought it over to her. "Would you call and find out?"

"What can I say?" *Uh, Wilson's disappeared and he was last seen with a murdered young woman, is he by any chance there?*

"Just tell them you and Dr. Streatfield have had a

small fight, and you thought he might have gone up to see them."

"They'll be upset."

"I think it's worth upsetting them, don't you?"

Julia nodded, the shock making her so exhausted she wanted to up and die herself.

His parents were more puzzled than upset by her call, and it was obvious that they were incapable of imagining anything really bad happening to their darling boy, Wilson. His mother actually ended the conversation by saying, "Lovely talking to you, dear. Kiss the kids for us."

When she pressed the disconnect button, Jones spoke immediately. "Anyone else you can think of?"

Julia straightened on the seat and swung her legs so that they extended to the floor. "He had no really good friends." She saw the expression on the security officer's face. "Not even me, but I guess I don't need to tell you that."

He bent forward, still sitting in her office chair, and reached with one hand across the open space. His large, black hand looked dry and inviting. She touched the palm of his hand with a slender finger. Just a touch and then she withdrew.

When Julia looked at him, he was smiling.

"We'll find him, I promise."

"Thanks." She couldn't smile back, but she knew he understood.

It was the only really good feeling she'd had in a very long time.

• • •

When Armand Jones had left, Julia did something rare. She closed the door to her office so that she could be alone. She offered no explanation to Margaret. She sat down at her desk and stared out the window. Her man across the way must be out to lunch, she thought.

Then she imagined, in vivid detail, that Wilson was making love to a research assistant from his lab. Only now it was a dead research assistant. She'd forgotten to ask the woman's name. Armand Jones had said she could expect the police to contact her at any time, and she'd be sure to ask them. She tried to see Wilson killing this woman. Stabbing her? Julia realized that she'd also neglected to find out how she died.

Though she could admit that Wilson must be involved, she also knew that he hadn't been responsible for someone's violent death. It was inconceivable. Still, she'd thought it inconceivable for him to be unfaithful, too.

He wasn't that type of man.

He hadn't been that type of man.

Something flared up inside her. At first she thought it was hatred, pure, fiery hatred. But, no, this wasn't hate.

This was love.

She wanted to hurl herself into his arms, lose herself in his body, possess him while he possessed her, clutch him to her heart with a great, moaning cry. Tell him, *Yes, I love you, Wilson.*

Still sitting at her desk, Julia hit a key on her computer and when the monitor lit up she began clicking her

way into Columbia University's system and then
Wilson's e-mail. The screen went dark momentarily
after she entered his password. Suddenly a terse message appeared: THAT ACCOUNT IS UNAVAILABLE. It
didn't say it was an incorrect password, or that someone was already logged on. No, this meant Columbia,
the police, *someone*, had taken control of Wilson's
e-mail. She stared at the message, realizing that whoever read his mail would also see the e-mail she'd sent
the night before.

She was alarmed that she hadn't heard from the
police. If Wilson was wanted in connection to a murder, and they couldn't find him, why wouldn't they
contact her the way Armand Jones had? Julia noticed
Mr. Jones's business card and she reached for the telephone. Her hand held the receiver and then carefully
replaced it.

She knew why she hadn't heard from the police.
They were watching her, probably tapping her phone
and computer, waiting for Wilson to send her a message. But she could call their bluff, go downtown and
file a missing person's claim. Julia's head dropped
forward, cradled by her thin hands, while her mind
swirled in a stew of murder and her husband's sexual
betrayal with another woman. She was incapable of
lifting her head, making a phone call, or deciding on a
course of action.

Julia wanted to be alone. To suffer.

Angela could tell that Dr. Streatfield had left home
because his toothbrush was dry and there'd been no

dirty clothes for three days. She'd also figured out that Julia had some idea of where he was and why he'd gone. It didn't take a genius to deduce that Dr. Wilson Streatfield had left his wife for another woman.

She felt like he'd broken *her* trust along with Julia's, though she admitted that was a ridiculous way to feel. But she'd been proud of "her" family, how generous, well-off, kind, and educated they were. She'd been a part of them, and they a part of her. Even if they'd not adopted her, she'd adopted them. They were in her hurting heart.

It was late Friday night, and Angela lay rigid in her bed, arms stuck out of the covers and stretched taut along her body. Julia had scarcely spoken all evening and she looked like a puff of wind would make her keel over dead. Angie worried about the files George had stolen from the Doctor's office. Were they connected to Dr. Streatfield's leaving? She couldn't see how or why missing files would cause him to leave Julia for another woman.

She sat up in bed, pulled on a robe, then opened her bedroom door slowly. The night was dark, and even the lights from other city buildings didn't penetrate much. Then she remembered how Julia had methodically wandered the large apartment to close drapes and lower blinds. Angela moved fast, her eyes already adjusted to the dark from staring up at the ceiling above her bed.

In the entrance hall, her hand carefully touched the cool brass knob of the coat closet. If you opened the door too quickly, it protested with a distinct squeak. She turned the knob slowly and then eased open the door. Angela groped for the hook hanging to the left and felt Julia's leather pocketbook. Inspired, she shut the closet door behind her, switched on the light, and sank to the floor, gently pushing away rubber rain boots and tangled scarves. She found Wilson's letter immediately, tucked down in an outer pocket of the purse.

She read it, paused, then read it again. When Angela returned to her bedroom, she crawled eagerly into bed, her conscience happy and relieved. He'd left Julia, he'd left Angela, and he'd left his kids, but not because she'd helped George do his dirty work. She turned on her side, tucking her left hand under the pillow and cuddling into the clean-smelling, soft cotton.

CHAPTER 23

T he very next night, Julia nearly kicked her out of the apartment, and Angela fought the worry of it. Perhaps Julia did blame her for Dr. Streatfield's disappearance. Perhaps she couldn't afford the salary anymore and she would put the kids in day care. Angela wandered along the blocks close to the apartment, trying to calm the panic in her. The thought of those children in day care was enough to make her cry. She'd do the job for nothing, room and board, that she would. Her heart calmed a little as she imagined the conversation with Julia and how Julia would be so grateful.

The November night was nasty cold, particularly the way the wind had whipped up. Angie heard there was a possibility of snow flurries later and she stopped walking to tip her head back and search the sky. She wore a raincoat with a wool lining, but such a coat wasn't enough on a night like this. She picked up her pace, nearly a trot, and plunged her hands deep in the coat pockets. She needed a plan for the evening. She could see a film, but she thought instead of the great store Bloomingdale's. She'd passed it many times since arriving in New York City, but she'd never had the courage to enter. Now she ran in earnest. An interior breast pocket of her coat held three one hundred dollar bills.

Lord, she knew she shouldn't and wouldn't spend the money, especially if she was going to be losing all her wages at the Streatfields. But it would do no harm to look, and if they stopped her, asking what business she had in such a fine, big store, she would show them her money.

She'd show them.

George perched on a stool in the window of O'Malley's Pub on Third Avenue, doodling in the steamy window on this cold night. He made a heart, an arrow diagonally piercing the heart, and wrote "George" in grandiose script. He paused and took a minute to sip from his warm scotch, the ice nearly gone. He wrote a plus sign and there he was staring at this empty heart, no one to link with his name, when Mother of God, he saw Angela rush by, all huddled into a long, flapping raincoat. He looked at the heart, leaned forward to stare out at where she'd passed, leapt to his feet, and ran out the door while flinging on his wool coat.

Julia thrust Jimmy into Lauren's arms, pretending the demands of child care and dinner preparation were too much for her, although Angela had actually left a leg of lamb, potatoes, and onions roasting in the oven and Julia had planted Emily in front of a video. For a long while, when Emily was a baby, Julia hadn't been sure whether Lauren wanted to hold a child. But Lauren, realizing Julia's acute sensitivity, had finally told her that to cuddle a baby was pure happiness to her.

"What would you like to drink?" Julia asked.

"Got a beer?" Lauren opened the refrigerator, Jimmy balanced on one hip, stuck her head in, and emerged holding a St. Pauli Girl by its frosty neck. "This'll be great."

"Can I help myself?" Bill said.

"Of course." Julia waved her hand toward the butler's pantry. "Would you make me a scotch and soda?"

Julia grabbed the beer from Lauren. "You want a glass?"

"Bottle." She bounced Jimmy and peered into his face, puckering her lips and making weird noises.

Julia found the bottle opener, popped off the top, and handed Lauren the beer.

When Bill brought her the scotch and soda, Julia picked up a plate of chopped liver and melba toasts, and led the way into the living room where they collapsed into the down-filled couch and armchairs.

"Can you tell me something?" Lauren said. "Why are you so perfect?"

Julia gave Lauren a shocked look.

"Pâté and crackers, drinks, roasting leg of lamb, full-time job, beautiful apartment, beautiful baby—" She stopped talking long enough to gaze at Jimmy, who was strangely content in her lap.

"And my husband's disappeared!" Julia interrupted. Fury made her voice tremble and she saw Bill's worried expression.

"I'm sorry," Lauren whispered. The normally white skin on her face grew mottled with pink and she chewed on her lower lip. "I hold Jimmy and something comes over me."

The two women looked at each other, neither sure of how to save the situation.

"I think Wilson will come back," Bill said.

Now the women glared at him, eager to blame someone else for the momentary discomfort in the room.

Bill's hands rose in the air, warding them off. "Hey, I *am* the only man here. I just might have a reasonable perspective."

Julia took her first sip of the scotch and was pleased that Bill had made it strong. She held the cold, yet burning, liquor in her mouth, then swallowed. "The woman he was with has been murdered."

"Jesus Christ!" Lauren jumped up and Jimmy started to wail.

Bill's face remained still, almost as if he hadn't heard, or didn't believe, her words.

Lauren frantically bounced Jimmy. "And he was so happy—now what?" She sent a beseeching look to Julia.

"Let's put him in the windup swing." Julia assembled the contraption folded in the corner of the room, plunked the screaming Jimmy in its vinyl seat, and then turned the timer crank. With a lurch and high-pitched squeak, the swing moved. Jimmy's legs kicked and the screams petered out.

"Remind me to get one of those," Lauren said to Bill.

"Will you please tell us *everything*?" Bill said.

Lauren sat down quietly, clutching her beer bottle, but instead of looking at Julia, she watched Jimmy.

Julia explained about Armand's visit.

"You mean the police still haven't *talked* to you?" Bill asked.

"I think they're watching me, probably tapping the phones too, with the hope that he's going to try and come home eventually."

"It's strange he hasn't been in touch," Lauren said. She slipped off her black flats and tucked her nimble legs up and under themselves, Indian-fashion.

Bill and Lauren looked at each other.

"What do you mean?" Julia said.

"It does suggest some kind of guilt," Bill said gently. "If he were innocent, he'd contact the police in order to help them find the killer. This is *Wilson* we're talking about."

"Exactly," Julia said in a high voice. "How can you possibly say that Wilson could be a murderer?"

Lauren sat up straight, her elegant back held an inch away from the couch. When Julia and Lauren first met, Julia had thought Lauren was like a black and white photo, with her pearl skin and pure black hair. But five minutes into their first conversation, Julia saw the colors: glints of blue in the black hair, burgundy lips, pink undertones of the white skin, dark brown eyes, black eyelashes with flecks of gold, and the hint of pale green in her earlobes.

"Everyone has that dark side," Lauren said, "that part of a person so unknowable and unimaginable."

Julia couldn't speak. The rage was beyond anything she'd experienced. Her best friends were saying that her husband, the father of her two children, had *killed* a woman. She felt panic explode in her chest and she saw her hands literally become claws, reaching for them.

"Get out," she said.

They jumped up, full of explanations.

Jimmy whimpered in his swing.

Julia's mouth split open in a wide scream of anger. "Get the hell out of here."

Bill grabbed Lauren's arm and tugged her toward the door. They snatched their coats out of the closet and opened the front door.

Emily ran into the living room and threw her arms around her mother's legs. Julia picked her up and whispered in her ear. "It's okay, sweetie, Mommy promises everything will be okay."

Still, the children's sobs echoed in the otherwise quiet apartment.

• • •

Angela edged toward the rack crowded with baby girl dresses of rich velvets and satins in the jewel colors red, green, and gold. Her right hand hovered and then dared to tug at the sleeve of a red and green velveteen paisley. The dress was ruined, to her mind, by an ivory lace collar cut in pointy triangles. She went on, more boldly now, flipping through the dresses and searching for the Christmas outfit she'd like to buy her own baby.

"Evening, Angela Byrne." George's voice, unmistakable in its Irish lilt and cocky tone, came from her left.

Though she was altogether shocked at finding him here, in Bloomingdale's, Angie didn't turn her head. Cool, she removed a dress, ugly as sin, and gazed at it.

"You don't have to hate me," he said.

She threw him a mean look.

"It's all over, so we can be friends now."

Angela rattled hangers and pushed the dress back on the rack. Her hands shook and her stomach seized from the dread of wondering what those words meant. *It's all over.*

"What's happened to Dr. Streatfield?" She turned on him, full-face and eyes sharp as she could make them.

"May I help you?" a silky voice inquired. The saleslady's eyes were icy.

"Thank you, no." Angela headed out of the children's department, dodging displays piled with holi-

day sweaters. The moving escalator beckoned and she
stepped down, clutching the smooth, undulating banister. Angie sensed George right behind her, looming.

"What kind of nonsense are you talking? Nothing's happened to the Doctor."

Angela ran a hand through her hair, gathering
stray ends and tucking them into the braid that hung
inside her raincoat. "As if you didn't know . . ." she
muttered.

His head moved close to hers. "Know what?"

She stepped off the escalator and walked with no
sense of destination, ending up in the glittering shine
of the jewelry department. Angela paused at a glass
display cabinet full of diamond rings.

"Has something happened to Dr. Streatfield?" he
asked.

She heard the innocence in his voice, and that
reassured her.

"The Doctor's gone away." Angela glanced at
George's right ear. "Another woman."

"Ahh . . . yes."

"I'm sure, indeed, you know about that." Her
hands opened flat on the display case and she found
herself imagining all those rings on each of her ten
fingers, a dazzle of diamonds.

"You make me out much worse than I am."

"Do I?" Finally she looked at him straight on. He
was too handsome for his own good, and certainly too
handsome for her to fuss with. She'd turned off forever from the good-looking man.

"You do, yes."

Suddenly he, too, placed a hand on the glass. His fingers stretched open, the baby finger only about two inches from hers. She heard his breathing, the sound of a man excited, and a hypnotic sensation stole over her. She couldn't move a muscle, and to her horror, her own breathing quickened. His baby finger inched like a funny worm toward her own.

Touch.

"Just leave me be," Angela cried out. She was mortified to feel the tears swim in her eyes.

"Why should I?" His whisper came low and urgent.

"Because," she said, turning on him furiously, "I only bring trouble. My name's Angela Trouble Byrne."

"And what about me? And isn't my name George Double-Trouble McDuff? We make a pair."

He stared into her eyes and Angela felt herself begin to melt. Desire flooded her chest and her lips grew numb with the wanting. Her right hand flew through the air and struck him hard across the cheek. "Leave me be!" And, desperate, she ran.

CHAPTER 24

George had just stepped out of the shower when the phone rang. His days and nights belonged to Mr. Wong again.

"Hello?" George said.

"Mr. Wong wants you."

"Does he need some girls?"

"No, just you. He'll be in the dining room. Waiting."

"I'll be there as fast as I can. You sure he doesn't need anything else?"

"You."

The phone at the other end disconnected.

Now what?

George rubbed his hair with a towel, trying to get most of the wet out, then dried his body off fast. He pulled on a dark blue Calvin Klein sweat suit, white running shoes, and a blue down jacket.

Eight A.M. and the streets were busy with rush-hour commuters. He got a cab quickly, probably because it was a sunny day and people felt like walking to work. He sat in the backseat of the taxi, drumming his fingers. The sick feeling in his stomach grew bigger, and for the fifty millionth time he wondered why he kept on with this.

But he knew why.

His finger was on the doorbell when the front door opened. Some new guy, tougher and stronger. That didn't exactly inspire confidence, George thought.

He turned left, into the dining room. Mr. Wong sat at the grand walnut table with his favored second in command, Mr. Mao. They were both dressed in their beautifully cut wool suits, and they were eating soup.

Mr. Mao glanced up, his soup spoon raised halfway to his mouth. He was a stout, bland-looking man, his graying hair cut close and nondescript, his wide face always without expression, even when George brought girls.

"George, I need a word with you," Mr. Wong said.

"Yes, sir."

"Would you like some soup?" he said. "Soup in the morning is one of the Chinese customs I actually like."

"Uh, no thanks."

"Stand over there so I can see you." Mr. Wong pointed to the head of the table.

George walked to the precise spot, his fluttering stomach calmer now. Mr. Wong wouldn't offer him soup if he'd screwed up, would he?

"We have a new guest in the house, the famed scientist, Dr. Streatfield," Mr. Wong said. He shot George a look.

"Yes, sir."

"I'm concerned about the Irish nanny."

"Concerned?"

"She's apt to alert the wife to papers being stolen," he said. "We've got it arranged that the wife will think the good doctor has run away with another woman, but I'm worried that the nanny will put two and two together."

"She's too stupid to think anything." Not true at all.

"We can't take the risk. Eliminate her within twenty-four hours."

"Kill her?"

Both Mr. Mao and Mr. Wong now gazed at him. They looked annoyed that the soup was cooling.

"Yes," Mr. Wong said.

"But if she disappears, too, Mrs. Streatfield will really get suspicious."

Mr. Wong smiled. "Excellent reasoning, Georgie-Porgie. What do you suggest?"

"I could threaten to kill her baby, the one she put up for adoption, if she says anything." He smiled at his own cleverness.

"I am very pleased with you." Mr. Wong bent his head and sipped his soup.

Mr. Mao bent his head and sipped his soup.

And Georgie-Porgie got the hell out of there.

George caught Angela at the playground later in the morning. She turned her back on him as he approached, her face all twisted.

"A fine way to say hello," George said.

"I don't care to talk to the likes of you."

Angela was looking worn and frazzled. Though her long red hair was neatly braided, the strands of hair on top of her head were bunched and greasy. She wore old blue jeans and a huge down jacket with sleeves that dangled over her hands.

"I gotta have a word with you," George said.

She glanced at him, then gave each swing a mighty heave. The children shrieked with joy and excitement.

"They've got the Doctor."

Angela gasped, then swallowed it.

"Nothing to worry you about."

"I thought you said if you got the papers, that would be it," Angela said.

"It's nothing to do with me, and nothing to do with you."

"Are they going to hurt him?"

"I've no idea, but I doubt it." George settled himself in a swing and pushed off with both feet.

"Stop that," she said.

"What?"

"The swings are for the children, don't you go swinging yourself."

"Spare me your lectures."

She turned on him, her face in a fury.

But he ignored her and began pumping with his whole body, as hard as he could. Soon he was sailing high.

The kids shrieked some more, so shrill that his ears ached from the sound. The cold air pummeled him and he felt his nose getting red and about to run with snot.

He felt like a small boy.

"Just keep your mouth shut," he yelled.

She said nothing and he glared down on her from way up high.

Still she said nothing.

He leapt from the swing as it came down, ran forward a few feet to steady himself, then whirled around. His breath came in ragged pants and heaves, his nose was running, and his hands were cold like his heart.

He felt like a small boy.

"I'll kill your baby if you say a word, you hear me, I'll kill your baby!" George said.

That thin white face of hers cut like a knife. Wide open eyes. He ran forward, wanting to shake the life out of her. She ducked between the swings, moving herself toward him and in front of the children.

And then he couldn't believe it.

She threw herself on the ground, right at his feet. She sprawled there on the cement and distantly he heard the children crying.

"Hey, get up." He leaned over and tugged under one arm.

She was murmuring something. He bent closer, trying to hear her words and still yanking on her to get up.

"Don't kill my baby. Kill me. Kill my Da, I don't care. But don't kill my baby." Her voice sobbed, begging.

George straightened and dropped her arm. She remained flopped at his feet. He wanted to kick her, to get her to stand up and fight.

And a part of him wanted to lie right down next to her, crying along with her.

He turned and left her there. He didn't look back.

As the swing slowed down, Emily inched forward and tried to touch the ground with her foot. She couldn't reach. The tears rolled down her cheeks, but she wasn't crying loudly now. She just needed to get to Angela.

Finally the swing stopped almost completely, and she jumped. Her right foot hit the pavement and collapsed. With a small yell, she followed her foot and collapsed onto the hard cement. One arm bent under her and the shock of it was terrible.

Emily crawled into the safety of Angela's arms, smelling her perfume and listening to her beautiful voice murmuring, "Darling, darling, darling."

CHAPTER 25

Wilson Streatfield emerged from a light sleep and couldn't understand why his heartbeat was so steady and strong. He could feel it in there, a reasonable, sane heart, no longer breathless with fear. He should be terrified, and indeed, had been terrified for the past seven days and nights. Now, this morning, he was grateful for all sorts of crazy things. He inhaled a deep, soothing breath and then sighed loudly, exhaling. Most of all, he was grateful that he hadn't consummated his relationship with Susan before they killed her.

Susan's last words were: "I hope you brought a condom." She'd just turned the key in the lock and stepped into her apartment, twisting around to look at him as she spoke. He followed her into the apartment, and the last words she heard were his own, saying, "No, I'm sorry, I've never done this before."

Then he'd felt a gun slammed into his right temple and he'd watched as a Chinese man leapt forward, seemingly out of nowhere, and shot Susan three times in the face. Immediately the man holding the gun on Wilson said, "Act cool, just act cool, and you won't be hurt."

The voice came close to his right ear, so close that he could feel the warm breath and smell the ancient, undigested garlic.

"What do you want me to do?"

During all these years in New York City, he'd never been mugged. Somehow he couldn't believe this was actually happening.

"We're takin' the elevator down to the basement. No funny nothin' or this gun goes off."

They turned and walked down the hall, the man holding on to his upper arm with a powerful grip, and the gun still pointed at his head. Wilson heard the door to Susan's apartment slam shut. When the elevator opened, the man hissed, "I'll have the gun right here in my pocket, all ready."

As he stepped onto the elevator, Wilson's eyes peered down, without moving his head, and he saw the man's coat pushing out around the gun's snout. The elevator sank to the basement without stopping. Though Wilson had no intention of doing anything that would risk not only his life, but someone else's as well, he still found the rapid descent unnerving. He would've preferred if the whole thing happened in slow motion.

"See that black limo up ahead," the man said.

"Yes."

"That's where we're going."

They moved quickly through the basement garage.

Wilson knew you were never supposed to get into a car. Television shows always instructed you not to get in the goddamn car. But a gun was rammed into him. No question they'd shoot him. And he'd probably die.

He ducked, the man's hand pushing his head down even farther, and climbed into the limo. Briefly, the gun no longer touched him, but across from him another man sat with a large gun pointed directly at his head. The man who'd been his escort in the elevator climbed in next to him, slammed the door, and the limo tore up the steep ramp and out into bright, sunny streets.

The windows of the limousine were tinted, and something about the way his view of the city streets was so oddly colored made Wilson think that the buildings of New York had never looked so gorgeous. Sunlight baked the stone, brick, glass, and steel, and it was as if the heat and color made the buildings rise like bread in the oven, puffing to twice their size and slowly turning golden.

Both men were Chinese, or Asian, and that surprised Wilson. He carried a peculiar bias toward the

Chinese, perhaps because of his love for music and how the Chinese people excelled at instrumental performance. It occurred to him, suddenly, that he didn't know of one famous Chinese composer. Odd. He'd have to think about that—surely there were several?

The men were relaxed, not quite smiling, but not quite serious either. Both guns remained pointed at him, the one across the way still at his head, and the one next to him at his side. The gun to his head was bothersome. You could threaten Wilson's legs, groin, chest, and back, and he'd feel only partially disturbed. But his head. Now, that was bad news.

Wilson looked at the man across from him, trying to decide if he dared ask that he point the gun lower. He was thickly built and squat, with muscles bulging out of a black leather T-shirt. His eyes gazed out the window, drifting over the people on the sidewalks, relaxed.

"Could you point that thing somewhere other than my head?" Wilson said.

The eyes flicked back to him, shocked. "What?"

"I just wondered if you'd mind moving the gun to my heart or something." Wilson tried a sheepish smile. "I'm nuts, I know, but that gun pointing right at my head is really, really unsettling."

"You *are* nuts." The gun remained where it was.

Silence settled on the limo and Wilson heard music playing low and barely audible. He strained to hear better. It was some jazzed-up version of a famous Beethoven sonata.

Wilson didn't dare turn his head to look out the

window, but finally he shifted his eyes to the right and
tried to see the guy next to him. This man was also
Asian, with straight black hair chopped off at ear
level. His hands were meaty and tough-looking, again
surprising Wilson. He thought of Chinese hands as
small and elegant, moving fast.

The men spoke briefly in Chinese, a quick volley,
and then it was quiet.

He concentrated, willing his mind to focus on
what could be going on. And then, just like that, he
knew it was something to do with the WS-100.
Something, but what? The chemical formulations
were out in the open, available to just about anyone
with a little ingenuity. The clinical trials had begun, so
there was no stopping the drug's formulation just by
stopping the inventor, Dr. Wilson Streatfield.

The limo pulled into a narrow, dark tunnel and
then into an underground garage. Wilson took a deep
breath. He had to be calm and he had to be smart.

"Let's go," the man to his right said. He opened
the door, stepped out and away.

The man across from him gestured with the gun,
pointing to the open door.

He emerged into a medium-sized garage, with
space for about five limousines, though there were
only two parked in a far corner. The walls and floor
were painted a pure and astonishing white. There was
no dirt anywhere.

The men led him to an elevator that stood ready.
They both got on with him, and the fit was tight. He
could smell their sweat. The one with longer hair

stood behind him, his coffee breath exhaling into the back of Wilson's head and then floating forward around his face. Wilson took a shallow breath and held it.

The elevator whipped them up two floors and its doors slid open without a sound. They exited into the elaborately decorated hallway of a mansion. Turning right, the men led him ten feet down the hall to a large mahogany door framed with a pediment above. One man turned the door handle without knocking.

A small Chinese man sat behind an enormous but empty mahogany desk. Bookshelves lined an entire wall to his left, and as Wilson entered the room, a small seating arrangement of puffy, down-filled couch and chairs was to his right.

The man stood, hands in the pockets of gray slacks. His gray jacket fell in perfect folds where the hands had disrupted its drape. Wilson was first aware of intelligent black eyes, a handsome face that seemed carved from golden wood, and the utter stillness of the man.

It was an immensely appealing picture and that, too, surprised Wilson. He felt no fear, only curiosity. Whatever was going on, it promised to be interesting, maybe even worthwhile. He actually relaxed, forgetting that they'd murdered Susan barely twenty minutes earlier. Perhaps Chinese scientists had heard of the WS-100 and they were following some rather unorthodox methods in trying to bring the substance to their country. The Chinese had always been way ahead of America when it came to utilizing and working with natural compounds, after all.

"How do you do, Dr. Streatfield? I am Mr. Luke Wong." He circled to the front of his desk and held out a tiny hand.

All of Wilson's hopes were lost when he heard the Southern accent. He was American Chinese, and that was a different story entirely.

He walked forward slowly, still conscious of the men with guns, and shook Mr. Wong's hand.

"I think we can do away with these guns, don't you?" Mr. Wong said.

"Yes."

Mr. Wong clapped his hands with a sharp, authoritative slap and spoke in Chinese. The men faded back and out of the room. There was a faint click as the door closed behind them.

"Let's sit down." Mr. Wong pointed to the couch, but he chose a matching armchair.

When Wilson settled on the couch, sinking deep into the cushions, he sniffed loudly, even rudely.

"What do you smell?" Mr. Wong asked.

"Wet dog."

Mr. Wong smiled, genial and pleased. "My poodle, Baby, was just sleeping there before your arrival. He'd had his weekly bath."

Wilson didn't reply. Somehow this wasn't the kind of situation where you made small talk. Anyway, he'd always been terrible at cocktail party chatter, leaving that up to Julia to handle for him.

"I'm sure you're wondering why we've brought you here." He stared at Wilson expectantly.

"Yes." Wilson didn't smile, although the sense he was getting from Mr. Wong was that this was all quite fun.

"You've made a very important discovery." Mr. Wong stood up again and walked to the desk.

He noticed that the desk's surface was not completely empty. A gold ball the size of a marble shooter stood alone and singular. Mr. Wong picked it up.

Wilson's heart began to beat fast, the way a hummingbird's wings move so rapidly that they all but disappear. He watched Mr. Wong toss the ball from one hand to another.

He wondered if it were a minuscule bomb, though he really didn't think they made bombs so small. His calm and focus had fled and he quickly worked to bring his mind back. *Pretend this is an experiment. Pretend you are formulating a hypothesis. Pretend.*

He didn't answer Mr. Wong.

"Isn't that correct?" Mr. Wong glided across the room, closer to Wilson. The ball bounced from hand to hand, as the hands moved farther and farther apart so that the distance became a greater and greater leap.

And then the ball dropped.

Wilson flinched despite an effort at control, half expecting an explosion.

"Sometimes you drop the ball—that's just the way, isn't it?" Mr. Wong said.

The round piece of gold glittered from the depths of the thick burgundy carpet.

Mr. Wong picked it up and slipped it into his right pocket. "You know, Dr. Streatfield, you must talk to me."

Still Wilson said nothing, testing his hypothesis.

"Otherwise we will hurt you." Mr. Wong's black eyes had gone flat, disinterested.

Wilson believed him. "I've made a fairly important discovery, yes, but I suspect you know all about it."

"I do, yes."

"So what do you want?" Wilson's voice was nearly a whisper.

Mr. Wong sat down on the couch, so close to Wilson that their knees nearly touched. "You can't guess, a brilliant man like yourself?"

"My conjecture is that you want me to stop production of the drug—" Wilson's voice rose with anger, "because without drug addicts you're out of business."

"But your drug is in human trials, surely it's too late for that." Mr. Wong's eyes opened wide with innocence.

"Precisely."

"We're back where we started—a neat circle." He held up the gold ball, turning it gently between two fingers so that they could admire its smooth global nature.

Sweat, like a single drip from the kitchen faucet, trickled from Wilson's right armpit, traveling down the side of his chest and settling at the waist of his pants. "Then, no, I can't imagine what you want with me."

Mr. Wong stood up again and crossed the room to where a thermostat was on the far wall. He touched the dial, moving it slightly to the left.

"What we're going to need, Dr. Streatfield, is an antidote to your extraordinary drug."

An antidote? How absurd. He supposed, actually, that it could be done, but it would be sick to try. And then his mind began to run with the idea, thinking of the various chemical conditions present in the WS-100, and how one might counteract them. It wouldn't be easy and there'd be no element of luck in it, not the way there'd been in his original discovery.

And it had been luck. Just finding that particular beetle grub, with that particular, specialized fungus, had been impossible to predict. And what followed were years and years of research, unsure what this fungus, whether in its sexual or asexual state, could do. He believed in luck for major scientific work, and so did most scientists; you couldn't get far without it. So now he was supposed to snap his fingers and make an antidote? Lady luck wouldn't be on his side for that. Anyway, the definition of the word *antidote* implied that it was a cure for a poison. How could a cure for the cure of addiction be called an antidote?

Mr. Wong, staring at him, burst out laughing. "I'm silly, aren't I?"

Wilson had the sense not to answer that one.

"But not all *that* silly," Mr. Wong said. "I have my undergraduate degree in chemistry from Princeton."

Wilson almost said, "What year?"

"It should be fairly simple to block your drug."

Wilson blinked. "I'm sure you realize that drug research now centers on combinatorial chemistry."

Mr. Wong's face stretched into a piece of melting taffy, long and thin with elastic tendrils. "I'm assuming a vast amount of preliminary work can be mimicked on the computer."

"Someone could presumably work on it, though there'd be no valid reason in the scientific community to do such a thing."

"Well, Dr. Streatfield, we'll let you get a little rest and then you'll start to work."

"I beg your pardon?"

"I own a majority holding in Pharmacopeia, in Princeton," he said with a grin, "so you'll have a library of approximately three point three million molecules."

Wilson leapt to his feet. "Nothing you can do, I repeat, *nothing,* could make me develop an antidote."

"Oh, I doubt that, Dr. Streatfield, I sincerely doubt that."

"My wife will call the police as soon as she realizes I'm missing, and Columbia University will certainly figure out my disappearance has something to do with the WS-100," Wilson said. "I was just having lunch with the president yesterday . . ."

"Yes, you've hit on something we need to deal with. Quite right. You must write Julia a letter," Mr. Wong said, "explaining that you've left because you're in love with another woman."

Wilson noticed the piece of thick, cream-colored paper and black fountain pen on the coffee table.

"Please write," Mr. Wong said.

"I won't."

"I suppose you noticed that we killed Susan?"

Wilson swallowed, but his mouth remained dry.

"We could easily do the same to your wife and children."

Wilson bent over the paper, the pen clasped in his hand awkwardly, as if he were just learning to write.

After he'd finished the letter, Mr. Wong spoke in a soothing voice about understanding how Wilson would need time to adjust to his surroundings before he could settle down to work.

They locked him into a small room in the basement. A switch by the door illuminated a fluorescent light fixture that hummed like summer cicadas. The room was painted the same alarming white color as the garage, but at approximately six feet by nine, it was still too tiny for a big man. Wilson lay on the bed and stared at the bright ceiling, which he could touch with outstretched hands when he stood up. His eyes roved the walls, watching the angles they formed at each juncture.

He rolled onto his side and closed his eyes, trying to sleep. The noise of the light fixture reverberated in his head. He pretended he was ten years old again and already tucked into bed. The insects buzzed in the summer night. He'd been running through the day, blueberry picking and swimming in the creek, and he was tired, but not sleepy. He wanted to sit up in bed to read awhile, but his mother was strangely determined that he go to sleep at eight-thirty, even on summer nights. Strange because she was such a reader herself. He knew that she and his father were downstairs on the screened-in porch, each with an iron lamp curved over their books, silent except for the insects and an occasional bird, reading away. It didn't seem fair.

Wilson's eyes opened. Then he rose stiffly from the bed, took one step to reach the switch, and turned off the light. Swiveling on the forward foot, he then took a careful step back to the bed. He lowered himself gently. He felt that if he was not gentle with himself, he would break.

He lay back down, on his left side, and bunched the pillow under his left cheek. The pillow was flat and made of foam, so it didn't lend itself to shaping. He straightened it out again and instead tucked his left hand under his cheek. He smelled his own smell. And, somehow, not meaning to, his face turned and his lips touched the palm of his hand.

The tears were slow, not like real tears, he thought. His mouth opened and he tasted their saltiness, and he kissed his own hand.

CHAPTER 26

A ngela had the day off, so she tried to sleep late. Instead she lay awake listening to Julia and the kids, and the sound of the rain pouring down. Finally she gave up completely and got out of bed. She ran a bath and soaked for a bit. Her stomach, under the bathwater, was moaning and groaning with hunger and she slapped at it playfully. "Hush, now, and I'll get you a bit of food soon."

With a large blue towel wrapped and tucked securely under her armpit, she went rummaging for the plain black wool skirt she'd bought right after her baby was born and a white silk blouse that Julia had given her. She sat in the blue armchair and pulled on black suede boots. Her hair had been tucked and pinned high up on her head while she bathed and dressed. Now she undid the pins and combed her fingers through so that her hair hung lose.

She picked up the wooden hairbrush, brought all the way from Ireland, turned upside down at the waist, then straightened fast, flinging the hair back, and brushed like a madwoman. Her red hair flew out, electric and sparky. But here in America it didn't frizz. Here in America her hair fell in long, graceful curls.

Julia insisted on loaning her a full-length Burberry raincoat and an umbrella. The doorman smiled broadly and wished her a pleasant day, despite the rain. She felt like quite the lady as she pushed out the entrance.

She stood at the curb, uncertain. In her pocketbook, she carried six hundred dollars. She supposed she could take a cab. But instead she opened the umbrella and discovered that the umbrella, also Burberry's, matched the coat.

Angela walked fast. Most people who were going to work were already there, and one would think this drenching rain might discourage pedestrians, but like Dublin, New York City wasn't discouraged by rain. A little smile curved at her lips and she eased into a dreamy mood. From the way men were glancing at her, some of them even leaning forward to peer under the umbrella, she was sure of herself.

Two blocks over, she turned deliberately down Amsterdam. She knew where she was going.

• • •

George almost didn't recognize her when she came out of the apartment building. She'd no kids with her and she looked quite the young lady. He'd had nothing to do, so he decided to stake out the Streatfields' place. You never knew what you might discover, and he felt safer pleasing Mr. Wong.

Not only did she look different, but she walked different. A long, graceful stride. She effortlessly avoided people and puddles, her body moving with balance and ease. 'Course, he'd follow her.

He saw the way men stared.

Julia stuck Emily and Jimmy in the playroom and rushed around the apartment, horrified by how much there was to do for Thanksgiving and the arrival of her parents the next morning.

Her head throbbed from a major hangover, and every minute she listened for the phone to ring, for it to be the police with news about Wilson, or Bill or Lauren to apologize.

The phone didn't ring.

In the library, she checked her e-mails. There were four new messages, but nothing from Wilson. She was about to go into his e-mail again and then, at last, to call the police, when she heard hysterical crying.

In the playroom, Jimmy lay on his back, rigid with fury and screaming loudly enough to pierce eardrums. Emily was lost in her drawing, hunched over a white sheet of paper.

"Did you do something to him?" Julia bent and picked up Jimmy.

"No," Emily said.

Then Julia smelled the strong, overwhelming odor of a dirty diaper. "He's made a boom-boom."

"He always cries then."

"I'm going to get him cleaned up."

"Okay."

Julia went out the gate and left it open behind her.

She plopped Jimmy onto the changing table. "No more playing around, Jim-Jim, Mommy's got work to do. We want everything nice for Grandpa and Grandma tomorrow."

Julia undid his diaper and made a face. Jimmy waved his arms like helicopter blades, and then he let out a shriek of joy.

She started to carry him back to the playroom, until she saw Emily in her bedroom, struggling to pull on boots.

"What are you doing?" Julia stood in the doorway of the room.

"Time to go out," Emily said.

"Sweetheart, it's pouring down rain." Julia crossed to the window and looked out. Yup, she was right, still raining.

"We *always* go out."

Julia turned away from the window, dread in her stomach. She didn't know if she could bear to leave the telephone and e-mail. Still, she needed to buy the turkey and other groceries, and arrange for delivery later in the day.

Emily stood in the center of the room, in her underpants and T-shirt, gazing proudly at her feet where the right boot was on the left foot, and vice-versa.

"But in the rain, do you go to the *park*?"

"Yeah, we swing in the rain. Angie sings a song about the old man dressed all in leather."

Julia sighed. "Okay, but we have to stop and buy the turkey and other food for Thanksgiving."

Emily nodded, still staring at her feet. "The California old people are coming tomorrow, right?"

"Grandpa and Grandma, you mean."

"Uh-huh."

"Yup, they'll be here."

And Daddy won't.

She felt sure of that now, though a part of her still couldn't believe it. What on earth was she going to tell her mother?

Julia was flushed and hot from the effort of dressing both kids, then equipping them for the rain and cold. She pulled on her rain jacket, a spiffy red number she'd picked up on sale at Searle last year, and left the apartment in a whoosh, trying not to think about the unmade beds, dirty diapers in the diaper pail, an unflushed toilet in Emily's bathroom, and the milk carton left out on the kitchen counter.

And the telephone ringing with no one to answer it.

The cold rain struck her bare hands where they clutched the handle of the double stroller, and she realized that she'd underdressed. Well, she'd make this as quick as possible.

It was strange to be pushing her kids along city sidewalks on a weekday morning, and she found it difficult to maneuver the stroller up and down the curbs. She usually went out with the kids only on Saturdays and Sundays, when Wilson took control of the stroller.

Julia tried to enter the largest grocery store in a twenty-block radius, but she couldn't manage to hold open the door and push the stroller through. She stood there, embarrassed, until an elderly man offered to hold the door for her. She smiled her thanks and he raised his wool cap to acknowledge it.

The world's worst day to enter a grocery store was the day before Thanksgiving. But enter a New York City grocery store on the day before Thanksgiving and you're asking for a mental breakdown. Within seconds she was again boiling hot, and when Jimmy began to cry, she knew he was, too.

"Get him a banana," Emily said. She grinned at her mother.

Julia rushed to the produce department and stole a banana. Just out and out stole the thing. She peeled it halfway and was about to thrust it in Jimmy's hands when it occurred to her that he didn't know how to hold and eat a banana.

"You have to feed it to him," Emily said, ever helpful.

"But how can I buy us a turkey if I'm feeding him?" She really wanted to know.

Emily squirmed around in the front seat and grabbed the banana from her mother. "I'll do it."

"Oh, you're such a wonderful child."

Emily beamed, then broke off a large piece of banana and mashed it into Jimmy's face.

"Tell him to open his mouth," Julia said.

"Jimmy," Emily said in a high-pitched voice, "open your mouth for the na-na."

Lo and behold, Jimmy opened his mouth.

Julia balanced a shopping basket on top of the stroller's roof and ripped around the store. She cut off old ladies, tripped a toddler, and interrupted a stout West Side matron at the butcher counter. The entire store sensed her desperation, her wild unhappiness, and they just stood back and let her go.

She paid the astronomical bill with a credit card, even adding the tip for the delivery person so that the groceries could be left with the doorman. This time she didn't even attempt to wrestle with the door. A store employee bustled over to hold it open. Glad to see her go, undoubtedly.

Just as they entered the park, the rain took a breather and she peered up at the sky from under her red rain hat to see that the clouds were still low and threatening. Julia moved faster, hoping to get the swinging done before it started again.

She sighed when she reached the swings. They were soaking wet, with small puddles in the seats and larger puddles on the ground under each.

Emily climbed out and ran for the nearest one. "I need the towel, Mommy," she called out.

Julia followed more slowly, Jimmy held backward in her arms so that he faced out, arms and legs

moving like he was an upside down insect. "I didn't
bring a towel."

Emily's horrified face stared back at her.

"I'm sorry, sweetie, Angie's better at swinging in
the rain."

"We'll just get wet, then." She plowed into the
puddle and sat resolutely down in the wooden swing.
Her boots splashed experimentally at the puddle.

Julia walked carefully around the puddle to the
back of the baby swing and then realized she'd have
to wade in if she was to get Jimmy into the swing.
She'd worn ankle boots and at the center of the puddle, water lapped over the tops.

Freezing cold water wet her socks immediately.
Oh, to hell with it, she thought. She shuffled her boots
and with some peculiar fascination felt the water soaking her feet all the way to the toes. Then she backed up,
grasping the swing tight, and let it go with a good shove.

"Me next!" Emily said.

"You next." And she sent Emily sailing high.

She pushed one and then the other, back and
forth, easily finding a rhythm and no longer aware of
wet feet. She was busy in her head, planning Thanksgiving dinner.

"Mr. Cunningham's office, please?" Angela spoke
clearly, trying to give the impression that, of course,
she had an appointment.

"Yes, miss, that'll be the eighteenth floor, Suite
1806," the guard said. He sat at a swooping marble
desk directly in front of rows upon rows of elevators.

Angela walked briskly toward the elevators. The guard's voice followed her, and she was frightened that he might be asking whether she had an appointment. But he was simply continuing his directions.

"Take a right off the elevator and follow the hall around to the right."

She turned to give him a swift, flirtatious look, almost a kiss of gratitude.

The elevator was crowded with professional men and women, and for a moment their suits and heels, jewelry and papers, intimidated her. But then she saw the men, lawyers they must be, looking at her. She smiled and straightened her shoulders. Maybe they thought she was a new secretary in the building.

Several people entered Suite 1806 with her, but she held back until they'd all gone their way. The reception area was hushed and lavishly furnished, reminding her of church. When she was a little girl, she loved going to Mass. The prayers and hymns, that special smell of old wood and stone, the soaring ceiling and the priests and nuns swaying in black and white, had fairly hypnotized her. It wasn't that she believed, not then and not now. Only that certain places could steal over you, seducing you and making you feel a trembling sickness inside. An erotic excitement, and when she thought of church, she thought of this terrible fear.

"May I help you?" the receptionist said. She was a black girl with her beautifully coifed hair swept into a French twist. Thin red lips were tight, revealing nothing. Mean.

Angela stepped forward, locking eyes with her, testing how mean she'd really be. "Yes, could you ring Mr. Cunningham, please?"

"Do you have an appointment?" Her eyes swept Angela.

"No, dear, but he'll want to see me." Angela leaned close to the other woman's face.

Both sets of eyes held steady.

"You know what I mean?" Angie said with a look of deliberate suggestion.

The receptionist dropped her eyes. "Who shall I say?"

"Miss Angela Byrne, about an extremely urgent personal matter."

She picked up the phone and pressed a button. "Yes, Mr. Cunningham, I'm sorry to disturb you, but a woman is here to see you, a Miss Angela Byrne."

Angie could hear the deep rumble of a male voice. She'd never met him.

"She says it's extremely urgent and—" the receptionist hesitated, "and *personal*."

More rumbling and then the receptionist hung up. "His office is down this corridor and on the left, number 1818."

"Thank you," Angela said, turning to head down the hall.

She felt the woman staring at her. She did her best to walk tall.

At number 1818, a man stood waiting, holding a sheaf of papers in his hand and looking unhappy. "Miss Byrne?" he said as she approached.

"Angela Byrne." She held out her hand.

Not so reluctant now, he shook her hand and checked her over. "Won't you come in?"

"I apologize for not making an appointment, Mr. Cunningham, but I was fairly convinced that you wouldn't see me if I tried to." She sat in a chair while he circled behind his desk. His computer, tilted at a right angle to his desk, glowed.

Just as he was about to make contact with the seat of his chair, he seemed to give himself a shake. "Forgive me, would you care for some coffee?"

She really couldn't believe her luck.

"Yes, please, that would be lovely."

At the doorway, he hung on to the doorjamb and looked back at her. "Cream and sugar, if I'm not mistaken?"

Goodness, the idiot was actually flirting.

"Cream and sugar."

Angela dashed around his desk and typed at the computer keyboard. She exited where he'd been working, found the logo FILES, clicked, and then entered the name Mary Casey O'Brien. She'd used a false name for fear of Patrick ever trying to trace her and find out what had happened.

Zip, zip, there it was. She memorized the name and address, pressed EXIT, and was just stepping back around his desk when Mr. Cunningham came in carrying two mugs of steaming hot coffee.

"Excuse me for prying, but I had to see the lovely picture of your wife and children," she said.

If he'd thought about it, Mr. Cunningham would

realize that she could have stood on the other side of the desk and simply swiveled the picture around to face her. But then, he *was* an idiot, thinking with his nether parts like so many men.

She took the mug and sat down in her chair again. "Ta," she whispered.

"Irish, right?"

She nodded, staring into the mug of coffee with a strange, wistful expression.

"How can I help you?"

Angela glanced up and noticed that he was again sitting behind his desk. He ignored the computer.

Dr. Richard Meyer, 836 Park Avenue.

"You arranged the adoption of my baby girl about ten months ago."

His face clamped shut, and his eyes looked wary.

"I gave you the name Mary O'Brien, to protect my privacy, you know? And I just wondered if you could tell me . . ."

"You signed a paper of confidentiality. The adoptive parents' identities are rigorously protected," Mr. Cunningham interrupted.

"Oh yes, I know that. I just can't sleep for worrying . . ."

"I understand it must be difficult, but if you'll excuse me, I have a great deal of work to do." He rose and moved back around to the front of his desk.

"It's just I was wondering, can you tell me how she's doing? Any health problems?"

"Look, I happen to know the parents personally.

The baby's in great hands. You can set your mind at ease about that."

He held out his hand, and Angela handed him the coffee mug.

Then she stood and headed for the office door. "I'm sorry to be bothering you. I had to know everything was all right, and if she ever needs me, for a transplant or something, I thought you should know my real name."

"I'll make a note of it."

Mr. Cunningham stood in the office door, still holding the two mugs.

She walked down the hall and then turned back. He was definitely looking at her bum. "Is she pretty?"

He stood upright, like a priest it seemed to her. And she thought he wouldn't answer, so she turned again and walked a ways down the hall.

"Pretty as a picture."

She bent her head to her chest. The sobs rose to meet her.

CHAPTER 27

The shock of the first morning had been terrible. In a way, he'd wished it was all over, that they'd shoot him and be done with it. He'd been quite still on the small bed, thinking of Julia reading the letter that morning and how hurt she'd be. It was unbearable. Then he'd remembered Susan, her exquisite face blown apart, her excellent mind gone. Yes, he'd like them to get it over with.

The door to Wilson's room had flown open and light splashed onto the floor. He turned, blinking violently, then covering his eyes with both hands.

"Who's there?" Wilson said.

"Who gives a shit?" A deep male voice, slightly accented, spoke.

Wilson dropped his hands and tried to see. It was a guard, standing in the open doorway with a gun pointing at him. His bladder was nearly exploding.

"Is there a bathroom?" Wilson said.

"This way." The small man wore a pointed goatee and a uniform of black pants and jacket. He stood aside and gestured beyond the door with the gun.

Wilson walked forward, almost stumbling as he emerged into the bright hall light. He smelled the odor of food cooking, and there were faint noises overhead, as if the house were waking up and stretching. Only a few steps away was a bathroom. He went in and turned to close the door.

"Door stays open."

"Okay." Wilson quickly unzipped. While the rush of urine streamed out, he looked carefully around the small bathroom, wondering why the door had to stay open.

A tiny window, too small for him to fit through, opened onto a window well covered by a thick grate. It was puzzling that they thought he'd be able to escape through such a minuscule window.

He flushed and went back into the hall. Again the guard gestured with the gun, pointing away from the room where he'd been sleeping. The walls were still painted in that dazzling, bright white color, and fluorescent lights shone like hot suns from the ceiling. The floor was covered with a flat industrial carpet in a gray and black tweedy design.

They emerged into a large room that continued the carpeting and white paint. At the far end, his lab awaited him. He could see the computer, and dozens of micro-titer plates and an equal number of pipettes. His chest tightened. This was a thoroughly professional setup.

"Breakfast." The guard pointed to a small table with a chair pulled up. A plate covered in aluminum foil, a glass of orange juice, and a mug with a lid on top were neatly arranged in front of the chair.

Wilson sat down. "As you can imagine, I'm not very hungry."

"Mr. Wong said you have to eat. Keep up your strength, get those brain cells working." With the gun, the guard tapped Wilson's head none too gently as he spoke.

"I'm afraid I'll be sick."

The guard stared at him, impassive. "You better eat."

Wilson thought maybe he'd better. Eating would help him make a plan and it had the added benefit of keeping the guard from hurting him. Not getting hurt was a priority.

Wilson peeled back the foil and found a plate of scrambled eggs, sausage, and home fries. Pieces of onion mingled with the potatoes, and it actually looked like dill had been mixed into the eggs. He picked up the fork and took a tiny taste.

This is so ridiculous, he thought, getting a breakfast as good as Angela might make at home. He chewed like a cow, slowly and steadily, trying to think at the same time. But for some reason, his thoughts wouldn't come. His mind turned off, in favor of his stomach receiving the hot, good food. He removed the lid of the mug, and steam rose in a welcome, insinuating curl. He sipped and tasted strong black coffee.

"I take cream and sugar," Wilson said.

The guard raised his gun, threatening. "Not now you don't, you dumb fuck."

Even Wilson couldn't believe he'd said something so stupid. The food was lulling him into complacency. He jerked himself back and looked deliberately at the lab.

He finished the breakfast, carefully placed knife, fork, and spoon in the center of the clean plate, then refolded his napkin and put it next to the plate.

When he stood up, he felt so relaxed that he stretched high overhead, his arms reaching for the ceiling and his hands clenching and unclenching.

The guard sitting on a stool by a heavy iron door leapt up and pointed the gun at him. At least this guy favored the torso gun pointing, not the head.

"I'm just having a good stretch."

The guard said nothing, but the gun didn't move.

"Would you mind if I did some exercises?"

"You're supposed to get to work." He shoved with his chin toward the lab.

"Could I run in place, or even around this room?" Wilson said. "I'm stiff."

"Get to work."

Wilson walked over to the lab area, pulling his knees up to his chest with every step. The guard frowned but didn't stop him.

He was carefully inventorying the supplies when he heard the door open. Every sound in a basement is magnified anyway, but combined with his nerves and the utter silence in the room, the noise of a door opening was real news.

Wilson whirled around.

Mr. Wong crossed the room toward him. He wore a white lab coat, and black trousers tumbled down to cover smooth loafers. He had small, elegant feet.

"Would you like one of these?" Mr. Wong plucked at his coat.

"No, thanks."

Mr. Wong pulled out a stool and climbed on. "You look pretty good." He cocked his head to the side, examining Wilson.

"I'm all right."

"What's your cholesterol—can you safely eat eggs?"

"I'm in excellent health."

"Wonderful."

"Your guard wouldn't allow me to do any exercises."

"But of course you may exercise." Mr. Wong turned his head and barked Chinese at the guard.

When he turned back, the two men briefly stared at each other. "You must call me Luke," Mr. Wong said.

Luke Wong.

"How will you begin?" Luke Wong said quietly.

"Either work with the dopamine genes, D2 and D4, or—"

Mr. Wong held up a hand. "Stop right there. Tell me about them." He didn't seem embarrassed to be asking for an explanation.

"D2 and D4 contain the blueprints for assembling the receptors, the minuscule bump on the surface of cells to which biologically active molecules are attracted."

Mr. Wong nodded.

"Just as a finger lights up a room by flicking a switch," Wilson said, holding up his finger and twinking an imaginary light switch, "so dopamine triggers a sequence of chemical reactions each time it binds to one of its five known receptors. If you can reduce the sensitivity of these receptors, or decrease their number, the sensation of pleasure achieved by any drugs would be minimized."

"But that doesn't—"

"No, of course not. You'd want to *increase* the receptors, flood the ventral tegmental portion of the brain so that even a small amount of drug would have an enormous affect."

Luke Wong frowned. "You must think I'm very stupid."

Wilson fell silent. His hands stroked the top of the lab counter, made of the same black material, an unpolished soapstone, all chemical laboratories used because of its nonporous nature.

He had a decision to make, that was obvious. Luke Wong was too knowledgeable to completely fool, but he could try to legitimize an approach that would be absolutely incorrect. After all, the WS-

100 was an untried and fantastically new drug—
Mr. Wong wasn't going to be able to grasp all of its
subtleties immediately. Wilson could probably buy
some time. But should he?

He wondered if he ought to just kill himself.

Very few scientists, other than himself, would be
able to find an antidote for the WS-100. True, the
clinical trials meant they had a couple of years. But
not really. Luke Wong knew that Wilson would be
missed by Columbia University within days, and he
knew that Wilson's wife, no matter what her sense of
humiliation and pain, would eventually try to find
him.

"I don't think you're stupid, but I do believe
you're overly optimistic about my chances here,"
Wilson said.

"Yes, of course you're right. But we've got the
perfect working conditions. You'll be able to concentrate—"

"I can't work without music," Wilson interrupted.

"You can't work without music?"

"I have to have classical music playing, it's just
one of those things."

Mr. Wong hopped off the stool and walked
rapidly over to the phone hanging on the wall next to
the guard and iron door. He picked up the telephone
receiver and spoke rapidly in Chinese for several minutes. At certain points, he stopped speaking and
seemed to be listening to the other person.

Wilson turned away and his eyes roamed the bottles containing various substances, which lined the

wall behind the counter. He could easily make an effective poison, though he suspected Wong didn't realize it.

"We're arranging the music. It will take some time. Meanwhile, perhaps you could check whether there's anything else you'll need?" Mr. Wong said.

Wilson wandered around the lab, opening every drawer and cupboard, noting all substances.

"As I was saying, you'll have the best possible environment. It is, though, a matter of luck. Perhaps we'll get lucky, perhaps not. We'll simply have to see what happens." Mr. Wong gazed at him. "Let me know when you need access to Pharmacopeia."

"How did you go from Princeton to this?"

Wilson busied himself by moving supplies, machinery, and glassware into different spots. In actuality, the lab needed reorganization.

"You have the question the wrong way round."

Wilson paused, thinking. "How did you go from this to Princeton?"

Mr. Wong nodded. "My father was one of the major smugglers of heroin and cocaine into the United States in the eighties. I knew I wanted to follow in his footsteps—well, I really had no choice—and we had to ask ourselves what was going to happen to the drug trade in the nineties and beyond."

Wilson stared at him, nonplussed by the matter-of-fact, straightforward way Luke Wong described his career decisions.

"Like a lot of Chinese immigrant kids, I was

smart, so I got into all the Ivy League colleges," Luke said. "You went to Stanford, right?"

"Yeah, my dad taught at a New England college, and I wanted to go far away."

"What college?"

"Middlebury."

He shrugged, dismissing it. "So I chose Princeton because Brooke Shields went there." He smiled. "And I majored in chemistry. I figured that it was just a matter of time before they found a way to attack drug addiction, and I wanted to be ready."

"But the discovery of that fungus was an utter fluke—"

"It was a fluke bound to happen," Mr. Wong interrupted. "If not you, Dr. Streatfield, then someone else. This country was determined to deal with the drug problem."

"And so they should, damn it!"

"You sound sure of yourself."

Wilson leaned forward, staring into Luke's eyes. He was a younger man than Wilson, and probably just as capable, but something must have happened to make him so . . . twisted.

"What do you see?" Mr. Wong was amused.

"How can you possibly feel good about millions of people losing their lives to drugs?"

"I don't feel good about it."

"You sure as hell don't seem to feel bad about it."

"People need escape and diversion. There's nothing wrong with that. I shudder at the idea of people *without* those sources of comfort." Mr. Wong jumped down from the stool and turned to walk toward the door.

"Comfort isn't something you know much about, I fear." Luke Wong heaved open the iron door and disappeared.

CHAPTER 28

J ulia prayed that Wilson would be asleep on their bed. She fantasized that he'd contacted a lawyer, maybe Bill, who'd convinced him that he had to tell the police everything and he'd found out that the police had already made an arrest of the man Wilson saw in this young woman's apartment. He'd be home waiting for them, and then she could yell and scream. She'd throw him out, of course, but first she'd know he was alive and innocent.

Innocent.

Doubt was creeping in and she felt crazy from it, utterly crazy.

Her husband had disappeared and was in some way implicated in the brutal murder of his lover; she seemed to have lost her best friend, Lauren; and her parents were arriving the next day to celebrate Thanksgiving.

She opened the door to their apartment and stood silent for a second, listening. Was he here, or had he been here? Had Angela come home? But the entrance hall was as quiet as the middle of the night. She saw into the kitchen, where the messy dishes were left out on the breakfast table. The light was dim and she heard spits of rain hitting the windows, and over that the distant roar of traffic rushing through puddles and the steady downpour.

Emily struggled to get out of the stroller. She kicked Jimmy's head as she leapt down. He wailed. But Emmy was gone, yanking at her pants as she flew down the hall to her bathroom.

Julia bent to pick up Jimmy, and then decided she'd have to let him cry until she got off her raincoat and boots. She sat right down on the floor in order to pull off the boots. Her head was level with his, and he stared at her, mouth wide with a cry about to explode.

"Hi, Jimmy," Julia said.

He smiled tentatively.

She stood up in her sock feet, dropped the raincoat on the floor, and picked him up. "Do you have a wet diaper?"

They headed back to his bedroom. He was, in fact, wet all over. "You poor baby." And she cuddled him close. He tucked his head straight into her shoulder and vigorously rubbed his face, particularly his nose, back and forth.

"Are you okay, Em?" Julia yelled from the changing table in Jimmy's room.

The bathroom, which was between the children's bedrooms, had a bright fluorescent light shining in the gloom of the dark afternoon.

"I made it," Emily yelled back.

"Good work!"

"I do good work." Emily stood in the doorway to the bathroom, naked from the waist down except for red socks on her feet.

"Are your feet wet?"

She looked down, studying them. "Yes."

Julia had stripped off all Jimmy's clothes and his drenched diaper. The apartment, as always, was warm. She stood him up, facing her. He dropped at the knees, bouncing and grinning.

"Let's give you guys a bath," Julia said.

"I'll put the plug in." Emily disappeared into the bright bathroom.

Julia perched Jimmy on her hip, one hand clutching his bare bottom and upper thigh. It felt wonderfully squishy and hot. She squeezed and for a very brief moment, too brief to remember, she forgot that the telephone messages waited, the red light blinking and blinking.

Forty-five minutes later, the kids were clean and in pajamas even though it was only two o'clock in the afternoon. She made Emily a bowl of Cheerios, settled with Jimmy in the crook of her arm sucking a bottle, and finally pushed the button on the answering machine.

The first message was from Margaret at the office, reporting that everything was under control. The second message was Bill, asking in an urgent voice for news and saying that Lauren really wanted to talk to her, when she was ready. The third message was a hang-up. Julia didn't like that. She stared at the machine, willing it to tell her its secrets.

"Can I have some more?" Emily asked.

"You want some cinnamon toast instead?"

Emily nodded, then pushed the empty bowl out of the way and put her head sideways down on the table. When Julia brought her the toast, she was asleep.

Still standing with Jimmy balanced in her arms, she ate the toast in swift bites, swallowing the pieces almost whole. If she tried to move Emily to her bed, she might wake up, so Julia decided to let her sleep right there.

Jimmy finished the bottle, and Julia heaved him up onto her shoulder, patting him for a burp while she walked slowly to his room. The burp burst like a balloon popping right in her ear. She kept him in her arms while she lowered the blinds, then gently tucked him into the crib, lying on his side with a stuffed zebra next to him. His eyes were closed before she'd left the room.

Out in the dim hall, she stood quietly for a moment, trying to decide whether she ought to clean house a bit. And she needed to put away all the groceries that had been delivered while they were at the park. But she didn't want to disturb the kids' naptime, so instead she went to the library and closed the door firmly behind her.

Julia turned on the computer and while she waited for it to boot up, she picked up the telephone receiver and listened to the dial tone. The line was open. Wilson's e-mails were still unread, and though she had ten e-mail messages waiting, none was from him.

She heard a gentle tap-tap at the library door. "Come in," she said.

The door opened a foot and Angela stuck her head round. "Am I allowed to come home now?"

"Oh, Angie, of course." Julia smiled. "Just please excuse the mess everywhere—the kids are napping and I didn't want to wake them."

"I'll take care of it."

Julia jumped to her feet and walked to the door. "Absolutely not. This is supposed to be a day off for you. Why don't *you* take a nap?"

"Can I be honest with you?" Angela's face looked tearstained and her upper eyelids were swollen.

"What? Is everything all right?"

"I'd really enjoy a little tidying up, Julia," she said. "I'll just have a cup of tea and change my clothes. Please let me help."

Julia searched her face, knowing something was wrong, but uncertain about prying. She'd realized for a while now that Angela was running from something, but it wasn't her business to ask.

"I'll make the tea while you change." Julia dropped her hand over Angela's hand, where it held the door open. A quick touch, that was all. She hoped it said enough.

Angela's face relaxed and she turned away.

When Julia went into the kitchen, she glanced at Emily. Her head faced in the opposite direction, but she was still asleep. Julia brewed the tea in a pot, and laid out cups and saucers, cream and sugar. Then she went into the butler's pantry and found the dark rum.

Angela was sitting at the kitchen table when Julia returned. She held up the rum bottle, questioning. Angela grinned and nodded.

They poured the tea, doused it with rum, and sipped for a few moments in a comfortable silence.

Julia shot a look at Angela and held her gaze. "I think you should know that Dr. Streatfield's gone away for a while," she said. "It wasn't really planned and it's a little awkward because my parents will be arriving tomorrow morning for Thanksgiving."

"What will you say to them?"

"I haven't figured that one out, if you want to know the truth."

"You will." Angela looked at her with admiration.

Julia's throat filled and she had to swallow more tea before she could speak. "I'm going to start some of the cooking tonight."

"I've not made a Thanksgiving dinner, but I'd be happy to help."

Julia shook her head, refusing the offer.

"I've nothing else to do and it's best for me to keep busy."

"We'll do it together then—I'll teach you how to cook a true Thanksgiving dinner."

Angela's eyes blinked once. "Great, though I'm a bit dubious about pumpkin and sweet potatoes."

Emily's head lifted and turned toward them, then dropped to the table again. An eye opened and closed. "Mommy forgot the towel," she said.

"Did she now?" Angela reached over and stroked Emily's hair.

Julia closed the door to her bedroom and crossed the floor on slow legs. She sat on the edge of the bed, back slumped, and she felt her racing heart thump against her ribs. Sometimes Julia had a sense of her body being too thin and frail. She imagined her muscles as long strips of tissue, already stretched to their outer limits, and with no resilience and snap. That was when a strong drink could melt her bones and inflate her muscles. But it was early in the day for a real drink, and she'd already had rum in her tea, so she would not. She picked up the phone.

"Lauren, I need you to help me." Julia watched bleached bony knuckles grip the phone. She heard Lauren start to cry.

"I'm sorry," Lauren said. "I'm just so angry at Wilson for hurting you like this."

"I know that, I really do." Sweat made the receiver slippery. She tightened her hand. "But Wilson isn't a murderer."

Lauren snuffled into the phone for a minute. "'Scuse me just a sec."

Julia heard Lauren blow her nose, then her voice again. "Bill and I talked about it, and I know you're right. Of course I know he couldn't kill someone."

"But?"

"But where is he? What's going on?"

"I think he must be protecting us." Julia quickly switched the telephone receiver to her left hand and wiped the right hand on a pillow case. "I don't deny he was with that woman. I'm furious about it, but I still need to talk to him, hear what he has to say, why the hell he felt it necessary to go to someone else."

"It's so unbelievable," Lauren said. "You're so beautiful and a wonderful person."

Julia felt sick inside, and she spoke quickly. "Maybe I am to blame. I never told Wilson my fantasies the way you and Bill . . ."

"Julia! Every couple is different," Lauren interrupted. "You have your own relationship, and *you* were happy."

"Was I?"

They were quiet.

"I guess you weren't completely happy," Lauren said.

"Right."

"Are you going to call the police? We think you should."

"My parents arrive first thing in the morning. Can you imagine a hullabaloo with the police and stuff on Thanksgiving?"

Julia stood up and stretched backward from the waist. Ah, her muscles were warmed up, probably because she wasn't fighting with Lauren anymore.

"We're still invited, aren't we?"

"Of course."

"So you want to wait just until Thanksgiving is over?"

"Maybe it's silly, but I can't deal with everything at once."

Another silence.

"Tell me again why you think Wilson is hiding?"

"He saw who the murderer was and he knows he'll try to kill him, too, so he's staying away to keep *us* out of danger."

"Makes sense."

"It does."

"So what can I bring tomorrow?"

"Nothing."

"I have to bring something, Julia."

"Would you make the flower arrangement for the center of the table?"

"I'd love to."

"See you at about noon tomorrow, okay?"

CHAPTER 29

Afterlunch, Wilson found a notebook and pen in a drawer. A smallish CD player had been plugged in and there were five classical music CDs from which to choose, one each of Beethoven, Mozart, Bach, Chopin, and Tchaikovsky. He started with Mozart, then opened the notebook.

He wrote the date on the first page, in an upper right corner. Then he dropped a few lines and wrote "The Antidote," centering the words on the page. Wilson looked up and stared at the guard.

The guard stared back, annoyed. "What you looking at?" he said finally.

"Nothing."

"You're supposed to do experiments, not stare at me."

"I stare a lot when I'm thinking."

The guard's hand fiddled with the gun in its holster. "Stare somewhere else."

"Mr. Wong would say I can look anywhere I want."

"Mr. Wong won't be back until tomorrow," he said. "So quit staring at me."

"Where'd he go?"

The guard glared, belligerent.

Wilson began making notes and sketches, combining properties haphazardly on the page, seeing where they went, what they became. The music calmed him. His sluggish mind, at first just pretending to play at thinking, kicked in and began to work. It was a relief, *his* comfort. He turned on the computer and fooled around some more.

He filled ten pages of the notebook with scribbled notes, and then the Mozart ended. He popped in Bach and again stared around the room. The guard glanced at him, then away. Wilson smiled and bent over the notebook again.

The Bach was three sonatas with harpsichord and three sonatas with basso continuo. They ached and moaned with longing, as if weeping from loneliness. He put the pen down and dropped his head forward, lost in the music. His breath came deep and searching, filling his chest with more air than he needed.

Panic.

The music seemed to say what he felt: that he would die.

"Hey, you okay?" the guard said. His voice was closer.

Wilson tipped his head sideways and looked at him. "No."

"You sick?"

"Yes, I need to lie down." He reached out with the right hand and shut off the CD player.

Standing, he teetered a moment, then walked slowly back to his room. He stopped to use the bathroom, door open and the guard standing close by. In his room, he closed the door, turned off the light, and felt his way to the bed. If Mr. Wong wouldn't be back until tomorrow, then he wouldn't work until tomorrow.

Wilson closed his eyes and fell asleep.

The kitchen's six burners were all in use, the electric mixer whirred with mashed pumpkin and sour cream, four pie shells lined the table, and Angela stood behind the counter, a mountain of peeled and sliced apples in front of her.

"They're both asleep." Julia came into the kitchen from the back hall. "Yikes, this is a mess."

"It's better to get as much done tonight as we can."

"Let's see, I'll just need to start the turkey at ten o'clock in the morning, and if you can set the dining room table at some point?"

"No problem." Angela's head was bent over the

apples, her fingers moving fast. "How many people, then?"

"You and me is two, the kids are four, my parents are six, Lauren and Bill are eight, and Margaret from my office is nine."

"Shall I open up the bed in the library and make it up?"

"You know, that would be great, let's just set it up like a bedroom."

"And if you don't mind my asking, but how long will they be staying?"

Julia glanced at Angela, her mouth turned down. "It is with great regret that I inform you that Mr. and Mrs. Fleming will be here until Sunday morning."

Angela laughed. "Not too bad."

"Next year we'll have *your* mother and father to visit."

"No, we won't!"

"Okay, I'm going to mash the sweet potatoes," Julia said. She ran both hands through her hair, sending it straight up in the air, and took a deep breath.

She figured that if she just kept cooking and moving, she wouldn't be able to spare a moment to think of Wilson.

George watched the women cooking. For the first hour, he'd stood at the window in his dark apartment, but he'd finally found them so mesmerizing that he poured himself an enormous scotch, pulled a chair close to the window, and settled himself down like he was seeing a movie in the cinema.

The only tormenting thing was not being able to hear what they said. Much of the time they didn't talk at all, but other times, their mouths motored along, fast and furious. He wasn't worried that Angela was saying anything about the Doctor being kidnapped because he knew she wouldn't risk her child. No, it was just his curiosity to know what women said to each other.

He was pretty sure she was tracking down her own baby this morning when she visited the lawyer's office. Silly fool, leading him right to the place. George leaned forward, cupping the glass of whiskey down between his legs and smoking up the window glass.

It got late, past midnight, and they were still at it. He was on his third whiskey and wondering what the hell they were up to, with all that crazy cooking. They dashed to and fro, bending and turning, twisting and reaching. Once the lady ran and then slipped along the kitchen floor, holding a spatula up like it was a sword. Angela threw back her head with laughter.

He wasn't a bad cook himself. Or so his gran always said.

All the other apartments grew dark and theirs glowed hot like a summer sun, jabbing at his tired eyes. His eyelids dropped, ducking the sun, and he nodded off.

CHAPTER 30

J ulia's bright red minivan inched forward, caught in a colossal traffic jam outside of US Airway's baggage claim area. Her parents had her car phone number and were going to call as soon as they'd picked up their luggage and were heading out to the street. But all the plans in the world seemed fairly irrelevant at this point. They were at the mercy of traffic.

Julia found it oddly comforting. This meant she might be as much as an hour late picking up her parents, which was a mercy right there. They'd just touched down five minutes before, according to the car clock, and she was already pulling closer to the pickup area. So she'd hit it exactly wrong and have to circle around again, killing another hour, at least.

Then she saw her mother, hard to miss usually, but in a crowd this size, Julia might have missed her. No such luck. She was waving an enormous blue velvet hat over her head in sweeping strokes. Double damn dog.

Julia put on her blinker and peered over her right shoulder, hoping to squeeze in front of a gold BMW. Her car phone rang. Oh Christ. She snatched it with her right hand and tucked it under her chin, still madly trying to get the BMW's attention.

"Sweetie, we're here. Your mother's on the sidewalk waving her blue hat," her father said.

"I see her, Dad, I'm trying to get over." Julia stuck her tongue out at the BMW, who took both hands off the wheel and threw them up in mock despair. Julia grinned.

Car friends, how nice.

"Okay, see you out there."

Julia let the phone drop into her lap, its cord stretching to its limit. Her mother caught sight of her and ran right into the street, in front of the BMW, who slammed on his brakes.

"She's mine," Julia mouthed to him.

He pulled a face. "Poor you," he mouthed back.

Julia turned her front wheels sharply right and cut in front of him.

Her mother opened the front door and leapt in. "There's your father!" she said.

"Don't worry, we'll just stay right here."

Her father pulled two rolling suitcases behind him,

crushing toes and luggage in his wake. He reached the minivan, slid open the door, heaved the suitcases into the backseat, jumped inside, slid the door closed, threw himself back on the seat, and let out a shuddering breath.

Julia put on her left-hand blinker, glanced in the rearview mirror, and saw her BMW buddy gesturing that she could pull out. She waved a little hand and he tooted farewell.

"This is the last time we make this trip, I swear to God," her mother said. "Your father's going to have a heart attack."

"Dad, are you okay?" Julia glanced in the rearview mirror. His eyes were closed.

"I'm fine," he said. "Just give me a minute."

"Julia, do you see that Mercedes?" Her mother slammed her right foot down on an imaginary brake pedal.

"I see it, Mom."

"And there's a Volvo in the right lane trying to get over," her father said.

"Can we have total silence until I get on the parkway?"

"Good idea," her father said.

Her mother took out a powder compact, clicked it open, and peered at herself. Then she pinched the powder pad between two fingers and resolutely began to powder every inch of her face with sweeping, sure motions.

Julia sneezed.

They hadn't aged at all in the four months since

Julia and the kids were out to California to visit in July. Though they lived in the land of sun, neither of them went outdoors without wide hats, long sleeves, and gobs of sunscreen. And they looked twenty years younger than anyone else, including those who were, indeed, twenty years younger. Their major form of exercise was walking, but they did it early in the morning, or after the sun set.

The rest of the time, since her father's retirement as an attorney at Fleming, Aldrich, and Winfrey, they worked steadfastly, in their separate studies, on their memoirs. This had been a brainstorm of her mother's, who had every expectation that their daughter would sell the memoirs for millions. She'd already worked out the packaging, a kind of *Mr. Bridge* and *Mrs. Bridge* idea, though the titles hadn't yet been chosen.

"How are the little ones?" her mother said when they were comfortably driving at seventy miles an hour on the highway.

"They're terrific."

"Isn't the speed limit still fifty-five in New York?" Her father's head was between the two front seats.

"Yeah, sorry." Julia eased off the accelerator.

She swallowed. This was the moment. She had to tell them before they got back to the apartment.

"Listen, guys," Julia said. "Things are a little tumultuous at home right now."

"*Tumultuous.*" Her mother rolled the word. "What a great sound. I must remember that." She dug out a tiny spiral notebook from her navy pocketbook, unclipped the matching navy and gold pen that attached to the notebook, and scribbled away.

Julia's lips thinned and tightened. Double damn dog.

"What do you mean?" her father said.

He already knew, she could tell from his voice. But her mother was busy putting away the notebook and pen, muttering under her breath.

"Wilson's gone away for a bit."

"What do you mean?" her father repeated.

"He's taking a trip at Thanksgiving?" Now she had her mother's attention.

"He's away, that's all." Julia put on her left-hand blinker and pulled into the left lane in order to pass a massive truck carrying live turkeys.

"It's a little late for them." Her mother pointed a finger at the turkeys. "You all should be in the oven, being cooked!"

The woman was nuts, always had been, always would be.

"Are you having marital troubles?" Her father leaned forward, pulling on the back of her seat for leverage.

"Yeah, a little."

"Wilson's *left* you?" Her mother's voice bounced around the red minivan.

"He just needed some time away, to do some thinking." She'd already decided not to mention the big announcement of the WS-100.

Her mother turned in her seat, stretching the seat belt. "What did you do, have an affair or something?"

"Mom, no, I'm not having an affair."

But when her mother continued to stare at her, Julia remembered how she used to recite an old nursery rhyme to her, "Monday's child, fair of face . . ." because she was born on a Monday and was a pretty little girl. Apparently Wilson had found someone else fairer of face.

"I always knew he had a roving eye," her father said.

"He's a handsome man, what can you expect?" her mother said.

"Handsome men always play around, is that what you're saying?" Julia snapped.

"So I'm right." Her father heaved a huge sigh and collapsed against the backseat.

Julia caught his eye in the rearview mirror and she shamelessly pleaded that he keep quiet. He ducked his head in a quick nod of agreement.

"Let me tell you who's coming to dinner." Julia shifted her voice into a cheerfulness she certainly didn't feel. She wondered whether she could find some leftover Valiums in the medicine cabinet. And she was going to start drinking the second they got home.

The apartment swelled with people simply by the addition of her mother and father, and Julia was grateful. They were predictably charmed by Angela, thrilled to see the kids, and they seemed willing to forget, for a while, that Wilson wasn't with them.

"Here's the cranberry sauce I promised." Julia's mother walked into the kitchen, holding out a plastic margarine tub.

"Great, Mom, thanks so much. Just put it in the fridge, okay?"

Her mother opened the refrigerator and peered inside. "I thought you said only eight were coming. There's a mountain of food in here."

"I know." Julia laughed and scrubbed the side of her face with her hand. "Angela and I went a little nuts."

"You're probably hoping that if you make a wonderful feast, Wilson will come home."

My mother, the shrink.

"I doubt that."

She pulled out a chair at the kitchen table. "Emily's watching the game with your father. It's so adorable, the two of them in that pullout bed . . ."

"Terrific."

"Is there anything I can do?"

"If I slide out the turkey, will you do the basting?"

Her mother leapt up and grabbed the baster. "Do you remember Thanksgiving when you and the boys were little?"

"Sure."

"That year we had twenty-five? My God, how did I do it?"

Julia opened the oven door with huge mitts covering her hands while her mother stood close by. Hot air blasted in their faces and they both reared back for a moment.

"Didn't everyone bring food?" Julia said.

"Sure, but I still did most of it. Fun, though, huh?"

"Loads."

Her mother reached into the turkey pan and began sucking up juice, then squirting it over the golden bird.

"You know, Julia, all marriages have their down times."

"Think so?" Her arms ached from holding the heavy turkey halfway out of the oven.

"Your father and I almost got divorced at least twice."

"I didn't know that."

"Well, obviously, I didn't tell you kids about it." She stood on tiptoe and reached to the back side of the turkey pan. "I'm convinced he had an affair with Regina Burroway."

Julia knew with absolute certainty that she didn't want to hear about the affairs her father might have had.

"But I just looked the other way, that's what you have to do."

"Not according to psychiatrists."

Squirt, squirt.

"They don't know everything. Just look at all their broken marriages."

"You can't prove that psychiatrists have more marital problems than other people."

"They just released a study about it. They *do* have more divorces than other doctors, at least I'm pretty sure it was doctors they were being compared to."

Her mother stepped back, one hand cupped under the end of the baster to catch the drips. She rushed to the sink and held the baster under the hot water.

Julia slid the turkey back into the oven and closed the door.

Jimmy suddenly started crying from his playpen.

"Mom, could you get him? Angela's arranging some flowers for the entrance hall."

When she turned, her mother was gone. And very soon Jimmy stopped crying.

She sank into a kitchen chair and closed her eyes. Wilson's absence had become horrifying. She couldn't bear not knowing where he was. But more than that, she couldn't bear not being able to comfort him, to say she was sorry for how badly their marriage had deteriorated, and that she'd try to do better. This day was a nightmare and she wouldn't wake up until he came home.

CHAPTER 31

At ten o'clock in the morning, George's eyes opened slowly. He still sat in the chair pulled in front of the window. His head lolled to the right and saliva ran down his chin from the corner of his open mouth. He jumped up and yanked the chair back to its spot next to the couch.

On the way to the shower, the phone rang. What now?

"Three girls by twelve forty-five today," Mr. Mao said.

"Okay." George tried to make his voice sound like he'd been awake for hours.

"Some special instructions, George," he said. "Young, Chinese, and beautiful."

"That may be tough, on such short notice."

"Oh, you can do it."

Mr. Mao always sounded like he belonged on a public radio station as an announcer for classical music. George found it disconcerting and unnerving.

"I'll do my best."

"That would be wise."

Click.

Bye-bye to you, too.

George stood still for a moment, knocking the telephone receiver gently against the palm of his hand, then he dialed one of his more infrequently used sources, placed his order, and said he'd be taking a shower, but he needed to hear back on availability in exactly fifteen minutes.

He was toweling off when the phone rang. He ran for the bedroom, dove across the bed, and snatched it up.

"Yo?" He'd heard American Italians say that. "How old are they? . . . Yeah, nineteen's fine . . . And they're gorgeous? . . . This is *very* important . . . Okay, great, thanks a million."

Americans also said "thanks a million" all the time, like they really had a million bucks.

He checked the clock next to the phone. Still an hour before he had to pick them up. Time for bacon and eggs at the local coffee shop.

After breakfast, Wilson ambled over to the lab. He'd exercised for an hour early that morning and now, with a full stomach, he felt sleepy again. He removed the Bach CD and stuck in the Tchaikovsky. Then he flipped through the pages of notes he'd made the day before.

The iron door opened and a man came in, carrying a suit on a hanger, a white shirt with a tie draped over it, dress shoes, underwear, and socks.

"Dr. Streatfield?" His voice was melodic and pleasant.

Wilson looked at him, then raised a single index finger of acknowledgment.

"Mr. Wong invites you for Thanksgiving dinner at one o'clock in the afternoon. You're free to use the shower and he's sent you these clothes, as the dinner will be somewhat formal."

Wilson's breath was shallow. He panted quickly, like a dog who's run too fast on a summer day.

Thanksgiving.

He'd entirely forgotten.

"I'll hang these in your room," the man said. "The guard will escort you upstairs at twelve fifty-five." He disappeared down the hall to Wilson's room, then reappeared shortly after. He did not look at Wilson again.

Wilson sat staring at a blank wall directly in front of him. Mr. Wong's behavior was strange. Why would he invite Wilson upstairs for Thanksgiving dinner? It was almost as if he believed Wilson would become a friend, and if so, that he expected Wilson would be staying here for quite some time. Perhaps Mr. Wong knew that Julia wouldn't be looking for him. Perhaps he'd told Julia some terrible lie. Perhaps he'd be in this basement for years and years. Such things had happened in political abductions, like those poor bastards in Beirut.

He stood up, stretched, and walked down the hall to the bathroom. A shower would feel great, and maybe he'd have some kind of epiphany in there. Maybe he'd figure out what to do. For the first time, the guard didn't follow him.

He must have decided that Wilson was harmless.

At one o'clock in the afternoon, Julia's kitchen shone. Side dishes warmed in two ovens and the cooling turkey was resplendent on its carving board. A Mozart oboe concerto played loudly on the stereo system, though it was barely audible over the murmur of voices from the living room.

Angela stood next to Bill in the pantry and glanced at him shyly before speaking. "Two bourbon and waters, a white wine, Chablis, if we have it."

Bill smiled at her and rubbed his hands together. "Okay."

He began pouring and stirring, not quickly, but he seemed to know what he was doing. Angela could mix a drink in half the time, but she buttoned her lip. She liked this tall man, his frizzy blond hair wild and silly around a thin face. And she liked it that he was married to an Asian woman.

"You haven't children, then?" she asked him.

"No, not yet." He scooped up ice cubes with his hand and dropped them in the glasses of bourbon. "We may adopt." His voice was low and shook slightly.

Angela flushed and her heart moved like a great fish. "That would be lovely."

Now it was his turn to look. "Are you all right?"

"Yes."

She saw his gentle eyes catch her and it was such a relief that she didn't move her gaze away. Their eyes locked.

"Can I do anything?"

Angela shook her head slowly. "You're very kind to offer."

"We'd be happy to help you if there were anything—"

"I'll remember." Angie grabbed the bourbons and left the pantry, moved through the dining room and into the living room.

The walls in this room were glazed a golden yellow and the drapes were a charming pattern of pale ferns on gold silk. Two couches done in greeny-gold velvet balanced on each side of the crackling wood fire. Though it was afternoon, and a wintry sunshine streaked into the room, Julia had lit the candles on the carved cherry mantel.

The bourbons were for Julia's mum and dad, and they were so full of gratitude when Angie handed them over that she wondered whether they might love their drink a wee bit too much. It would explain the mum.

Angie turned and started back. Bill was behind her in the living room, handing the sherry to Margaret.

"What would you like?" Bill asked Angela.

"I'll get it, don't you worry," she said. "If you just want to do yours and your wife's."

She made both herself and Julia gin and tonics, squeezing in plenty of lime, and adding only two small ice cubes. Bill worked quietly next to her, pouring two red wines. Gin in each hand, she fairly skipped back to the living room.

Everyone was chattering like they didn't miss the Doctor at all, for which Angie was grateful, though it was puzzling. She sat on an upright chair that was over by the window, off by herself. She was glad to be included, but she didn't want to presume.

Emily appeared at the far end of the living room, clutching a book. She stared around the room, a slight frown on her face until Angie waved for her. She dashed across, dodging people's legs, and landed triumphantly in front of Angela with her book stuck straight out in front of her.

"You want a story, do you?" Angela said.

"Please?"

She'd taught the child well.

"I'd be delighted." Angie hauled Emily up on her lap, opened the book, and began to read in a whisper, hoping not to disturb the conversation flowing around her.

The living room quieted, not that either Angela or Emily noticed, and soon the only sounds were Mozart and Angela's voice. Finally Angie glanced up, curious about what was wrong.

"Don't stop," Margaret said. "You sound so lovely."

"We all want to hear the story," Bill said.

Yes, yes, the others chorused.

Angela blushed a deep red color. She felt it shoot up her neck and into her face, and then the prick of sweat dotting her forehead. They stared at her, expectant, and she found she couldn't disappoint. When she finished reading the story, they all clapped, and Angela leapt to her feet and gave small curtsies right and left.

It was lovely, this Thanksgiving business.

CHAPTER 32

Though Wilson was no expert, the dark blue suit was definitely cashmere. So were the socks. He sighed at the sweet softness as they slid over his toes and then the way the buttery brown shoes eased on. He ambled down to the bathroom to use the mirror for the tie. His freshly washed hair flew gently around his face, so he took the brush and worked at it vigorously for a few moments until it fell straight back behind his ears in large curls.

He stared at himself in the mirror, trying to believe it was actually Thanksgiving, that he'd been kidnapped and was being held in the basement of a New York City mansion by a drug lord who'd graduated from Princeton.

Wilson gripped the sides of the sink and leaned into the mirror so that he could see only his eyes and nose. "Thank you for sparing my life and the lives of my wife and children. Please, God, please let me go."

He left the bathroom and walked down the hall to the main room.

The guard checked his watch. "Five minutes."

Wilson stood still, staring at him. It was the same guard as the day before.

"I said not to look at me."

"What else am I supposed to do?"

The guard took out his gun and pointed it at him. "Look somewhere else."

Wilson dropped his head and gazed down. "Nice shoes, huh?" He stuck out one shoe, heel digging into the carpet.

No answer.

He pulled the shoe back and unbuttoned the jacket of the suit, then plunged both hands into the pockets. "I don't really care if I stretch the material."

"Shut up."

"Okay."

They were dead quiet. The guard shuffled his feet. Wilson's head hung down so that he wouldn't look at the guard's face by mistake, but he glanced sideways along the carpet and saw a thermos under the guard's chair. It was pushed back against the wall, and if Wilson hadn't been looking at such an odd angle, he wouldn't have seen it at all.

"Time to go," the guard said.

They marched out the iron door and up a long,

thin stair also made of iron and covered with a thin strip of black carpet running down the center. Wilson's stomach flip-flopped and he felt lightheaded. He could smell roasting turkey and other wonderful cooking odors as they came up into a back hall. He looked right and glimpsed the kitchen.

"Left," the guard said.

He turned left. This hall was paneled in cherry wood and carpeted in a lush red, black, and green floral design. Delicate brass sconces lit their way, and the coved ceiling was painted with fluffy white clouds in a blue sky.

Wilson took a deep, deliberate breath.

They came to the end of the hall, where it spilled into the entrance to the house. Black and white marble, splashy green ferns in a corner, an ornate carved table with a gold marble top. It was empty. He stepped farther into the entrance and heard voices to his right.

The dining room glowed. Gold velvet drapes were drawn and a double-pedestal candelabra flickered with candlelight in the darkened room.

Mr. Wong appeared in the open doorway. "Dr. Streatfield, thanks so much for joining us." He held out his hand.

Wilson stepped into the room and shook Mr. Wong's hand.

"Let me introduce you," Mr. Wong said. "I believe you know Mr. Mao, and then we have Josephine, Jennifer, and Jean."

Three beautiful young Chinese women glided forward and shook his hand shyly. "How do you do, how do you do?" Wilson said.

"I'm sorry, but our lady friends do not speak any English," Mr. Mao said.

"And though I know you're an accomplished man, I don't believe you speak Chinese, am I right?" Mr. Wong said.

Wilson nodded and grinned a large, fake smile. It was absurd, but he felt an obligation to behave correctly, especially because the women were so extraordinary looking. They each wore a long silk gown of a different color, red, blue, and green, with the traditional tall Chinese collar. On their feet were high heels, matched to the color of their gowns. One woman's long hair cascaded straight to her waist, another's was twisted up and pinned on top of her head, and the third had cut her hair to chin level where it swayed evenly and methodically every time she moved.

They were exquisite.

"Shall we take our seats?" Mr. Wong said. "I believe there are place cards."

Wilson felt as if he were in a Kafka novel as he moved around the table and searched for his seat. He was in the center, with one woman next to him, Mr. Mao and Mr. Wong at the ends, and two women opposite. The woman with the shorter haircut was the one to his left, and instinctively he knew that she was his.

And when he knew that, he knew the rest.

His wine glass was full and he reached for it with a trembling hand. Would he be forced to sleep with this woman? Could he be forced? He swallowed the delicious wine, French and old.

Maybe he'd even like to sleep with her.

Outside Mr. Wong's mansion, George stood still for a moment. The day was cold and lit with weak sunshine. He buttoned his new camel overcoat and pulled on brown leather gloves, then removed a pair of sunglasses from his coat pocket. When he'd tried them on at Bloomingdale's, he'd been seduced by his own appearance and he was determined to wear them, weak sun or no.

He'd figured out that it was Thanksgiving, and his heart was sick with having no place to go. George wandered the streets for endless blocks, walking aimless and slow for miles, bored by the closed shops and empty streets. He passed some high-class bars, this was the expensive part of town after all, but even they looked too quiet to give him much company.

He meandered down Fifth Avenue, finally stopping to sit on a bench at the entrance to Central Park. He removed a handkerchief from his back pants pocket and blew his nose. The cold was getting to him, and there was a damp in the air that made him want a cozy fire, whiskey, and his gran. He looked across the street and saw a church, and then the sign standing out in front announcing a Thanksgiving service at three o'clock in the afternoon.

He didn't allow himself to think as he walked across the street and entered the church. Thinking, in his experience, was deadly difficult and would get him nowhere. It was a Catholic church and he made the sign of the cross by habit, then muttered a Hail Mary. Candles flickered, and a handful of people were scattered throughout the cold, echoey interior. Pretty depressing, truth be told.

George sat in a pew about halfway back. A priest entered from behind the altar, took his place at the pulpit, and stared out at the measly pickings.

"Thank you for joining me today, and God the Father, as we bow our heads in thanksgiving for the bounty and love that is ours on this earth."

The priest was Irish.

George's heart almost stopped beating, so shocked he was. His eyes slid sideways, checking out the rest of the congregation. Irish faces, every last one of them. How had this happened? Why'd he end up here? Maybe God sent him, though he wasn't even sure he believed in God. Still, this was an oddity to be sure, and it would need some explaining.

The predictable service continued and George's heart settled down to its usual beat, ta-dum, ta-dum, ta-dum. He tried to pay attention, figuring that was why he'd been sent here, but his mind wandered as badly as ever it used to when he was a child.

He left before the service finished, found a bar quickly, and started drinking. Thanksgiving in America, lost in the drink.

The first course was a lobster consommé.

"This is sublime," Wilson said, meaning it.

The women raised their eyes, looked at him, and

returned their gaze to their soup bowls.

Mr. Wong took a sip, and closed his eyes. "Yes," he said finally.

A long silence descended as they ate the soup, the kind of silence in a social situation that signaled difficulties. It made Wilson nervous. Was he the one responsible for conversation? Well, damned if he'd do it. He finished the soup, and carefully placed his spoon in the middle of the bowl.

"Cook has noticed your excellent table manners," Mr. Mao said. "It's very gratifying."

"But I've only eaten downstairs, with the guard."

"You place your utensils correctly after finishing a meal."

Wilson turned from Mr. Mao to Mr. Wong, helpless at knowing what to say.

"It's clear you were raised in an upper-class environment," Mr. Wong said. "That makes it so much more pleasant for us here, since we can welcome you upstairs."

"Imagine if he'd been a Jew," Mr. Mao said.

"Yes." Mr. Wong rang a small silver bell, which was to the right of his wine and water glasses.

Wilson wanted to scream that he sure had fooled them, that he'd actually been brought up in a trailer park and simply by dint of hard work and scholarships he'd managed to get to Stanford. But it wasn't true. His pedigree, back hundreds of years, was indeed what would be called first class.

He looked across the table at one of the women. A tiny smile hovered on her lips and it occurred to him that they understood English very well, that they were probably American college students earning their way through Hunter, or even his own university, Columbia.

A young man moved soundlessly around the table, collecting soup bowls. Wilson tried to catch his eye, but without success.

"So you grew up in Vermont?" Mr. Wong said.

"Yes."

"Are your parents still alive?"

The wine was good, giving him an edge. "No, they died about five years ago in a car accident." The lie was easy.

"Did you have brothers and sisters?" Mr. Mao asked.

"I was an only child."

"Very good, and a male child," Mr. Wong said.

"Surely you no longer believe that it's better to have a male child?" Wilson couldn't help himself.

Mr. Wong's eyes were amused. "It's obviously more advantageous for a family to have male children."

"I don't think that's true."

"Do you believe men and women are equal, exactly the same?" Mr. Mao said.

"Yes."

"This lovely creature is the same as you and me?" Mr. Wong reached to his left and held up the limp, white hand of the woman with hair piled on top of her head. She didn't react.

The door swung open and the same waiter

entered with two plates. Wilson and Mr. Wong were served first, but the others quickly followed.

Sliced turkey, dressing, mashed potatoes, glazed carrots, and a dab of cranberry sauce were artfully arranged on the plates. It looked like a still life, too good to eat, but after the first taste Wilson found he couldn't stop. He did make a crazy effort to handle his fork and knife perfectly, since he had his upper-class background to uphold.

God, he thought, I'm an idiot.

They served dessert and coffee in the large, cold living room where the fire was unlit and the furnishings too Victorian for comfort. Wilson imagined his own living room, the fire crackling and the golden walls warm with light.

A mahogany rolling table held a selection of four different kinds of pies: apple, pumpkin, pecan, and sweet potato. A huge silver bowl billowed with whipped cream and small turkey-shaped chocolates clustered in a smaller bowl.

Wilson tried to decide which pie to have and then thought to hell with it, and actually ate a piece of each. At six three and a hundred and eighty pounds, he'd always been slim, so he figured he'd take the opportunity to put on weight. The coffee was rich and marvelous, especially in that cold room.

"I hope you like Jennifer," Mr. Wong said.

He looked at the woman with the chin-length hair.

"She's beautiful."

"She's for you, to take the sting out."

"Usually you clean a cut with antiseptic, stinging the sting."

"Very clever." He sipped his coffee. "But I want good work from you, that's our priority, and so I think a little TLC will do wonders."

"Thanks for the offer, but I can't."

Mr. Wong leaned over to place his coffee cup down on a rickety side table. "You must try." He picked up the bowl of chocolate turkeys and offered it to Wilson.

"If I eat anything else I'll be sick." He avoided Mr. Wong's eyes, wondering what to do. Perhaps he'd go to his room with the girl and tell her he just couldn't do it and that they'd have to keep it a secret. Or perhaps he'd just do it.

Mr. Wong went over to Jennifer and whispered in her ear. She nodded and then turned to walk toward Wilson.

His heart actually had the audacity to speed up, as if she were a person he really wanted to make love to. He'd never simply "had sex" with someone, though he knew he'd been about to with Susan. He could no longer really remember why he'd wanted some strange woman when Julia, his gloriously beautiful wife, waited at home.

Jennifer linked her arm through his and gently tugged him to the living room door. When they stepped into the entrance hall, Wilson's guard was there, his gun drawn and ready.

"Back to your place," he said.

It sounded like a bachelor pad or something.

They walked quickly and did not speak along the back hallway, down the stairs, through the iron door, and into the lab. He saw her head jerk up and stare around with interest.

"Are you taking any science courses this semester?" he said.

"Organic," she said, then stopped, horrified.

"Don't worry, I knew and I'm not telling." Wilson walked toward the lab. "Would you like to see?"

She nodded.

The guard behind them shut the door and locked it, then sat heavily in his chair.

Wilson walked her around, pointing things out. He didn't try to get her to talk again because the guard might overhear.

"Let me show you something interesting," he said. He pulled out the stool that Mr. Wong had used, and she hoisted herself up on it, the long red skirt of her gown trailing beautifully to the floor.

He poured various chemicals into one test tube. "Do you know what happens with this?"

She shook her head, no.

"Check with your professor next week when classes begin again," Wilson said.

"Hey, you guys are supposed to be in the bedroom," the guard said.

"But you're always telling me to work."

"Should I call Mr. Wong, Doctor?"

"No, no, we're going." Wilson offered her his arm and they walked together down the hall to his bedroom. "It's not much, I'm afraid."

She sat on the bed and bounced a bit.

He closed the door and his mind zipped along, trying to decide whether he could tell her anything and trust her to help him. But he knew she'd be killed if he did. Mr. Wong would ask her questions when she went back upstairs, and he'd see she knew something. And then this young woman would attend no more organic classes.

He couldn't risk it.

She patted the bed. Her smile was enchanting, demure and lively at the same time.

But he needed her to talk. "I think if you whisper, it'll be all right."

Jennifer shook her head and placed a finger over her lips. Then she pointed up to the light fixture, eyes wide and knowing.

He crossed the room and sat down on the floor at her feet. She jumped up and grabbed his hands, tugging for him to sit on the bed.

"I like the floor," he said. "When you're as tall as I am, furniture doesn't always fit that well."

She smiled and collapsed to the floor next to him, her skirt flowing up as it caught the air and then deflating across his lap. He touched the silk with a finger, then two fingers.

So slippery and gorgeous.

Julia noticed that a strange hilarity settled over the table as the dinner began. She supposed it had to do with all the alcohol they'd been consuming, but it was as if no one noticed that Wilson, her husband, wasn't

with them. His place at the far end of the table was
taken by her father, and though she'd urged him to sit
there, she still felt furious when she looked at him.
She was a big believer in toasts, but not much for
prayers said at the table. Suddenly, though, she
thought that maybe prayers were what they needed.

"Angela, would you say a prayer?"

"But I'm Catholic," Angie said. "Is anyone else?"

"That's all right. Any kind of prayer will do."

They bowed their heads, and Julia felt the numb-
ness from two drinks fill her mind with thick swirling
clouds.

"Our Father, who art in heaven, hallowed by thy
name," Angela said. "Thy kingdom come, thy will be
done, on earth as it is in heaven."

What is thy will for me, then?

"Give us this day our daily bread; and forgive us
our debts, as we also have forgiven our debtors."

*Wilson, you are not blameless, I think you know
that even at this moment.*

"And lead us not into temptation, but deliver us
from evil."

*Deliver you from evil, oh yes, deliver you to me
again. Come home, Wilson, come home.*

Wilson's arm circled around Jennifer's thin shoulders
and her face turned to him. Her eyes stared into his,
and he could see that she wanted him. And he knew
that her desire was real. He started to kiss her, urging
himself to do it, but as his lips brushed hers, he
couldn't continue.

He heard Julia's voice. *Come home, Wilson, come home.*

His eyes flew open and he looked about the small room, desperate and shocked.

"Are you all right?" Jennifer's whisper was barely audible.

He held his finger to his lips, still staring about the room. Then he leaned toward her again, pressed his mouth against her ear, and spoke. "I can't do this. Forgive me. We need to make noises as if we've done it."

Wilson pulled back and looked at her searchingly. She nodded.

There was a long moment of silence, and then Wilson made a loud moan. She clapped a hand over her mouth, stifling the giggles.

He grinned and pointed a finger at her.

She moaned, much more convincingly than he had. Then she spoke in Chinese, obviously words of passion. Her eyes closed slightly and she undulated from side to side.

His grin faded and he wondered, briefly, whether he wasn't making a mistake. But then her eyes popped open and she winked at him.

They moaned and groaned, he swore in English and she swore in Chinese, they rustled clothes and leapt up and down on the bed, pulled out the sheets, moaned and groaned some more, and finally, in an explosive burst of noise, they stopped. Together.

They had to stuff the sheets into their mouths to block the manic laughter.

When she left, he kissed her tenderly on the forehead and smiled a big smile. He wanted to reassure her that he was fine and that she need do nothing about his situation.

In the hall outside his room, he risked speaking. "Say nothing."

She nodded and trotted away.

He cleaned up the bed and then sat down, staring at the open door. Nothing happened. He stood up, closed the door, turned off the overhead light fixture, and lay down on the bed. Time to think.

CHAPTER 33

The test tube of poison was still in its rack the next morning. Wilson knew timing was vital. This would not be an efficient way to kill, and he had no way to predict how long it would take. He needed not only the opportunity, but also, perhaps, several hours for the poison to work.

He waited two days, until Sunday morning. He figured Sunday would be quiet, and he'd seen nothing of Luke Wong, which suggested he was away. Sunday morning wouldn't be a time he'd return.

He got up an hour earlier than usual, and was at his place in the lab before breakfast was delivered. Fifteen minutes later, the phone rang, the guard answered, and then hung up immediately.

The guard opened the door and slipped out, and Wilson heard the key turning.

His heart beat fast. He picked up the test tube, rushed across the room, unscrewed the guard's thermos, poured the test tube's contents into the thermos, replaced the top, repositioned the thermos in its exact spot, and tore back across the room.

The key in the lock clicked almost immediately, and the guard reentered, carrying a plate covered in foil. He carefully locked the door behind him and then strode over to the small table, putting the plate down with surprising delicacy.

"Breakfast." He swiveled on his heel and headed back to his chair.

Wilson crossed to the table slowly, watching the guard out of the corner of his eye.

He sat down and peeled back the foil. The plate was piled with blueberry pancakes, four links of sausage, and two sunnyside-up eggs. The cook was obviously thrilled to have such an appreciative and large eater. Wilson glanced at the guard, who sat upright in the chair, arms folded across his chest, his face wearing a grumpy expression.

"Don't you get something to eat?" Wilson said.

"Later."

"How about that thermos?"

The guard looked surprised. He leaned over at the waist and stared under the chair. "I forgot about my tea."

Wilson didn't answer, instead picking up a knife and fork and carefully cutting a piece of pancake and sausage. The food was, as always, delicious, but Wilson had difficulty swallowing and chewing.

He was killing a man. It was unbelievable to him that he would be the cause of a man's death. Unbelievable and utterly terrible.

His hands shook and the pancake turned in his stomach.

The guard poured out a large cup of tea and held it up to his lips, blowing.

Wilson knew it was irrational of him, to care what happened to his guard, a man who'd been unpleasant and nasty for days and who'd probably shoot him in the head without a second's hesitation.

The guard gulped the tea. Thank God he wasn't a sipper.

Wilson cut another piece of pancake and sopped it in the egg yolk. He raised the fork slowly to his lips and watched the guard.

Nothing.

He tipped the cup again and gulped another healthy swig of tea.

Then he actually smacked his lips in satisfaction.

The guard took an hour to die, which surprised Wilson. He thought it had something to do with the heat of the tea, and of course, every person's metabolism is different. The guard fell off the chair, sprawling loose and splayed, then crumpled tightly inward. He tried to vomit, but by then rigidity had set in, and he couldn't.

Wilson wanted to cross the room and stand ready

for when it was all over, but squeamishness kept him in the lab area. He looked down at his hands, flat on the black soapstone. Even spread out on the countertop, they shook. He had to get control of himself. Taking a deep breath, he popped the CD player open, removed Beethoven, and put in the Bach, which he hadn't dared to listen to again. The bittersweet music filled the room. He bowed his head to his chin and began to chant to himself.

God, let me go. God, let me go. Let me find the courage. Let me go, God, let me go, God.

He heard the final grunt, glanced quickly, and saw that the time was now.

Wilson shoved back from the counter and ran across the room. He had to turn the guard over in order to reach his gun, but something was fevered and frantic in him now, and the man whose arm he touched, still so warm, was nothing human to him. He grabbed the gun, then didn't know what to do with it while he searched for the keys.

Bach soared through the room.

Carefully Wilson placed the gun down on the floor, pointing it away from himself. He reached into the man's right pants pocket, and now he felt the terribleness of what he'd done, for he was close to the man's genitals and that seemed, despite everything, horrific. He found the single key, reached for the gun again, stepped fast to the door, and inserted the key into the lock.

It turned smoothly. Right outside was the small, dimly lit anteroom. He started to climb the stairs, as slowly as he could and still remain balanced. The gun was raised and pointed ahead of him. He had no doubt whatsoever that he'd use it, though he'd never fired a gun in his life, much less at a person.

Then Wilson heard the distant ring of the telephone and knew in the racing wildness of his heart that it was the telephone where the guard lay dead. He thought momentarily of running back down and answering. Maybe he could trick them. But the language was a problem.

He leapt up the stairs, frantic at the repeated sound of the ringing telephone. At the top, he opened the plain pine door and turned left to run down the long hall that led to the entrance. Kitchen noises were loud. It sounded like the breakfast dishes were being cleaned.

Wilson started running as fast as he could. He could see daylight spilling into the open doorway at the end, and he knew that was the entrance to the house. In the entrance was the door.

The door to the outside.

Wilson blocked out all sounds and thoughts and feelings as he continued to run. He didn't pause to wonder who would be in the entrance hall, but instead simply ran into the center of the black and white marble floor, his eyes on the heavy mahogany front door. He was vaguely aware of black figures dotting the circumference of the room, but he didn't think of the possibility that he might be shot.

Like the most beautiful woman in the world to him, Julia, the door beckoned. And he ran to her, praying that Julia's arms would open to welcome him.

Fool that he was, naturally the front door was locked. His hands yanked on the doorknob, desperate, the panic rising until he thought he might go berserk with the craziness he felt.

And so, because he was such an idiot, they had no need to shoot him. Instead, three men closed in quickly, grabbed his gun, and tied him up. They pulled him across the enormous entrance hall to where Mr. Wong stood on the third stair, waiting.

He'd been home after all, though not yet ready for the day. He was dressed in an elaborate pair of pajamas and dressing gown. In his arms, he held a small poodle.

Five more men rushed in from the hallway that led to the basement stairs.

"The guard's dead," one man reported to Mr. Wong.

"How did you do that?" Mr. Wong said calmly to Wilson.

"Poison."

Mr. Wong nodded slowly, his face turning almost white. "Take him to the lab." He took a step down.

Two men grabbed him and pushed him toward the back hall. But Wilson walked in that direction with no fight left in him, and soon their hands were looser and more accommodating.

The guard had already been taken away.

When they got to the lab, Mr. Wong spoke in Chinese. One guard stood by the door and two others followed Mr. Wong. The dog was let down and went running wildly through the place, sniffing and snorting. Mr. Wong walked up and down the lab area, searching for something.

"You understand about stereo speakers?" Mr. Wong said.

Wilson started to answer and then, seeing the expression on Mr. Wong's face, chose not to.

"Two speakers separated by some distance and playing slightly different sounds trick the mind into creating a sense of three-dimensional sound."

Wilson took a tentative step backward, and the two guards moved in. They grabbed both arms and held tight.

"It's much the same way that the mind creates depth perception from binocular vision. With only one speaker, you cannot create that sense of three-dimensionality, and the music seems flatter and less interesting."

Mr. Wong picked up a particular bottle and nodded to the guards.

They forced him to his knees and held his head against the countertop, his left ear pressed to its warm surface.

Mr. Wong approached, the bottle tilted, and carefully poured several drops of what Wilson knew was sulfuric acid in his right ear.

He screamed in agony and struggled against the guards.

Suddenly they let go and he fell to the floor, clutching both hands over both ears. He could not hear his own moans, or not at first. He tumbled to the right, so that the right ear pressed to the carpeted floor. Both hands now cupped that ear. The pain slowly receded.

"If there is any more nonsense such as we've had this morning, you'll lose the hearing in the other ear, Dr. Streatfield."

Wilson sat up slowly, balancing himself with both hands. Nausea and a light-headed sensation. "I won't do this research. It would be—" He stopped speaking, searching for the word.

"Sacrilege?" Mr. Wong said.

Wilson closed his mouth, fury making his eyes water. He blinked several times. "I won't work on an antidote. You may as well just kill me."

"Dr. Streatfield, I can assure you that you'll get to work by tomorrow morning. You'll work like you've never worked before. In fact, I suspect you'll be so inspired that you'll have a major breakthrough. After all, what we're talking about is not really that difficult."

"If it's so easy, get some other crooked scientist to do it for you," Wilson interrupted.

"I wish I could. You're certainly proving to be a lot of trouble, but a scientist with your experience and insights into this particular research problem is not the kind of person one can so easily find, especially in my professional circles."

Mr. Wong laughed. "Put him in his room."

The men jerked him away and tossed him into his room. They closed the door and he heard the lock turn.

He cuddled his deafened ear into the pillow.

Julia, he thought, I need to talk to you. Listen now, listen carefully. You need to call the police. Call the police. Call the police. Call the police.

CHAPTER 34

W et snow fell so thickly that Julia wondered if her car's windshield wipers were going to be able to do their job. She didn't even want to think about the possibility that her parent's flight might be delayed.

Or canceled.

"Sweetheart, your father and I are very concerned about Wilson and you," her mother said.

"Yes, we are." Her father leaned forward, again leveraging himself by grabbing the back of her seat.

"I know."

"Why haven't you called him?"

"You just have to say you're sorry," her father said.

"Don't you mean *he* has to say that?" A scream burbled up inside.

"What he means is, it doesn't matter who says it first. After all, it takes two to tango. Just say you're sorry and get him back," her mother said.

"You don't even like him that much."

"I beg your pardon," her father said. "I've always been very fond of that man, very fond. He's just a little quiet is all."

Like someone else I know. Julia didn't think she'd ever had a truly personal conversation with her father. She leaned over and turned up the heating system, then pressed the button for the back window defroster.

"Well, you'll do what you want, of course," her mother said. Her white fingers picked and plucked at the ribbon of her navy hat. She'd worn the blasted hat every time she stepped outside, and Julia hated the sight of it.

"I love Wilson very much and I have every expectation that we'll work things out," Julia said.

"The kids sure are wonderful," her mother said. "But they need a father."

Julia's foot pressed the accelerator. She couldn't wait to get to the airport.

George was tired of Mr. Wong's office. It was always dark, strangely and abnormally dark. Why didn't he open the drapes and shutters, let the sun shine in? This morning a thick, wet snow was falling, but even that would've been more attractive than this burial plot of a room.

He was alone, waiting to see Mr. Wong. He sat on the love seat, urging his mind to go blank. He didn't like to think negative thoughts about Mr. Wong, for fear that he'd read his mind. It was ridiculous, but that was the nature of Mr. Wong's power. He thought about playing ball in the streets of Dublin when he was about eight years old, and in his imagination he gave the ball a great kick and it flew over all the boys' heads.

"Good morning, Georgie."

Lord, he wished he'd stop calling him Georgie. That was his gran's name for him.

He jumped up. "Good morning."

"I have a real quick order for you."

"Yes, sir."

"Kill the nanny today."

"I'm supposed to . . . what?"

"You got a hearing problem?" Mr. Wong's face wore a weird smile.

"You said to kill the nanny. But . . . why?"

"It's an order. No questions, no discussion. Now, out of here. Mr. Mao will issue you a gun."

"What if she doesn't leave the apartment today— some days, she doesn't."

"You're wasting my time. Just take care of it."

George headed for the door.

"Georgie-Porgie?" Mr. Wong said.

He turned.

"Either she's dead by tonight, or you are, understand?"

"Yes, sir."

He left the room, pulling the door shut behind

him. His legs were jelly as they descended the grand staircase.

Mr. Mao was at the bottom, waiting for him. "Dispose of the gun afterward."

"Yes, sir."

"It's very important that the gun be lost."

"I understand."

In a daze, he placed the gun in his waistband, pulled on his camel coat, and left Mr. Wong's house. The snow whirled around him and he yanked out the wool cap that was stuffed in his coat pocket.

Two policemen stood waiting for Julia in the reception area of her apartment building.

"Julia Fleming?" said the white one, his crisp black hair slicked back beneath his cap.

Snow dotted their uniforms. They'd only just arrived then, she thought.

"Yes, I'm Julia Fleming."

They both flashed their IDs. "I'm Officer Callahan," said the white one. "Could we speak to you privately, please?"

"How about my apartment?"

"Fine," he said.

In the elevator, the black police officer eyed her. "I'm Officer Smith." He paused. "You don't seem surprised to see us."

"My husband's missing and implicated in the murder of a young research assistant who worked at his lab." She tried to keep her voice steady. "I'm not surprised."

"How do you know that?" Callahan asked.

"Armand Jones on Columbia's security force came to see me before Thanksgiving."

They stepped off the elevator and Julia looked carefully at each of them.

Smith pulled out a small spiral notebook and a pen. He spoke while he scribbled in the notebook and they walked, three abreast, down the long hallway. "He shouldn't have done that." His tone was mild.

Julia stood with the key in the lock of her apartment door, waiting before she allowed them in. "Please stay here until I ask the baby-sitter to take the kids to the playroom. I don't want them upset."

"No problem."

Angela had tidied up the apartment, the washing machine hummed with the sheets from the pullout couch, the Sunday paper stood neatly stacked on the living room cocktail table, and a fresh pot of coffee dripped into its glass carafe.

"Where is everyone?" Julia called out.

"We're in the playroom," Angela said.

She stood outside the room, at the guardrail. "Could I speak to you for a moment?"

"Of course." Angela put Jimmy in the playpen and walked over to Julia.

"The police are here," Julia whispered.

Angela's face blared white.

"It's about Wilson being gone. Nothing to worry about, I just wanted to file a report since I'm not quite sure how to reach him."

Angie nodded her head quickly.

"Can you manage to keep the kids in here while I talk to them? I don't want Emily—"

"Absolutely," Angela interrupted. She grabbed the doorknob and began to shut the door.

"I'll let you know when they've gone."

"Right."

Callahan and Smith accepted mugs of the freshly brewed coffee and then perched on the couch in the living room.

"What else did Mr. Jones tell you?" Smith said.

"I don't want to get him in trouble."

Smith stared at her, unspeaking.

"I know that my husband had lunch with a young woman and then they went to her apartment." The red flush stained her cheeks and she looked briefly out the window, watching the snow fall thin and steady now. She leaned over and groped for her pocketbook, removed Wilson's letter, and silently handed it to Smith.

He and Callahan read together.

"When did you get this?" Callahan asked.

"That next morning, after he'd been to the lunch."

"Were you surprised?" Smith asked.

Julia tried to control the tears. She nodded quickly rather than risk words.

"Nothing like this had ever happened before?"

She shook her head.

"We understand he's made an important discovery."

"That happened years ago," Julia said. "The clinical trials are beginning and there'll be a public announcement soon, but the scientific community has known for at least a year."

Smith wrote in his notebook.

"I don't think Wilson's work had anything to do with this, do you?" she said.

"Never know," Callahan said.

"Do you have any idea where your husband might be?" Smith asked.

"I called his parents because that seemed the most likely, but it was clear they hadn't a clue," Julia said, "and he doesn't really have any close friends."

"A bit of a loner?"

Julia's eyes opened. "Yes, that would describe Wilson."

"We need to search the apartment." Callahan stood and placed the empty mug on the coffee table.

"Do you have a search warrant?"

"No, should we go get one?" Smith snapped.

Julia knew that Wilson wasn't in the apartment and she knew there was nothing to hide. Still, she wondered if she ought to call Bill. They looked at her with impassive expressions. Her lips tightened and the lump in her throat swelled. "What about my kids?"

"Can the baby-sitter take them somewhere?"

"I guess." Julia glanced out the windows again, where the icy snow flew about.

"Why don't you tell them the police are doing a safety check on all the apartments? That'll make them feel okay," Smith said.

Her eyes warmed. "Good—I'll be right back. You

can start." She waved her hand toward the library.

When Smith and Callahan finished their exhaustive search of the apartment, they stood stolidly at the front door. Julia ached for them to go.

"We have an arrest warrant out for your husband, Mrs. Streatfield, so if you hear from him, it's imperative that you contact us."

"There's no way—"

"We know," Callahan interrupted.

"Nevertheless," Smith said.

Julia found Angela and the kids in the playroom. "Okay, you get going. See a movie, anything."

Angela smiled. "I don't mind."

"Sorry the weather's so dreadful."

"Oh, I love the snow."

In her room, Angela thought of taking a shower, but decided she didn't have time. She changed into a skirt, blouse, and sweater, then pulled on the black suede boots. The snow would probably stain them, but after today, it wouldn't matter. She checked that she had her passport, and then found all her money, more than three thousand dollars at her last count, in its hiding place behind the toilet. She stuffed most of the money in wads down the legs of the boots, some into the center of her bra, and the rest in her pocketbook.

She tried to block the sounds of Emily and Jimmy, but when Jimmy started to cry, probably a dirty nappy, she felt a seizure of pain across her chest. The hardest part was going to be leaving the apartment without crying. She stood at the door to her room, her hand on the doorknob, and she deliberately thought of something nasty. She thought of George, pushing on her eyeballs that first day in the park. She closed her eyes, feeling the blackness and sharp shootings of light. Deep breath, and she turned the knob.

She pretended to be in a great hurry to make some sort of appointment. Afterward, even an hour later, Julia would wonder why Angela was in such a tear, the woman with no friends and no place to go. But by then it'd be too late.

She made it to the elevator without crying. The elevator doors slid closed, and her eyes closed too, still trying to keep the tears from spilling over.

She failed at that, like it seemed she failed at everything.

CHAPTER 35

George waited across the street from the Streatfields' apartment building with his umbrella tipped to keep off the sharp, biting snow. On a Sunday, there was a reasonable chance she'd either be coming or going. And either way, he'd get her. He was going to give himself a couple of hours of waiting, and after that, he'd have to think of a different plan to bring her out.

There she was.

Angela paused just outside the door and looked up at the sky. Then she carefully opened her umbrella. She stepped out onto the sidewalk and took off at a fast clip. She seemed to have no hesitation, walking so fast, but every now and then, she looked up and checked a street sign. It was obvious she was going somewhere particular, somewhere she'd never been before.

After ten blocks, she stopped at a hot dog stand and bought herself a Coke and a hot dog. She leaned against a building, the umbrella wedged forward to protect her, eating and drinking fast. He wanted one himself, but didn't dare stop right in front of her.

Instead he crossed the street and walked up and down. The sea of umbrellas and thick snow meant she'd never notice the way his own umbrella marched back and forth, going nowhere.

She tossed her trash in the receptacle next to the hot dog stand, and started off again, and he followed her. She stopped at a glassed-in phone booth, folded up her umbrella, went into the booth, fished out a quarter, and punched in some numbers. He saw her body go rigid, at attention, and the way her face changed as the flow of words came out of her mouth. She looked all charming and sweet, not the least bit worried or anxious. Her head nodded up and down, as if in agreement.

She pressed to disconnect, found yet another quarter, and made another call. Her lips moved rapidly.

She dug into her pocketbook, searching, probably for another quarter. She started pulling up big items, a wallet, a glasses case, a zippered makeup case, even her passport, balancing it all under her chin and arms. Finally, at the very bottom of the pocketbook, she found more change. Now she was in a hurry, tumbling everything into the bag and quickly putting in the third quarter, still her lips moving with the number like she was saying the Hail Mary.

And suddenly George whispered the words. "Hail Mary, full of grace, the Lord is with you. Blessed be . . ."

There she went, off like a flash, running with her bag flung over her shoulder, struggling to put up the umbrella, and checking the street signs at the next corner. They fairly tore through Central Park. She moved so fast that George thought he might lose her. She trotted a little, but George could keep up by lengthening and quickening his stride.

At the corner of Park and Seventy-fifth, she slowed down. She looked at the number of the first building, then quickly crossed the street without paying sufficient attention to the traffic, to George's mind. He sauntered, peering into doorways, but it was tricky because this was a residential block and there were no shop windows.

Angela stopped all of a sudden, leaning back against a building. Her umbrella was still open, but instead of tilting forward, she held it high and straight.

She was staring at an apartment building directly across the street.

George waited in the center of the sidewalk, trying to figure out what to do. If he went up to her now, he could just shoot her and run. He knew that was what he had to do. But he was finding it hard to contemplate. His legs were wobbly and he felt sick to his stomach.

She looked wild, her red hair crazy around her

face and her eyes wide as if with fright.

He ducked into a doorway that led to steps down to a basement door. Water seeped through the soles of his shoes, and his socks clung wet and cold to his feet. It reminded him of being on the streets after school every day, just hanging around in the misty rain, his breath puffing cold and wet out of a dry mouth, nose running like the rain itself, hands red and chapped.

His gran didn't like him to be home. They only had two rooms, and she kept the place neat and clean. A dirty boy didn't fit too well, and there was nothing to do anyway. She cooked on a hot plate, a single chop if he was lucky, but usually a mess of eggs, with some baked beans and fried bread made in the same pan after. But it was warm there, and if he was sleeping, it was okay. His gran liked him sleeping.

Angela moved, stepped out from the building's protection just a bit, and her attention was drilled to across the street.

A woman in a long wool coat, black boots, and a large rain hat pushed a pram out the door held open by a uniformed doorman. Actually, it wasn't a pram, but an enormous blue carriage with a gold curved handle arching to meet the woman's hands. A clear plastic tent covered the carriage from the hood to its end.

George looked back at Angie. She'd tilted her umbrella to hide her face and she was walking down the sidewalk, away from him and in the direction that the woman across the street moved.

He left the doorway's seclusion, opened up his umbrella, and followed.

• • •

Angie thought her heart would catapult out of her chest it was beating so hard. My baby, my baby, my baby, her brain sang.

At the corner, the woman and carriage turned left. Angela ran across the street against the light, panicked that they'd get too far ahead. A taxi blasted his horn at her, and she made a final leap onto the curb. She tried to keep the umbrella tucked over her face, but she kept peeking out to check on their location.

My baby, my baby, my baby!

They moved fast over three blocks, and Angela was about to panic. What if they didn't stop anywhere? She knew from her own experience that once you were out with a baby, you nearly always found some errand that needed doing.

She sped up, making a plan as her boots splashed recklessly in large sidewalk puddles. She'd pretended to be Dr. Meyer's secretary calling to request that the nanny get some groceries. But what if the nanny had other ideas?

In the middle of the block, the woman steered the carriage into a grocery store. She had trouble with the door, and Angela came up right behind her so fast that she held it open.

The woman flashed her a smile of thanks and Angie saw that she was not young. Her face was lined and white, and the hair flying out from under the hat was also white. So her baby had an *old* nanny. What a shock.

Angela followed her into the grocery store,

quickly folding up her umbrella and tucking it, wet or not, into her oversized pocketbook.

Ready for action.

The woman pushed the carriage down one aisle, turning at the far end to the right and walking past several more aisles before turning into the one loaded with baby supplies. She parked the carriage and began reading the fine print of the baby food jars.

Angela meandered by, acting as if she were in search of an item on the opposite side. She stopped level to the carriage, reached for the baby powder, and began to read the can. She saw the woman take two steps, then three, away from the carriage.

She turned, still holding the baby powder, and moved between the old nanny and the carriage, immediately crouching down to the lower shelf so that the nanny wouldn't be alarmed. Angela picked up a large can of formula and rose slowly, as if deeply engrossed with reading the ingredients printed on the label.

Her eyes slid left and strained to see the baby through the plastic covering. *You must be hot in there. The nanny ought to fold it back so you get some air. Except that must keep germs from getting in. Probably the doctor-father insisted on being careful about germs.*

One leg suddenly kicked, boom. Entranced, Angela leaned forward and stared. The baby's eyes were open.

"Isn't she darling?" The nanny's voice was low and pleasant.

"I can't see her too well, but she certainly looks sweet."

The nanny folded back the plastic curtain. "I love to show her off." She reached in and picked her up out of the carriage.

Angela's throat filled, closing as if she were being choked.

Her baby was the picture of Father James.

His hands were smooth and white, not like any man's hands that she'd ever seen or imagined. They didn't look real, more like they'd been carved out of marble. But they were warm, stroking her arm just above the elbow.

"The Virgin Mary had a baby, Angela, what do you make of that?" he said.

She stared at his cassock, the simplicity of black and white, and then slowly looked at his face. He was the most beautiful man in all of County Donegal. Everyone said so. She remembered the jokes and whispers about what a terrible waste and shame it was, to have a man so beautiful being a priest.

"We can pretend, Angie, that I'm God and you're the Virgin Mary." He leaned forward and his face moved closer to her.

And he kissed her. His lips were not so smooth as his hands, and they smelled a bit, if the truth be known.

She leaned back, away from him. His hands drifted up from her elbows to her shoulders where they rested for a moment, kneading and massaging.

"You are a virgin, aren't you? Because if you're not—" His eyes flashed anger.

"I am, Father, you know that. I'm a good girl."

"My beautiful Virgin Mary," he murmured.

Then he pushed her back against the confessional, lifted her skirt, and raped her.

Angie knew enough now to call it rape, but she hadn't known then. She hadn't cried out or tried to fight him off. And she'd tried to forget it by immediately letting her boyfriend Patrick have his way with her.

Oddly, and it was something too strange to understand, she'd enjoyed being with Patrick. Maybe she hadn't loved him, but she trusted him. He'd thought he'd given her a baby.

Her baby was not Patrick's, though, she knew that now.

"May I hold her?" Angela said, trying to control the trembling in her voice.

The nanny looked at her for a moment, checking, then handed the baby to her.

"What's her name?"

"Rachel, after her grandmother."

Angie cradled the head close to her cheek, wallowing in the clean baby smell of her. She closed her eyes against the tears.

George stood at the end of the aisle, studying a display of molasses, brown sugar, and canned pumpkin, leftovers on sale from Thanksgiving.

When he saw the nanny give the baby to Angela, his feet got twitchy. He took a step forward. She was crooning to the baby, but he saw her body straighten.

And he knew what she was going to do.

George rushed down the aisle and was standing next to her as she stepped backward. She bumped right into him.

The nanny's arms were out, reaching for the baby, but Angela clutched the baby tightly even as she turned, horrified, to see that George was blocking her way.

The nanny pried at Angela's hands, and when she could not loosen them, she yelled for help.

Their eyes held for only a second.

"Give her back," he whispered.

"She's mine."

"I know, but you must give her back."

"You'll kill her."

"I won't, I promise." George looked deep in her eyes.

The baby was crying now, and several women were at the end of the aisle, holding back the way New Yorkers have learned to do.

"She's stealing my baby!" the nanny cried.

The women swarmed down the aisle toward them.

Angela looked wildly around, thrust the baby into the nanny's arms, and took off down the aisle in the opposite direction.

George followed her out of the store and as she ran for more than three blocks.

Finally he caught her by the arm. "I'll get a cab— we need to leave this area. She might call the police."

Angela was limp, and he easily steered her to the side of the street. They stood in a puddle several inches deep, and he flagged down a cab.

George gave the address of his building.

Angela felt the shakes hit just as they crossed the threshold of his apartment. Her head was light and dizzy, and suddenly she couldn't stand up. She bent forward at the waist, almost toppling over.

George's arm reached around her shoulders and then tucked into her armpit to help her walk without falling. He guided her to the couch in the living room, and she collapsed into the corner, her head resting on the arm of the couch.

She closed her eyes.

George left the room and she heard him rummaging around in the kitchen, the unmistakable clinking noise of a bottle touching a glass. She wanted to just disappear, swallowed into the couch like it was a great coffin.

He returned to the living room and sat on the coffee table directly in front of her.

The glass of pure amber liquid was held right in front of her lips when she opened her weary eyes. "Take a sip, you'll feel better," George said.

She shifted her weight so that her left arm still leaned heavily into the couch's corner, but her head was straight. She took the glass, tipped it into her mouth, and with four huge swallows she downed the scotch. Her eyes filled with tears and she gasped.

"Nice job," he said.

Angela nodded, risking a glance into his eyes.

They twinkled. Typical Irishman, she thought.

"Now, why'd you want to take that baby?"

"I told you, *my* baby."

"Even so."

"I was going to take her back to Ireland with me," she said. "I've nothing to lose."

"What kind of talk is that?" He leaned forward and kissed her quietly on the lips. "You're a gorgeous great lass, you are. You've got everything to gain."

She shook her head, no.

His left hand ran down the slope of her head and then into the tangles of her long hair. "Shall I brush it out for you?"

Tears again rushed to her eyes, and these spilled over.

"I'll be right back." He stood and removed the empty glass from her limp hand.

She dropped her head into the crook of her arm.

George returned holding a hairbrush, and he sat down next to her on the couch. He touched her shoulder and she straightened up. Then he pushed one shoulder away so that her back was to him.

He worked slowly through the knots, wet from snow, his touch hypnotic, and she found the anxiety easing away. Maybe the scotch helped, too, she thought idly. When the brush ran smooth, without a catch, he pulled the hair back into a tail, divided it into three, and began to plait.

"Have you got an elastic, by any chance?" he asked.

She reached into her skirt pocket and found an elastic, which she held up for him to take.

"A little lopsided," he muttered, "but not bad for a first try."

She laughed quietly. It felt a little lopsided.

His hands rose to her shoulders and gently pulled her toward him. Her back curved gratefully into his chest while his hands slid down her arms and then covered the backs of her hands, picking them up to wrap them across her waist. He rested his chin on her shoulder, his lips close to her right ear. He spoke words of love.

He couldn't kill Angela. He'd rather die himself, truth be told.

CHAPTER 36

J ulia took the kids out in the snow before their nap, hoping to get them wet, cold, and exhausted. She also stopped for a video, a rare treat for Emily. When they returned home, they went right to sleep.

She glided through the apartment, soothed by how organized and beautiful all the rooms were. In the library, she crossed to where the CDs were lined up, found Puccini's *Turandot* and put it on. Then, curled into a miserable bundle on the couch, she began to cry.

Emily must have heard her even from the depth of her nap. She appeared in the doorway. "Mommy?" she said.

Julia raised her face, covered with tears. "Hi, sweetie." She tried a wobbly smile.

Emily ran across the room on little tippy toes. She threw her arms around Julia. "Don't cry, Mommy."

"Okay," Julia said. She blew her nose into a tissue and then pulled Emily onto her lap, holding her so tight and close that they felt like one person.

At seven o'clock that evening, she tried to put the kids to bed, but they'd begun to sense her mood and they were restless. Finally she settled in the rocking chair in Emily's room, with Jimmy hiked up on her shoulder, and read a long Winnie the Pooh story. The familiar words, with their old-fashioned cadence, moved her as well as the children.

When they were asleep, she walked quietly around the apartment, tidying up. She left a small light on in the entrance hall, and even went into Angela's room to turn on her bedside lamp and close the blue velvet drapes over the window.

Julia started a bath for herself and while she waited for it to fill, she searched through the medicine cabinet until she found the dusty bottle of Valium way in the back. She took two small pills, ten milligrams, and by the time she lowered herself into the bath, a marvelous lassitude filled her.

She climbed into bed at eight o'clock and shut off the light and the ringer on the telephone next to her bed. She fell into sleep as if sleep would somehow solve everything.

• • •

Angela crept through the dark apartment and into the kitchen. She stood at the light switch and quickly flashed it on and off. An answering flash from the apartment opposite made her smile.

She went to her room, noticing immediately that Julia had left the light on and closed her drapes. Her heart warmed. She thought of the children, and even though it was midnight, she decided to go check on them. Sometimes Jimmy kicked off his covers, and Emily often liked a drink of water.

At first she thought the teddy bear in his crib was Jimmy. Her hand moved slowly through the dark, and rested on the cold, empty sheet. Then her stomach flip-flopped.

Quickly she walked to Emily's room, but the sensation tearing through her body already warned her. The bed was empty.

Now she headed down the hall toward the master bedroom. There was a chance that the children were asleep in bed with Julia. It was embarrassing to even think of knocking on her door. She stood still, wondering what to do.

Well, if she woke her, Julia would think it was sweet of Angela to be worried.

She knocked quietly, then listened.

No answer.

She knocked again, more loudly now. She heard a moan from the bedroom, not really a "come in," but she opened the door anyway. The bed faced the door, and she saw a figure struggle to sit up in bed.

"What?" Julia's voice was husky with sleep.

"It's Angela, Julia. I'm so sorry to bother you, but I had to check that the children were with you."

Julia began patting the bed, frantic. "No, they're not. I put them to bed at seven o'clock!"

"Oh Jesus, Mary, and Joseph," Angela whispered. "They're gone."

Julia leapt from the bed and rushed forward, pushing roughly past Angela and dashing down the hallway. Angela heard her small cry in Emily's room, and then the wail of anguish when she got to Jimmy's.

Angela ran and grabbed her arms. "Look, I think I've an idea what's going on. Has Dr. Streatfield returned?"

Julia stared at her, eyes wild and red. She shook her head, no.

"Before you call the police, we've got to talk." Angela led Julia to the kitchen.

Julia collapsed at the kitchen table, her head clasped in her hands.

Angela ran to the light switch and began turning the lights on and off rapidly. "George, George," she muttered.

"What are you doing?"

"I'll tell you everything in a minute, but I need to get George's attention. He's going to help us."

"Is George your boyfriend?"

"Yes, I suppose he is now."

The lights across the way suddenly flashed several times. Angie left her lights shining and ran to the window, waving madly with a swooping motion to indicate he must come over.

George pointed to himself and then moved his fingers as if he were a figure walking. She nodded vigorously up and down. He turned and disappeared.

Angela picked up the phone that linked with the doorman. "Yes, Bernie, when my friend George shows up in a few minutes, send him right up, okay? Thanks awfully."

In a fluid string of words, Angela told Julia everything. At the end, she stared at Julia, scared of her reaction.

Julia's expression was blank. "You think they've got Wilson and now the children?"

Angie nodded. "I think so. But we'll ask George, maybe he knows."

The doorbell rang and Angela ran to let George in. She grabbed him by his jacket and shook. "They've taken the Doctor and the children, *my* children," she shouted.

He looked first one way, then the other, not believing it.

"We have to go after the children. Do you know where they are?"

"I didn't know, Ange, you have to believe me."

"Hello, George," said a voice from behind Angela.

He looked over her head to where Julia leaned in the kitchen doorway.

"Are you the motherfucking bastard who's responsible for the fact that my husband and kids have been kidnapped?"

He moved toward her.

"Watch it, buddy." She raised one hand, brandishing the portable phone. "I'm real close to dialing 911."

"I got them the research papers, that's all. And then I guess they took your husband—I didn't even know about that—but I'm sure they haven't hurt him because they probably want him to do some kind of research." George stood still, in strange contrast to the flow of words from his mouth. "They didn't tell me anything else. Just I did a good job, so I figured that was it."

"So you're stupid."

"I was."

She blinked.

"I know where they are, with a Chinese drug lord called Mr. Wong," he said.

Julia stared stupidly at both of them.

"I've got the idea we need," George said.

Wilson lay still on the bed, eyes closed and about to drift back into sleep, when the door was again flung open.

"Mr. Wong wants you."

The guards stood in the doorway, their guns drawn and pointed directly at him.

Wilson stood slowly and wondered if he should raise his hands up in the air, but it seemed foolish since there was no way he could overtake two men with guns. He kept his body crouched and loose, hoping he appeared unthreatening.

They marched him back up the same flight of

stairs, but they poked him to turn right down the long corridor. He came into the kitchen, which was dark except for a light shining over the cooktop.

Mr. Wong sat at the black granite island in the center of the room, his small elegant hands holding a cup of tea.

He pointed toward a door. "Your children are in the maid's room, just there."

Wilson gasped. Then he leaned forward and vomited on the floor. Tears streamed from his eyes and mucus from his nose. He lifted only his head to stare at Luke Wong.

"Would you like to see them?"

Wilson rushed forward.

Mr. Wong held up a warning hand. "Hold on a minute, Dr. Streatfield. We must have your assurance that you'll not wake them—they've had a disruptive night as it is—surely they need their sleep."

"I won't wake them." Wilson's voice was strangled in his throat and it came out thickened with emotion.

Mr. Wong turned the knob and held the door open about two feet.

Wilson walked over to the door and then felt the barrel of a gun in the small of his back. Mr. Wong nodded to the other guard, who leapt forward and pointed his gun into the room where Emily and Jimmy slept.

"I won't," Wilson said.

"Just making sure," Mr. Wong murmured.

A night-light shone in the small room and a woman sat on a chair facing the door, between two white cribs. The room was silent and calm with deep breathing.

"I can't see them clearly," Wilson whispered.

"Go in quietly and look."

He tiptoed forward, remembering how he and Julia had checked them every night before they, too, went to bed. He peered over the crib on the right and saw distinctly the small shape of Jimmy with his stuffed zebra clutched in his arm. He swallowed hard.

Then he looked into the left crib. Emily had crammed herself up into the top half of the crib, her head bent awkwardly. Her face was pressed against the pillow in the upper right corner. She was terrified even in sleep.

Carefully he turned and walked back out.

In the kitchen, Luke Wong waited for him. "Do you suppose *Mrs.* Streatfield would like to join us next?"

Wilson's heart galloped and fury blazed up inside his head. He felt as if his eyes burned with yellow flames. "Her name is not Mrs. Streatfield," he gasped.

"Ahh, a liberated woman. Did you meet at Stanford?"

Wilson glared, wondering if he had the courage to spit in Luke Wong's face. "She's liberated, smart, and also happens to be stunningly beautiful."

"What does she do? I assume she works, given the nanny?" Mr. Wong held up his hand, stopping Wilson's anticipated words. "Let me guess." One elegant finger tapped his nose and his eyes narrowed.

Wilson thought how much he'd like to wrap his

hands around Luke Wong's neck and squeeze the life out of him. It would be a sensual pleasure, better than sex. The kitchen smelled heavily of garlic and peanuts, from the dinner hours before.

"Stockbroker," Mr. Wong said.

Wilson had had enough. He worried that their voices might wake the kids, and even that Emily would recognize his. "She's a literary agent," he spit out. "A very successful business of her own, the Julia Fleming Literary Agency."

Luke Wong showed surprise by a rapid blink of the eyes.

"Can I get to work right away?" Wilson said. "I think I know what to do."

"How marvelous that your creative juices are flowing. Would you like something to eat before you begin?"

"Just a Coke."

They led him back down to his lab, where the lights were brilliant and unforgiving.

He moved with such fluidity and economy that he astonished himself. Yes, his creative juices were flowing. Overflowing.

CHAPTER 37

Julia went back to bed at three o'clock in the morning. She'd taken another Valium an hour earlier, but as her body stretched straight under the sheet, arms at her sides, even the toes of her feet pointed like a dancer's, the drug barely touched her. She could feel the palpitations of fear in her chest, small flutterings like a baby bird poised on the edge of the nest, about to jump. Her breath came fast and shaky and she had to breathe more quickly to get enough oxygen.

The biggest fear was whether she ought to be trusting George, a young man who'd so obviously been untrustworthy. And what about her sweet, innocent Angela, involved with such a character? But then she imagined the police surrounding this Mr. Wong's house, and the negotiations between Mr. Wong and the police, and Mr. Wong's inevitable threats, and finally Mr. Wong killing her children. Oh God, the pain was too much. If she thought of Emily and Jimmy, alone and terrified in that house, it was excruciating.

She started to pant like a rabid animal, and her hands clutched at her thighs, the nails digging in so that she felt the sharp tear of her skin.

Abruptly she fell off the cliff and into sleep.

"I think you should stay here," Angela said.

"If you don't think Julia would mind, I'd like that," George said.

"It's okay."

They were sitting in the living room, crushed close together.

Angela pushed harder against him. "You're done with it for good, are you?"

He needed no explanation for what "it" meant. "I'm done for good."

She turned and kissed him on the cheek. Such a clean, beautiful face he had, not the face of a gangster or criminal.

"We could die," he said.

For a moment, nausea rushed into her chest and she had to swallow. "I guess."

"Don't be foolish now, don't take stupid risks. You do what you can, but leave it up to me."

"We'll be together."

"No, now, I mean it." George turned and grabbed her shoulders. "Stay out of the way if it gets rough. I'm the one deserves to die, not you. You've done nothing in all this." He was shouting and his eyes glittered.

Angela felt the anger rise in her until her face exploded red, and she grabbed his shoulders and shook him back and forth. He moved like a rag doll, with no resistance. "Don't tell me what to do, bloody hell, don't you tell me what to do."

Her right hand flew down in a sharp slap across his cheek. Sobs and tears burst out, but she yelled. "I will save those children and I will save you and I will save the Doctor and no *man* is going to stop me!"

She grabbed a pillow at the opposite side of the couch and clutched it to her middle, arms tight and trembling. Her voice deepened and became almost apologetic. "I'm so tired of men telling me what to do."

George sat still, right where he'd been, his hand touching the cheek she'd slapped. "Am I the first man you've hit?"

Angela shot him a hard glance, but then she saw his gentle face.

"That you are."

"Then I'm honored, indeed."

She thought he must be joking, and she stared at him again. The twinkle in his eye was all twinkled out and the dimple in his cheek swept clean by her blow. Then she could see he meant it, and relief rushed in so fast that she had to take a great breath and let out a huge sigh of air.

"I guess I love you, George McDuff."

"And I you, Angela Byrne."

The next morning, Angela cooked an enormous breakfast for George and Julia, but they just picked at the food.

"It's been four days since he called for girls and he never goes longer than that, so it's likely to happen tonight," George said.

"What should we wear?" Angela said.

"Fancy—the house is elegant, and he'll be very taken with such high-class ladies."

They trooped to Julia's bedroom and George took a seat on a chair in the corner while they modeled every formal dress Julia owned. As they went in and out, twirling in front of the full-length mirror, George told them about Mr. Wong and Mr. Mao. He tried to think of small details that could be of use, but there were actually few things he knew about them.

"Let's go in the kitchen and I'll draw you a map of the house," he said when they'd made the dress decisions.

He got a little carried away by the map. Soon he was drawing in every piece of furniture and writing the colors of the paints on the walls.

"You're good at this." Julia peered over his shoulder at the beautifully drawn map. "Do you like interior decorating?"

"Oh, sure."

"Why don't you become a designer?"

"Right," he said in a voice of dismissal.

"You're going to have to do something to earn a living."

"I *know* that."

Angela was staring at him. "So what are you going to be?"

"I've no idea."

He looked up from the map, surprised to see them giving him such direct, searching looks.

"You go to school to become a designer," Julia said. "They've got scholarships, but first you could apprentice with someone, and learn and save up your money."

"Who'd have me?"

"I could ask around," Julia said. "I've got a client who's a designer. He wrote quite a good book five years ago, about painting your walls with faux finishes."

Julia and Angela peered at him, trying to see the face he'd carefully tucked low and out of sight.

"I'd . . . I'd like that," he finally said, his voice dropping as low as his head.

Angie reached over and ruffled his hair. They were quiet for a moment, all of them thinking whether they'd be alive to do any worrying about their futures.

George stood up and went looking for the knives. He put six of them out on the kitchen counter. "Have you got a stone so I can sharpen them?"

Julia stood up. "Yeah, I think it's pushed way in the back of this drawer." As she yanked at the drawer, she was struck with a dizzy spell and she grabbed onto the counter. Angela's arms went around her and guided her back to the kitchen chair.

"I think I'd better try eating something, after all," Julia said.

George began sharpening each knife, whish, whish, whish.

Julia picked up a piece of bacon from the platter at the center of the table and nibbled a small piece off the end. The deep smoky flavor tasted good and she felt her stomach rumble in appreciation. She took a larger bite and stared without seeing out the kitchen window.

She would probably have to kill a man, either that, or be killed by him. Each alternative was terrifying. What she felt in the pit of her stomach was just this tiny round ball of courage, no bigger than a marble. And the bacon, weird though it sounded, the bacon was curling itself around the ball, thickening and enlarging it ever so slightly. Julia took a larger bite of bacon and she concentrated on the ball, willing it to grow, watching its shape change until it filled her stomach and pressed against her rib cage.

"I just thought of something," Julia said.

George stopped the rhythmic knife sharpening, and they both looked at her.

Julia explained to them about the police's interest in Wilson's whereabouts. "I'm sure they're watching me," she said finally. "So they'll follow me to Mr. Wong's and wreck everything."

"We need to fool them," George said.

"I could go out earlier and lead them away, but I'm not fast enough to lose them after that."

"We need you," George said. "They've never taken just one woman."

"I know," Julia said.

Emily asked for Cheerios, but they didn't have any.

"I make pancakes for you," said the little man, all hunched over and strange.

"Okay." She glanced at Jimmy, who was sitting in a high chair and picking up pieces of cooked rice and eating them. He was slow and methodical. "Good boy, Jim-Jim."

"You call him Jim-Jim?" asked the old woman.

"Just me, no one else."

"Hey, Jim-Jim," the woman said, bending over the high chair tray and sticking her face into his.

Emily needed to go to the bathroom, but she'd just gone. Her legs tightened. She looked carefully around the kitchen, trying to find something to like. But it was a huge room and hard to really see. She smelled her mother in bed, not pancakes, and her eyes filled with tears and she rubbed them away with small fists. When she looked up again, her eyes stopped at the telephone by the back door.

She knew her telephone number. She'd recited it a bunch of times for her Mom and she had a little song that went with it.

"I need to go," Emily said.

"You just went." The old woman frowned.

"Otherwise I'll wet."

"You remember where it is?"

She nodded.

"So go."

Emily looked down from the high kitchen stool. She couldn't just hop down like it was a chair. She bent over, clutched her arms around the seat of the stool, and carefully let her legs dangle toward the floor. She couldn't see how far it was and the terror she felt was horrible. Should she just drop? Would she break her legs?

She dropped.

And landed smoothly, no problem. She trotted down the long hall to the first door on her left. The knob was shiny and gold and when she touched it, the cold shocked her like a spark. She opened the door wide and looked up for the light switch. Click, and there was light. She shut the door carefully and thought about locking it. Her mother said never to lock the door, though.

Quick, before anyone came in, she yanked down her underpants and sat on the toilet. She waited, feeling an unbearable pressure to pee and nothing happening. Her mind drifted and now she thought of Thanksgiving dinner, and how the candles flickered and flamed like in a fairy tale. The piddle was small but helped make her feel better. Since she was still worried about being interrupted, she jumped off, pulled up the underpants, flushed the toilet, and grabbed the doorknob.

Whoops, forgot to wipe.

Too late.

She opened the door and carefully turned off the light, and then she ran down the hall in the opposite direction from the kitchen. She had to find a telephone.

She knew that. If she could just find a telephone, they'd be okay and Mom and Angie would come for them (where *was* Daddy?). At the end of the hall, where light spilled from the entrance hall, a dark figure suddenly appeared.

She screamed at the top of her lungs and tried to stop running, but she couldn't stop right away and the person moved forward, grabbed her, and tucked her under one arm. He strode back toward the kitchen.

Emily went dead. She drooped like wet spaghetti.

"Look what I found running away," the man said.

The old woman made tsking noises.

"Shall I teach her a lesson?"

She screamed again, kicking her legs and flailing with her arms. He swept her forward, and began beating her across the bottom. She screamed and screamed, feeling as if her head would fall off from the power of her own voice.

Then he carried her back to the dark room off the kitchen, threw her in a crib, and walked out, shutting the door behind him. She cried herself to sleep and woke later so hungry she thought she'd die.

Emily climbed out of the crib and walked over to the window, pulled aside the curtain, and stared at the bright day. One puff of white cloud drifted across the sky and she imagined an angel forming from the cloud. Angela had told her about angels, because Angela's name was like an angel, and now this cloud angel flew with great white wings toward Emily, arms stretched out to her.

Angels would come and save them.

• • •

Wilson was at the lab, writing in his notebook, when he heard Emily's first scream. He leapt to his feet and ran to the door. The guard was up and pointing his gun before he was halfway across the room.

"One more step," the guard said.

Wilson stopped. There were no more screams. He stood still, listening, while the guard walked toward him.

"Get back to work," the guard said.

"That was my little girl."

And then the screams began again. Horrifying screams. Wilson threw back his head and screamed with her.

The guard took a last step, raised his right hand, and slammed the gun against the side of Wilson's face. He fell immediately, knocked out.

He woke about thirty minutes later, lying in the same spot. His deaf ear was cradled in his hand, pathetically still trying to find protection. He moaned and opened one eye.

The guard sat on his stool, looking at him with an expressionless face.

Then Wilson remembered Emily's screams. He tried to think if there was anything he could do. If he killed himself, would that save his children? Would Mr. Wong calmly return them to Julia? No, of course not. If he found the antidote, would that save his children?

He turned his head, hiding his face in the crook of his arm, and wept.

CHAPTER 38

L uke Wong perched on top of his massive mahogany desk, speaking into an impossibly small telephone. His poodle, Baby, scrambled around on the desk, peering over first one side and then another, trying to work up the courage to jump. He yelped, high and whining. Mr. Wong scooped the dog up under the stomach and tossed him to the carpeted floor where he sprawled, momentarily shocked into silence and stillness.

Mr. Wong clicked the phone shut and absently fingered the large gold ball in his left hand. It was two inches in diameter and beautiful. Luke Wong rose to his feet, so that he was standing on top of the desk.

Baby barked, circling the desk and staring up at Wong.

He tossed the gold ball gently from hand to hand, gazing through the open doorway and into the adjoining bedroom. A little nap on his big bed, he thought, just the ticket.

Armand Jones looked surprisingly comfortable as he sat in the center of Julia's couch. At first he'd refused anything to eat or drink, but since he'd heard the whole story and figured out that any sort of professionalism could be kissed good-bye, he now watched with pleasure as Angela and George carried in a platter of turkey sandwiches, dill pickles, sour cream potato chips, and a selection of cold beers.

They ate as if this might be their last meal. Nerves no longer mattered.

Armand took a huge bite and smiled while he chewed with a closed mouth. He rolled his eyes at Julia, and she rolled her eyes back. They were becoming friends, the four of them, and Julia felt the tears that were never far away sting her eyes.

George left the room to call in at Mr. Wong's, explaining over the telephone that because he wasn't at his apartment, he wanted to check whether Mr. Wong needed any girls. A long silence followed.

They sat still and listened.

"Right, sure thing," George said. They heard the receiver being replaced.

He appeared in the open doorway leading to the living room, where they waited.

"We're on," he said simply.

Armand went down to the street five minutes before Julia. She stared at her watch, then back at the door to the apartment. Angela paced with her, up and down the entrance hall, their high heels hammering. Julia's stomach boiled with acid. She was terrified of being sick.

Suddenly the phone rang, a loud blare of sound that made them jump.

"Lauren, I can't talk right now."

"You sound weird. What's going on?"

Angela gestured and pointed to her watch.

Julia took a deep breath, debating. "The kids have been kidnapped and I'm going to get them. It's all to do with Wilson's disappearance and this drug he discovered."

"For God's sake, call the police!"

"They'll be killed if we use the police. We've got a security officer from Columbia with us, who's going to divert the police."

"We're coming over right now."

"I'll be gone," Julia said. "Say a prayer."

"Tell me where you're going," Lauren begged. "I promise I won't tell the police, but maybe . . ."

Julia hesitated, then blurted out Mr. Wong's address. She slammed down the phone and ran out the door.

"See you in fifteen minutes," Angela called after her.

Julia balanced herself in the descending elevator and took deep breaths. She tightened the white mink stole around her shoulders and walked out into the cold, snowy New York City night.

She walked as fast as possible, but negotiating ice and snow in high heels made for slow going. Armand had told her that it was vital she move quickly, and her breath came heavily from panic and effort. In desperation, she slid her feet like ice skates, or cross-country skis, and she found a distinct rhythm.

Julia skated through the night, dodging pedestrians, yellow cabs, and dogs, a woman possessed. She was going to get her children and her husband. Let Armand deal with the police.

Fifteen minutes later, she trotted on tiptoes down the concrete ramp leading to the apartment building's garage basement. The heels, now that there was no snow beneath them, were again a hindrance to speed. She ran toward her minivan, relieved to see the heads of George and Angela in the front seats.

She'd agreed to George's offer to drive. The show she needed to put on at Mr. Wong's was more elaborate than George's, and she wanted to prepare for her performance, not deal with city traffic. She sat alone in the backseat, the beaded red silk cocktail dress creeping up to midthigh. When she crossed and then recrossed her legs, she gave the dress a little tug.

Angela was in the front seat, next to George. She wore a deep green velvet dress that Julia had bought at Loehmann's twenty years before. Her coat was Julia's full-length black mink. Angela and George had actually argued with her about that. She'd snapped that she'd willingly rip the coat into shreds if it meant getting Wilson and the kids out of there safely.

But she wasn't at all sure whether minks and tight dresses with high heels could save them, Wilson, or the children.

George hadn't told Julia that he'd never driven in the States, so the wheel on the left, and the lanes on the right, were a challenge. Sweat trickled down each cheek, dripping onto his coat. He maneuvered out of the garage with no mishap, and more relaxed, he eased carefully into the stream of evening traffic. He glanced in the rearview mirror and saw the headlights of a car pull out fast, crowding close to him. George looked forward again, concentrating on all the dangers in front and to the sides. A block later, he again looked in the rearview mirror.

The lights from the car behind bore into them, harsh and bright.

"What's that guy's problem?" Julia turned in her seat and stared out the back window.

The lights rushed forward and slammed them before the car. The bump was enough to fling Julia against the back of the front seats. Her hands shot out and she caught herself.

"Fuck!" George yelled. "It's Mr. Wong. He's figured out I didn't kill Angela. Probably thinks I just took off."

"You were going to kill me?" Angie screamed.

George honked his car horn desperately. "I'll tell you about it later—just get going now."

"Angela, duck down, open your door, and crawl

out," Julia screamed. "George, we'll meet you at Wong's."

Simultaneously, as if they'd practiced this routine many times, both women crouched to the floor of the car, groped for the door handles, threw open the doors, and tumbled out into the street. Julia clung to the side of her car, praying not to be hit by another automobile in the next lane. She sidled along the car, waiting for a chance to run across the street.

Her minivan groaned and lurched forward, struck once again by the automobile behind them. Julia hoped that George had the sense to just abandon the car.

She leapt forward, straight into the path of a taxi. The driver's face collapsed into a terrible expression of anger and fear, eyes wide and lips drawn back. Julia saw his arms lengthen and straighten on the driver's wheel as his foot slammed the brake. She kept running and made it to the opposite sidewalk. Angela followed two seconds later. She grabbed Julia's hand and pulled her down the sidewalk at a full run. They slipped on snow, but managed to hold each other up, and to keep going.

They tore around the first corner.

"Let's take a cab." Julia darted into the street and hailed a taxi half a block away. The cabbie screeched across the intersection where, now out of their sight, horns blared.

Angela and Julia threw themselves into the back-seat of the cab, their dresses twisted like candy canes. Julia was surprised that their urgency didn't make the driver floor it.

He turned around, a bearded Sikh in a ratty red turban, and glared at them. "You ladies in some kind of trouble?"

"Four fifty-nine Park Avenue," Julia snapped. "We're in a hurry."

Lazily he faced front again, carefully shifted from park to drive, checked rearview and side mirrors, and pulled out into the traffic. Then he floored it. Julia looked back and saw a Chinese man skidding around the corner and running in their direction. His head jerked right and left, trying to locate them, and she realized he didn't know they'd grabbed a cab.

Julia leaned toward Angela, one shoulder touching hers. "Did you bring any money?" she whispered.

"A hundred dollar bill in my shoe."

"I don't think this guy will have change."

Their eyes met, peering sideways, and Julia felt the giggles coming. Both women resolutely looked out opposite windows.

Angela sniffed.

Julia swallowed desperately.

Giggles boiled in small bubbles high in her chest until, in a wild heat, her laughter overflowed. The cab rocked with their snorts.

"We're going to ruin our makeup," Angela said, swiping at her face with both hands.

"We mustn't be messy for Mr. Wong and Mr. Mao."

They fell away from each other, against the cold doors of the cab, and then careened back together again. Suddenly Julia noticed that it was snowing.

"Look." She pointed.

"We may have a white Christmas, ladies," the cabbie yelled through the plastic partition.

They were quiet, thinking of Christmas.

George had felt the second slam of the car behind him in every bone. He glanced to the right and saw that Angela seemed to be running right in front of two yellow cabs. The urge to close his eyes overwhelmed him, but George pinned them open. Somehow, against absurd odds, neither Julia nor Angela was hit. In the rearview mirror, he saw a man leap from the car and take off through the traffic, chasing Angela and Julia.

George wrenched his door handle, jumped out of the minivan, and left it still running. He darted to the sidewalk and glanced behind him. The driver of the car behind leapt out of his car, slamming the door. In a glance, George recognized one of Mr. Wong's men. George wore laced shoes with crepe soles, but even so the sidewalks were slick with mushy wet snow and ice. His breath puffed out full and urgent, clouding his view as he ran. It was almost as if he were blind. When the snow began, George nearly shouted for joy. Suddenly, with the thick, lazy flakes and his soaking frigid feet, he was again a boy in the streets of Dublin. Maybe ten years old, quick and lean, he'd grabbed a package of hot chips right out of a child's hands, then flew through the alleys and back streets, cramming the salty fries into his mouth as he ran.

George ducked down this street and that, leading the man in a maze of false starts, turns, and feints. He looked around and saw the man was still there, but he also noticed that now, at this distance, he couldn't see his chaser's face. Mr. Wong's man wouldn't recognize him. They were after Angela, clearly. If he could just bloody well lose the bastard, he'd show up at Mr. Wong's and no one would know the difference.

He slowed deliberately, until the man was half a block away, then sped up and ran into a McDonald's. He tore right around the counter and into the kitchen, straight out the back door, climbed the side of a Dumpster, and hurled himself inside. George lay still, trying to hold his breath, which was impossible. Instead, he panted rapidly, like a small animal.

Shouts spilled from the kitchen. The door clanged open and a man's footsteps pounded outside, then stopped for a millisecond.

George could imagine the man searching left and right for a sight of him.

A yell from the kitchen. "Police on the way!" Then the door slammed shut.

George heard the man's heaves of breath and finally the sloppy sounds of feet running and slipping through slush.

It was quiet.

He found Angela and Julia half a block from Mr. Wong's mansion. Angela's arm, holding open her mink coat, enclosed Julia, trying to keep her warm.

"Everyone straight on the plan?" he said.

"What happened?" they gasped.

"No time to tell you now." They started walking down the street. "Just, are you ready?"

He looked at both women. Finally, together, their heads nodded.

They climbed the steps to Mr. Wong's mansion. The arched, ornate lamp over the front door sent glittering light tumbling over them.

His hand reached out and he rang the bell.

"Hey, Butchie," George greeted the man who opened to them.

Butchie grinned, staring with open admiration at Julia and Angela. He stood back to let them in. "You done good tonight. I thought you were cracked with those two a couple a' weeks ago."

"Yeah, well, you win some, you lose some."

They clustered in the entrance hall. George dared to look at Julia and Angela now in the full light of the house. They were dazzling, red lips arched up into full smiles and hips jutted to one side. Julia tapped a high heel impatiently.

"He said to come to the living room for introductions," Butchie said. He snorted at such nonsense and then escorted them to the living room.

Dim lights were scattered here and there, and the gas fire burned. Still, the room was damp and formal.

Mr. Wong and Mr. Mao came forward. Their eyes clung to the women.

"Welcome," Mr. Wong said. "May I help you with your coats?"

He shot a look of pleasure at George after their coats had been removed and the full extent of their figures could be appreciated.

Julia began strutting around the room, showing

off a little while peering at paintings. Her long, thin, shapely legs flashed in the shimmery stockings she wore. Mr. Mao followed her. "May I offer you a drink?"

Mr. Wong asked the same of Angela, who softly nodded. They'd decided she should speak as little as possible, for fear that her Irish accent would cause suspicion. And if she did have to speak, she was to do her best with an American accent.

When Mr. Wong wanted to know what kind of drink she'd like, her voice was barely above a whisper. "Whiskey," she said, biting the word in two.

They remembered George when the drinks were made. "Wait in the kitchen," Mr. Wong ordered.

George turned to leave and Mr. Wong spoke again. "I'll just have a word with you in the other room."

In the entrance hall, Mr. Wong grabbed his arm, the first time he'd touched him, and spoke quietly. "Word from my men says the nanny is alive."

"She's very dead." George looked indignant.

Mr. Wong stared at him, eyes sharp.

George snapped his fingers, as if realizing something important. "The wife has a friend she sees a lot."

"The nanny's been killed, absolutely?"

"Of course."

"Excellent." Mr. Wong turned and disappeared back in the living room.

George sat quietly at the kitchen table, listening. He saw the door that led to the cook's room and it occurred to him that the children could be right there.

He was supposed to wait until the couples had gone upstairs, but he wanted to get moving. The faster he went, the less likely that Angela would be compromised.

He tapped on the closed door, ever so quietly. In seconds, the door opened a crack and the barrel of a gun emerged. "Henry, it's just me, George," he said.

The door opened wider. A tiny, shriveled Chinese woman stood in the doorway, the gun in her hand lowered.

"Ssh," she said, stepping out and closing the door behind her. "They're sleeping good."

"Who's sleeping good? I was just hoping Henry could make me some eggs."

"Henry way upstair. I make you egg if you quiet." She gave him a warning look, half-mocking and half-serious.

"Sure, I'll be quiet." George whispered. "But what's going on?"

"Just some children visiting. Don't wanna wake 'em."

He felt a tiny flicker of excitement.

"How you want egg?"

"Scrambled. And have you got any bacon?"

She raised her eyebrows at him. "'Course we got bacon." She shuffled over to the refrigerator.

He sat down at the kitchen island, his back to the cook's room, watching the old woman. She was a sweet old lady and he didn't want to hurt her. Still, she must've known those kids weren't just visiting.

She began whipping the eggs in a small, deep

bowl. Butter sizzled in one cast-iron skillet while bacon curled into its fat in another. Sizzle, sizzle, he thought. And he rose, walking slowly across the kitchen. He felt sick at what he was about to do, but there was nothing for it.

He raised his right hand, holding the snout of the gun, and hit her on the back of the head with the gun's butt. Her knees sagged and she was out. He stooped to pick her up in his arms and carry her to the cook's room.

She was light as a child, and he easily opened the door to the room and placed her carefully in the chair between the cribs. Then he quietly scooched the chair over to the right and jammed it against the crib with the baby. He hitched the backs of her sleeves over the top of the chair, so that she was held in a sitting position, then carefully arranged her head against the crib.

He turned without looking at the children.

He knew what they'd agreed: whoever found the kids should get them out safely before anything else. But if he took them out by the back kitchen door, what could he do with them? He wouldn't be able to leave them in the cold, all alone, and that meant he wouldn't be able to help Angela and Julia.

CHAPTER 39

Julia sauntered around the bedroom, acting tough and brave. But her legs wobbled from fear and a couple of times she lost her balance and had to grab onto a piece of furniture. She stole a look at Mr. Mao. He was seated on the edge of the king-sized bed, his legs spread and steadying himself.

She didn't think this guy was half so interested in sex as he was pretending to be. He looked exhausted and worried.

He *should* be worried, Julia thought. Real worried.

"Would you like me to give you a bath?" She made her voice calm and soothing.

His eyes lit up. "That's a Chinese custom. The girls wash their men."

Julia went into the bathroom and paused, while she was alone, to take several deep breaths. Her head was light and she felt like she could pass out if she wasn't careful. She turned the faucets of the bathtub full force and in the tumult of noise, she quickly lifted her dress and removed the knife tucked between her shoulder blades, held in place by her bra strap. She slid the knife under the small bathroom rug centered on the tub.

When she came back into the bedroom, the man was trying to tug off his shoes. She placed a steadying hand on his knee, crouched down, and rapidly began untying the shoelaces of both shoes.

"Nice," he said.

"I hope so." She tilted her head back and gave him a big smile. His eyes were mild. He didn't look at all dangerous.

Angela had at first thought she could interest Mr. Wong in an elaborate striptease, one which took quite a long time. But that's not what he had in mind.

"I think I should marry you," he said.

She sat on the edge of the bed and he crouched at her feet. Her shoes were off and he was rhythmically stroking one foot, ankle, and the calf of her leg.

"Umm," she murmured. She'd been trying to get by with inarticulate moans and groans.

The knife was tucked into the back of her garter belt, so she sat up straight. George had wanted to wrap it in a handkerchief, but she'd refused. She might have very little time, and having to unwrap the knife could be her end. She'd rather risk a few knife nicks in the hollow space of her buttocks.

She was so scared that she could hardly breathe.

His head bent over the arch of her foot, kissing. She reached with her right hand, curling around to her back. The skirt of the dress pulled too tightly where she sat on it. Why hadn't she flipped it out when she sat down?

She'd have to start over.

"Bathroom?" she asked, drawling the word.

He looked up, surprised, but stood back so that she could go.

"Right over there, beautiful." He pointed.

Angela sashayed across the room and into the bathroom. She shut the door but didn't lock it, although that's what she felt like doing.

She pulled up her skirt and grabbed the knife. Holding it in her hand, she stared at it. Now what? Then she had brilliant, if extremely risky, idea.

She stripped off her dress and bra, leaving on only the garter belt, skimpy panties and stockings. She returned the knife to the small of her back.

Then she opened the bathroom door.

George gently closed the door on the old lady and sleeping children. He searched for a lock, but there wasn't one. He grabbed the gun and then noticed the black smoke spiraling up from the pans of bacon and butter. He ran around the island and turned off the burners.

George headed down the corridor, toward the entrance hall, his gun tucked out of sight in the waistband of his pants and behind his suit jacket. He glanced to the left, at the plain pine door leading to steps to the basement. He was pretty sure the Doctor was down there. But, again, he kept going.

First the women and children. And that meant, first, killing Mr. Wong. His heart thumped like mad and he had to swallow against the nausea of fear. He'd never killed anyone, and despite everything, he didn't want to kill now.

The entrance hall was empty, its marble floor again maddening him with the dancing squares of black and white marble, and he heard no sounds from the living room. He peeked in, just to be sure. The fire burned, strangely cheerful in the silent, empty room.

He turned back and stood still at the bottom of the grand circular staircase. From the other times he'd brought whores here, he knew the rendezvous lasted several hours and that the house pretty much closed down. The guards were dismissed to their bedrooms at the top of the house.

He climbed the stairs slowly, glad that he'd thought to wear soft shoes. George opened the door to Mr. Wong's office with a slow twist of the knob. He slid through the open door in the space of only a foot. The room was nearly pitch black except for a tiny lamp that shone onto the mahogany desk.

Quiet. Too quiet, for George. Quiet wasn't good.

He reached for the gun with his right hand, while gently closing the office door. He crept forward and then heard a low growl. Fear so hard and cold that it was like a drowning clamped around him. He turned and saw a small dog standing on the cushions of a love seat tucked into the corner of the room. Its ears were cocked and the growl was getting louder.

It came to him out of nowhere. Mr. Wong called the dog Baby.

"Here, Baby," he whispered.

The growl stopped, but the ears stayed up and the body was taut, ready to leap off the couch, tear across the room, and sink its sharp little teeth into his leg.

"You wanna treat?"

Baby's tail began to wag. He landed on the thick carpet without a sound and came running over.

George held out his hand with two fingers pinched together. "I've got a treat for a good Baby," he murmured.

When he got close, George said, "Sit, Baby, sit."

Baby sat.

George scratched his ears, cooing at him, and the dog flopped over, giving him his belly, the little tail curled and wiggling between his legs. George scratched his belly carefully, raised his head, and looked around the room. He saw the large round gold ball sitting in solitary glory on top of Mr. Wong's desk. He reached for the ball and held it in his left hand. The pleasure for Baby became too much. The dog leapt up and began to tear around the room, barking like mad.

When Mr. Mao was in the tub, Julia stayed dressed and began soaping him with a washcloth. She started with his feet.

"Don't you wanna come in with me?"

She thought quickly. She'd been worried about whether she'd have the strength to kill him, even with surprise in her favor. He'd fight like a crazy animal.

Julia unzipped her dress and put it carefully across the toilet.

"Hang it up in the bedroom closet," Mr. Mao said.

"Thanks, sweetie." She tripped out of the bathroom.

She could hardly breathe from the panic sweeping up her legs and into her belly. Deliberately she made herself think of the terror Emily must have felt, must still be feeling. She hung up the dress and tore off the rest of her clothes.

As she crossed the room, naked, she stood tall. She walked with a wide and deliberate step. Her breath came in short pants.

His head lolled back against the tub, eyes closed. She knelt and pulled the knife out, but left it on the floor of the bathroom. Then she straightened, and using her toes, edged the knife to the far end of the tub, where his head so peacefully rested.

"Hey, sleepyhead," she whispered in his ear.

He woke and sat up with a splash. She gently pushed him farther forward and climbed into the tub behind him, her legs extending forward around him when she sat down. Then she pulled him against her so that his head again lolled backward, but this time resting on her shoulder.

She sang in a whisper, soothing and stroking him. Her hand reached for the knife.

• • •

Mr. Wong stood at a small, built-in bar on the far side of the room, his back to her. He turned when he heard the bathroom door click.

The dog was barking, and he glanced toward the door.

"Wow." He raised his drink glass as if to toast her.

The fear was gone, replaced by modesty and shyness at revealing her body.

"Ta," she said.

His eyebrows arched. "What?"

"Thanks, I mean."

"You've got red hair like the Irish."

She didn't say anything, just stared at the suspicion crowding his small handsome face.

Julia slit his throat. Then she pushed his head down under the water. His knees at the opposite end of the tub popped up like turtles. The water turned deep red, splashing around her. But he didn't even struggle. She thought that he'd been asleep. She wanted to believe he'd been asleep.

With one hand still keeping his head under the water, she rose from the bath and stepped out. Red water flowed off her body and she felt a terrible heat filling her. Tentative, she released his head and moved back. The water still lapped against the sides of the tub, but Mr. Mao was utterly and forever still.

Julia grabbed a towel and dried herself off. Then she rushed back into the bedroom. She was still damp and the silk stockings kept sticking as she tried to slide them over her legs.

"Shit, shit, shit," she swore.

Suddenly she leaned over and vomited. Her head whirled with dizziness and she was sure she would faint. Desperate, she plunged her head even lower, down between her legs, and she panted deliberately, sucking in the oxygen, begging God for the strength to go on.

When she could, she straightened up and ripped off the stockings, skipped the underwear, and pulled the red dress over her head. She looked down as she slipped on the high heels and saw her legs streaked with pale red blood.

Julia ran for the door, and then hesitated before opening it. She willed herself to slow down. She stood in the open doorway and listened. The house was dead quiet.

George had guessed that the children would be in a bedroom on the second floor, or in the basement. But she thought the basement more likely because noisy, crying kids wouldn't be so annoying down there.

She skimmed down the stairs, barely focusing. Turning right in the entrance to the house, she found a long hallway that led to the kitchen. She trotted in the high heels, surprising herself with how fast she could move.

She passed the plain pine door, but then caught herself and turned around.

As soon as she opened the door, she saw the guard sitting on a chair at the bottom of the steep stairway, the location he moved to at night.

"Hi," she called out.

He'd been asleep.

"Hi," he said gruffly, sitting up straighter. "What do you want?"

"Mr. Wong sent me to show you a little fun, 'cause you're working so hard."

"Mr. Wong?"

She started swaying down the stairs, her hips moving. Don't let him notice my legs all streaked with blood, she thought.

The guard shifted from foot to foot, embarrassed and surprised.

"You don't like me?" She moved closer and touched his cheek with one finger.

"Well, sure I like you." He grinned.

Both her hands cupped his face, then ran down his neck and shoulders, to his chest. She gave him a playful push. "You don't like me."

He grabbed her around the waist. "I do," he protested. He pulled her close, trying to kiss her.

Her hands slid lower and she felt the gun. Then her left hand slid even lower.

He moaned.

In a swift motion, she grabbed the gun with her right hand, jammed it into his waist, and fired.

The retort was so strong that her hand jerked up and she dropped the gun. He collapsed over her. Julia toppled him sideways, reached for the gun, and pointed it at his head. But he lay still.

There was no dizziness this time, only her legs like jelly.

The key was in his pocket and she quickly turned the lock. Desperate, desperate. The sound of the gun had been loud. She didn't have time to waste. No time, no time.

Julia threw open the door and saw Wilson sitting on a lab bench staring with horror in her direction.

"Oh my God, what are you—" he said.

"Wilson!"

He ran across the room and pulled her trembling body into his arms. She slumped against him and he thought she may have fainted. "We have to get the children!"

Her head rose from his chest and pressed up against his chin.

Wilson pushed her away, grabbed her hand, pulled her out of the room, and tugged her up the stairs.

"This way," he said, turning to the right. He let go of her hand so that he could run. "There's a guard in the room with them, a little old lady." His voice was a hoarse whisper.

They tore into the silent kitchen. Julia handed him the gun.

"Open the door and then jump back so I can shoot," Wilson said.

George pushed the door mechanism, which he'd noticed discreetly hidden on the desk's surface, and then darted out, springing across the room as Wong's bedroom door slid open.

Mr. Wong waited for him, his gun ready. George leapt sideways, rolling to the ground as Mr. Wong fired. He felt an agonizing burn in his lower leg. Still, he kept rolling.

Suddenly the dog was on him, leaping all over as he rolled. He thought the animal was trying to bite him, and he curled into a ball, head tucked in his hands. But then he realized Baby was playing. He glanced at Mr. Wong and saw the gun in his hand moving, trying to fire without hitting the dog.

And then he saw Angela.

What the hell was she doing?

She'd leapt up on the bed, knife raised, and she looked about to jump.

He wanted to shout, "No, Angela, no, take care of yourself." But then he remembered.

"Kill him, Angela, you can do it!"

Mr. Wong whirled around, and the gun fired as he turned, but Angela was already flying through the air and the bullet missed her.

She landed full on top of him. The dog, Baby, barked wildly and ran to Mr. Wong. His teeth sank into Angela's leg.

George aimed the gun, but he couldn't shoot Mr. Wong without risking Angela. Suddenly his left hand tightened on the gold ball. As a boy, they'd all practiced with both hands, and he was nearly as good with the left as the right. Nearly.

He heaved the gold ball at the back of Mr. Wong's head.

Angela had the knife at his throat, but he was far

stronger than she and he threw her off. Baby still clung to her leg.

The ball crashed into his skull and Mr. Wong crumpled.

George stood up, carefully aimed, and shot Luke Wong in the chest three times.

They heard a gunshot, and now the noise of pounding feet reverberated through the house.

Julia threw the door open and crouched in the doorway. She wanted to get into that room.

Wilson blinked, trying to see clearly so that he didn't shoot his children.

But the room was still.

Suddenly they heard Emily's voice. "Mommy?"

"I'm here, sweetie, come to get you." Julia stood and ran into the room.

They saw the still figure seated by the crib. "I think George was here before us," Julia said.

Wilson wanted to ask who George was, but he could hear the men coming. Shots ricocheted off the corridor walls.

He switched on the light and slammed the door. No lock, damn it all to hell.

"Take the kids and get out the window with them!" He started pulling one crib over to place across the door.

Julia grabbed Jimmy out of the crib and Wilson picked up the old woman. He dumped her into the crib and then began yanking the second crib over.

He heard the window fly open. He picked up the

second crib and piled it on top of the first.

Wilson turned and grabbed Jimmy out of Julia's arms. "Climb out and I'll throw them down to you."

Her eyes were wide and blank. But she quickly placed one leg and then another up onto the windowsill. She bent forward, angled her head out the window, and dropped from sight.

Before even checking on her, he'd thrust Jimmy out the window. Then he, too, ducked his head out the window and looked down.

She stood below him, her arms outstretched.

He hesitated.

It wasn't easy to drop your baby through the air. What if she didn't catch him?

"Daddy," whined Emily.

He heard the racket of the men beating down the door. He dropped Jimmy, and without waiting to see whether Julia caught him, he turned and lifted Emily up onto the windowsill.

"Jump to your mommy," he said.

To his amazement, she actually giggled.

Julia had put Jimmy down on his back, where he flailed, screaming at the top of his lungs. Suddenly Bill appeared from the shadows of the house. He picked up Jimmy.

"Here I come, Mommy," yelled Emily.

And she jumped, arms open like the wings of a baby bird flying home.

"Run as fast as you can!" Wilson screamed to Julia.

Still, he didn't wait. His legs were through the window and he'd turned onto his stomach, sliding out, when the door to the room burst open.

They shot him right in the head.

CHAPTER 40

George heard the office door crash open and the pounding feet of men approaching. He turned back to the bedroom door and began shooting. The first two were easy, but the third had his gun pulled and ready. Still, George felt his two seconds of advantage. The man hadn't expected the two before him to fall so quickly.

George dropped to the ground, his gun still pointed high, and he fired rapidly. The man fell with a thud.

Now George leapt to his feet and turned wildly toward Angela and Mr. Wong.

The only sound in the extraordinary quiet after the gun's firing were Angela's whimpering cries and the dog wailing over the body of his master.

George's arms circled Angela. "Come on," he said, "we've got to hurry."

She stood on wobbly legs, the blood from the dog bite dribbling into her shoe, and ran with him past the three men in the outer office and out to the hall. At the top of stairs, she stopped.

The entrance hall just below them was filled with police. Walkie-talkies squawked and the hubbub was like an open air market in summer. She realized she was almost naked.

"Go put your dress on," George said.

Angela turned and retraced her steps, shifting her eyes away from the dead men. In the bathroom, she suddenly collapsed onto the toilet and stared at the dark green velvet dress flung over the bathtub. She grabbed a towel and pushed it against the dog bite, then pulled it away. It was a shallow bite and the bleeding had almost stopped. She heard the dog, still whimpering over Mr. Wong's body.

She got dressed quickly and rushed back out. Several feet away from Mr. Wong, she crouched and crooned to the dog. "Come here, sweetie, come here. I'll take care of you. Come to Angie."

The poodle turned and Angela's heart hurt when she saw the anguish in his eyes. "Come here, sweet boy."

He tucked his tail between his legs and began to grovel along the floor, his belly dragging, inching closer to her. She didn't reach for him. She waited. He was six inches from her hand; then his cold nose touched her fingers and she gave a start. He pulled back.

"It's all right, your nose was just a bit chilly. Let me warm you up."

He pushed his nose out again, and this time Angela rubbed the space between his nose and eyes, the bridge of his nose, with her thumb. Harder and harder she rubbed until he flopped over, legs loose.

She scooped him up in her arms, stood, and walked out of the room. He cowered against her. She felt a tentative lick on her hand, and she smiled.

At the top of the stairs, she looked down at the mass of people and searched for George. He was talking to three policemen in a corner of the entrance hall. A couple of feet away, she saw Julia sitting on the floor, both children in her lap. Lauren and Bill were crouched next to her.

She flew down the stairs and pushed her way over to them. Julia's white face stared up at her. Jimmy was crying hysterically.

Emily jumped up and threw her arms around Angela's legs. "I knew you'd come, I knew it!"

"Did you now? Well, of course you were right." Angela's left arm still cradled the poodle, but her right hand settled onto Emily's head.

"I knew you were an angel."

Julia and Angela looked at each other. She could see that the Doctor wasn't there, but she thought better of asking in front of the children.

She knelt next to Emily. "Do you think you could take care of this wee doggie? He's a little upset and needs some cuddling."

"Oh, please, yes."

Angela carefully put the dog into Emily's arms. She heard Emily begin to croon to the dog.

Now she leaned over and took Jimmy from Julia. When she stood up, she placed him carefully into the space between her neck and breast. He snuggled, still crying, and she whispered in his ear. "Jimmy, my boy, I love you." Then she started to sing one of her traditional lullabies, and the crying quickly spiraled down into hiccups and an occasional heaving sob.

Emily sat down and leaned against the wall, the dog still in her lap, all her attention now focused on the dog.

"Where's Dr. Streatfield?" Angela asked Julia in a low voice.

"They shot him in the head." Julia's voice was dull. "I'm just grateful Armand got the police here so soon."

"Oh my God." Angela glanced around the crowded room and spotted Armand's massive body in a far corner, where he was talking to the police.

"I've got to get to the hospital."

"We can take Angela and the children home," Lauren said.

"But you have to talk to the police before you go to the hospital," Bill said.

"Yes, all right."

"I'll go speak to the lieutenant over there and make the arrangements," he said.

Angela hugged Julia for a moment. "I'm praying for him."

Tears wet Angela's blouse, but Julia straightened her head only moments later.

The women's eyes met. They did not speak because they'd gone beyond words. Green, wet, wide eyes stared into green, dry, dark eyes. It was enough.

They put down newspaper in the children's bathroom for the dog, whose name they now knew was Baby. Emily sat on the toilet watching him sniff around the room. He kept returning to where her bare feet dangled, giving them a quick lick. She giggled and pulled them up.

She got into her nightie all by herself, then scooped up Baby and tucked him in, under the covers, her arms holding him against her chest. He turned his face to hers, and the licking began again. Her face got a good wash.

Emily waited for Angie, who was feeding Jimmy a bottle, doing a diaper change, and then putting him to bed. On the bureau, one dim light shone. She stared around the room, her eyes getting heavy. She was home and in love with a dog named Baby.

She fell asleep.

ONE YEAR LATER

"I confess that I already know much of your story," Dr. Ellis Maurer said.

Julia thought Dr. Maurer's features, wide elegant nose, mahogany skin, and strong, liquid brown eyes, every detail, formed a man too handsome to be a marital counselor. She didn't want to stare at him, but she also didn't want to look at Wilson.

Her green eyes roved around the tidy office.

"Thank God we're not in the news anymore." Wilson sat straight in the wheelchair, but even so, he looked smaller. Julia knew that he felt smaller.

In the year since the kidnapping, they'd lived apart. Wilson convalesced in Vermont, under the care of his mother and father. Julia often drove the children up for the weekend, although those visits had stopped a month ago when the papers and evening news reports screamed the latest: Wilson's miracle drug was a failure. Clinical trials had been halted abruptly because of massive, deadly side effects.

Suddenly Wilson looked directly at her. "Your hair is so long."

She met his eyes briefly, and then darted to Dr. Maurer. Help, she thought, please help. Wilson's head had been shaved, and kept shaved, for six months. A sharp buzz of white shone like snow crystals.

Julia wondered whether they really understood why grief or age made hair turn white, and she wondered what Wilson's white hair said about him. Where had he gone on this terrible journey, and was he going to come home again?

Dr. Maurer gazed at her with a kind of bored impassiveness, which Julia found extraordinary, given the circumstances. One of his eyebrows arched, as if to echo Wilson's question, though there was no reason why *he* should care about the length of her hair.

She looked again at Wilson. "I'm growing it out."

He nodded.

"Why?" Dr. Maurer said.

Julia considered a loud, uncontrollable yell. She spoke in a rush. "For strength, I'm growing it for strength."

She peeked at Wilson.

"You were always such a pisser," he said.

"Me?"

They stared at each other.

"*You* were the pisser," Julia said.

"Aren't you both pissers?" The doctor glanced at them.

"We used the past tense." Julia uncrossed her

legs, and she noticed that Dr. Maurer wasn't paying attention to her legs. A tiny sense of relief snuck through her.

"You're still who you were," Wilson said. "More so."

"Why more?"

"Christ, Julia, you saved our lives."

"Not just me. It would've been hopeless without George and Angela."

Ellis spoke to Wilson. "I understand, just from the news accounts, that you got Julia and the kids to safety, and then you were shot at the last moment."

"That's right!" Julia said.

Wilson's head hung low and Julia saw the long mark of his incision curl across the top and then disappear down the back of his skull.

"If it hadn't been for me . . ." Wilson trailed off without finishing.

"The price you paid was enormous," Julia said.

"Fuck!"

She went rigid and noticed that even Dr. Maurer looked surprised. They were quiet, waiting for Wilson to continue talking.

The wait was so long that her nails dug into the palms of her hands. When she peered at Dr. Maurer, he gave her a pointed look, which she read as warning: *Don't say a word.*

In the year they'd lived apart, they talked more than the previous ten years of their marriage, but the words of their talking floated like particles of dust in the air around them. Nothing came of them. She figured that she'd never known Wilson at all, or the other alternative, that her husband had been unutterably changed by his loss.

It was not a question of whether she still loved him, but try making him believe that. Julia was devastated by his decision to return home to Vermont from the hospital. He needed her, or so it would have seemed, but he couldn't allow her to care for him.

"What do you feel right now?" Dr. Maurer said to Wilson.

"I don't *feel* anything." Wilson spat out the words. "But I can tell you what I *am*."

Julia's legs wound around the chair and tied themselves into knots. She uncurled them and deliberately placed them squarely in front of her body, toes lined up like soldiers. Squiggles of confusion about her relationship with Wilson glowed in phosphorescent colors, and she thought she couldn't do this, that it was too hard to make this marriage work again.

Julia had realized that they needed counseling if Wilson moved back to New York, and her. You'd have to be inhuman not to need counseling after what they'd been through. But when the drug failed, he withdrew completely. He didn't allow her to bring the kids up, although he spoke to them on the telephone once a week. Julia watched Emily become more and more frantic, crying several times a day and waking often during the night.

Finally, to protect her children, Julia insisted that Wilson see Dr. Maurer with her. She only got him to agree by first approaching Wilson's mother and begging for her help in convincing Wilson.

"I'm a failure." Wilson shifted in his wheelchair. The full force of his angry face slammed into her. "So you win. Are you happy now, *satisfied*?"

She leapt up, hands clenched. Her voice trembled when she yelled, "You selfish, cold sonofabitch!"

"Julia, could you please sit down?" Dr. Maurer said.

She collapsed.

Julia had never seen Wilson cry before. She tried to go to him, but Dr. Maurer gave her another one of his looks—she was beginning to know them well—and so she remained rooted to her chair.

Finally, when the sobs had ended, Dr. Maurer turned to Julia. "Can you explain a little more about why you're so angry at Wilson?"

She felt foolish. How could she be angry at this poor man, whose greatest sacrifice had been an utter waste? Julia flushed. "I'm not angry."

"You called him a selfish, cold, sonofabitch."

Both men's eyes were on her and it seemed like they were in cahoots to push her into a corner, to make it all her fault. Her voice came from her stomach, buried deep, and it rose to a shout. "You made our whole marriage into a fight. Who wins? Who loses?" She took a shuddering breath. "Who the fuck cares, Wilson?"

"I care!" Wilson's clenched fist slammed the arm of the wheelchair.

"So now that you think you've lost, you want out of the game, huh? You want to take your marbles home to Mommy and Daddy."

Wilson glared at her, and the bristles of his white hair screamed with frustration.

After a moment's silence, Dr. Maurer spoke to Julia again, this time more gently. "Make us understand more of what you mean," he said.

"Our marriage shouldn't be a competition, with you and me on opposite sides," she said. "It's like when I found the fungus on the beetle." She glanced at the doctor. "*I* found the fungus, but Wilson adamantly refuses to believe that. Since it promised to be such an enormously important discovery, *he* had to have found it himself."

Dr. Maurer held up one small, delicate hand in a stop sign and turned to Wilson. "What do you say about this?"

"You mean who found the worthless fungus?"

The doctor nodded.

"I remember finding it, what else can I say?" He shrugged. "It's irrelevant anyway."

Julia thought her head would explode with the pressure.

"But you say you found it?" Dr. Maurer looked at Julia.

Suddenly Wilson sat up straight and pointed a shaking finger at her. "I didn't do this alone, God damn it, you never really loved me, never really wanted me. You're the cold sonofabitch!"

She reached across the distance between them and hooked her finger around his accusing one, looping them together in a gentle hold.

His eyes, without the long black hair that used to frame his face, were huge.

"Say you're sorry," she whispered.

"Sorry for what?"

"For that other woman, the research assistant."

His finger tightened around hers. "But I didn't . . ."

"Wilson," she said.

"I *am* sorry, I'm sorry for absolutely everything."

Dr. Maurer stood up. "If you'll excuse me. I'm just going to grab a cup of coffee."

They nodded and he slipped out the door.

"I think we're boring him," Wilson said.

"Probably." She tried a small smile.

"Julia."

"Yeah?"

"I can't saddle you with this." He gestured to the wheelchair. "You should go out and find someone else. You have your whole life ahead of you."

"Now you're boring me."

Wilson grimaced. "I mean it."

"You know Angela and George's wedding is this weekend?"

"I was planning on just going back home to Vermont tonight."

"Home is here, with me and the kids."

He stared out the window.

"Angela wants you to take her down the aisle."

"Oh, that would be interesting!"

"Better than boring." Julia poked her toe against his leg. "She could either push you, or you could wheel yourself alongside. Emily's the flower girl and Jimmy's the ring-bearer."

"And if I'm the Father of the Bride, what are you?"

"Matron of Honor." She grinned. "Stay, it'll be fun."

"Maybe I will."

"Stay forever, Wilson."

He peered at her, shy. "You're my only hope," he whispered.

Julia felt the gentle flush of pleasure sweep up her chest and neck. To be Wilson's only hope, how extraordinary for him to believe such a thing. She wanted to rush across the room and cradle his body in her arms.

Instead, she stood up and pushed Wilson backward so that his wheelchair was lodged against the far wall's bookshelves. "There's one thing we gotta get settled," she said.

Quickly she turned over her chair and plunked it in the middle of the room.

Dr. Maurer appeared in the doorway to his office, holding a steaming mug of coffee, just as Julia lowered herself to the upside-down chair.

"This was the log." She patted the chair and then balanced herself on its arm. "I dropped down to the ground." Julia fell to the floor on the other side of the chair and then stretched full-length on the carpet.

She crawled forward on her belly. Suddenly she pressed her nose to the carpet. "I remember how the earth smelled so rich it made me dizzy." She inched along so that her head was beneath Dr. Maurer's desk chair. Julia reached out a hand, lifted the piece of wood, snatched the beetle, sat up, and turned around.

"'Wilson,' I called out.

"'What?' you said.

"'I think I found something.'"

Julia turned around and stared at Wilson. Dr. Maurer raised the coffee mug to his lips and took a loud sip.

"I think I found something," Julia whispered again.

She opened her hand and let the beetle fall back to the earth, rose slowly to her feet, crossed the office to her husband, and found him waiting.

If you enjoyed this book,
try these other acclaimed thrillers. . . .

COLD WHITE FURY
Beth Amos

This gripping supernatural thriller recalls the chilling mood of Dean Koontz's *Watchers* and the pulse-pounding tension of *The Client*.
ISBN 0-06-101005-7 • $5.99/$7.99 (Can.)

THE DEPARTMENT OF CORRECTION
Tony Burton

When a string of vicious, but apparently unrelated crimes leads a reporter on a quest for the truth, he uncovers a conspiracy of unspeakable evil. . . .
ISBN 0-06-101309-9 • $6.50/$8.50 (Can.)

THE PARDON
James Grippando

"Powerful. . . . I read *The Pardon* in one sitting—one exciting night of thrills and chills." —*James Patterson*
ISBN 0-06-109286-X
$6.50/$8.50 (Can.)

THE PRICE OF BLOOD
Chuck Logan

This riveting suspense novel reads like a thrilling treasure hunt with a murderous legacy that echoes down from the past.
ISBN 0-06-109622-9 • $6.99/$8.99 (Can.)

 **HarperPaperbacks**
A Division of HarperCollinsPublishers
www.harpercollins.com

Available at bookstores everywhere, or call
1-800-331-3761 to order.